'You might marry again, perhaps?'

'I doubt that, sir.' Annabella sounded subdued. They were back on dangerous ground.

Sir William allowed the curricle to slow down, and half turned towards her. 'You seem very certain, ma'am! How is it possible to tell what the future holds?'

'It is not, of course,' Annabella allowed, permitting herself to meet those perceptive blue eyes for a brief moment. 'But I do not think...'

'Perhaps,' Sir William said thoughtfully, 'when one has been married happily once, it is difficult to imagine such good fortune occurring again.'

Nicola Cornick is passionate about many things: her country cottage and its garden, her two small cats, her husband and her writing, though not necessarily in that order! She has always been fascinated by history, both as her chosen subject at university and subsequently as an engrossing hobby. She works as a university administrator and finds her writing the perfect antidote to the demands of life in a busy office.

Recent titles by the same author:

THE VIRTUOUS CYPRIAN
TRUE COLOURS

THE LARKSWOOD LEGACY

Nicola Cornick

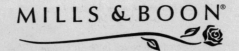

MILLS & BOON®

First published in Great Britain 1999
Harlequin Mills & Boon Limited,
Eton House, 18-24 Paradise Road, Richmond, Surrey TW9 1SR

© Nicola Cornick 1999

ISBN 0 263 81525 0

Set in Times Roman 10½ on 12 pt.
04-9904-74968 C1

Printed and bound in Great Britain
by Caledonian International Book Manufacturing Ltd, Glasgow

Chapter One

'Annabella! You graceless girl! Why, I declare, you are as clumsy as an elephant!' Lady St Auby brought the phrase out triumphantly, for she had seen such a creature in Lord Eaglesham's zoological collection. The words were delivered in a sibilant hiss, unlike Lady St Auby's habitual hectoring tone, but they were hurtful nevertheless. Annabella St Auby bit her lip and a flush came into her pale cheeks.

This time, her transgression had been small. She had stood aside to allow her mother-in-law to enter the Taunton Assembly Rooms first, as precedence demanded. Unfortunately, Lady St Auby had been so deeply engrossed in gossiping with her bosom-bow, Mrs Eddington-Buck, that she had not realised that Annabella had stopped and had cannoned into her back, setting her hairpiece askew and dropping her fan in the process.

It had been a disastrous way to re-enter Taunton society after a year of mourning. It seemed to Lady St Auby, in her anguish, that every head had turned in their direction and every conversation was suspended. The coiffure, which had taken her maid five-and-forty minutes to prepare, was slipping irretrievably over one ear. She knew that she had flushed an unbecoming mottled puce, and to make matters worse, her husband was gaping like a drunken fish and her daughter-in-law was hanging her head like a shy debutante. She dug Annabella viciously in the ribs.

'Well, don't stand there gawping, girl! Oh, that Francis ever chose to throw himself away on such an ill-bred little miss!' It was not the first time she had uttered such a remark. Lady St Auby made no secret of the fact that she considered her only son to have married beneath him, and Annabella had damned herself beyond redemption by failing to be the heiress she had promised to be. Hard-won self-control helped her to ignore her mother-in-law's vulgar observation, even when Mrs Eddington-Buck tittered behind her hand.

The Taunton Assembly was unlikely to be the epitome of high living, Annabella thought, as she followed Sir Frederick and Lady St Auby through the crowded ballroom to find a vantage point opposite the door. Bath would have had more society to offer, but the St Aubys were too poor to travel there. The company tonight would no doubt consist of the usual hunting and shooting set with whom Sir Frederick in particular had always mingled, and the evening would drag along with no hint of excitement. The Assembly Rooms were shabby and in sore need of a fresh coat of paint. Annabella sighed. She felt like they looked. Her evening dress might have been fashionable three years previously, but even then it had been run up by

her father's housekeeper, based on a faded pattern
from the *Ladies Magazine*. At the time it had been a
rather pretty shade of mauve. Now it was a faded
lavender, and served as the half-mourning appropriate
to one who had lost her young husband so tragically
a year before.

They had paused several times whilst Lady St
Auby tried to find the most advantageous position in
which to wait to be seen and greeted by the great and
the good. Unfortunately, several early arrivals had
taken the best spots and it was a while before her
ladyship was satisfied, elbowing some poor unsuspecting young lady out of the way and moving a pot-
ted palm slightly to the right so that it did not obscure
her field of vision. The St Auby party took up their
stance, but almost immediately Lady St Auby's eye
fell on Annabella with disapproval. She tugged at her
evening gloves so viciously that the seam ripped.

'Smile, girl! No one will believe that you have a
desire for entertainment if you stand there with such
a Friday face!'

Several heads turned at the hissed undertone. Annabella flushed scarlet.

'I beg you, dear ma'am—'

'Lady Oakston! Sir Thomas!' Suddenly Lady St
Auby had no time for Annabella's faults. She was
fulsome, wreathed in smiles. 'A pleasure to see you
again!' Now she was gushing like a mountain stream
and Annabella turned to scan the ballroom again. It
seemed very crowded that night, but perhaps that was
because she had become unaccustomed to such bus-
tle... Lady St Auby was simpering now as another
set of acquaintances came up to greet them. It re-

minded Annabella of the rather unpleasant way in which her mother-in-law would melt girlishly when Francis had put on the charm, trading on the fact that his mother could never refuse him anything...

'Such a sad loss to us,' Lady St Auby was saying to Lady Oakston, wiping away a surreptitious tear. 'My dear daughter-in-law was so overcome we feared she would become a recluse!' The insincere smile was turned on Annabella, with Lady St Auby waiting for her to echo her sentiments. Annabella was silent. She had her faults, but hypocrisy was not one of them. Lady St Auby turned her back on her.

'Simple creature!' Mrs Eddington-Buck said, with an artificial trill of amusement, and she did not mean it kindly.

After spending a sequestered year in the rotting manor that the St Aubys called home, these bright lights and loud voices were almost shocking to Annabella. As a young girl she had craved excitement, but knew well enough now that it was not to be found amongst the hard-drinking, hard-riding hunting set. Before her brief marriage, her life in her father's ostentatious home had been empty and dull, and she had briefly thought that her marriage might introduce her to a wider society. It had done so, but she had not been accepted into the gentry any more than her father had been before her. And now both her husband and father were dead, and she was stranded, a poor relation, in a county society which had once regarded her as a curiosity and now thought of her scarcely at all.

But it seemed that the whole of Taunton society was on show tonight and one could not but wonder why. The hard eyes of these bejewelled women were raking Annabella contemptuously, dismissing her old faded lavender half-mourning with small, self-satisfied smiles. The looks of the men were more equivocal still, appraising, familiar… Annabella knew that it was Francis she had to thank for this disrespectful attitude, for when he had been in his cups he would talk loudly and unreservedly about matters which were best kept between husband and wife. His cronies, gleefully recognising this weakness, had encouraged him to the hilt until the whole of Taunton appeared to know intimate facts about Annabella that could only add to her embarrassment.

Annabella sighed again as she thought of Francis. She was guilty of the charge that she had entrapped the St Aubys' pride and joy, for she had set her cap at Francis as the only means of escape from her father. Weak and dissolute, Francis St Auby had had a penchant for women and gambling, and Annabella had gone into the marriage with her eyes open, aware of the threat to her future posed by both. She had bought Francis with the promise of her fortune, for she had known instinctively that he would have no other interest in her. Sure enough, he had set up a mistress in the town before the banns had even been read, but Bertram Broseley's wealth had been rumoured to be immense and this had at least been sufficient to prompt Francis to go through with the wedding, his mistress prominently on display at the ceremony itself. Annabella, who had known full well that Francis's character was unlikely to improve, had smiled all through her wedding day until her face ached, grimly aware of the price she had chosen to pay in order to avoid her father's alternative plan for her future.

At first, matters had not been so bad. Bertram Broseley gave them a generous, if grudgingly granted, allowance, and they lived in tolerable comfort. Annabella rarely saw Francis, who spent his time with his mistress or in the low town taverns he frequented. Then, eighteen months previously, Broseley had died unexpectedly and disaster had struck. There was no inheritance. The legendary fortune had proved illusory, swallowed up in all the debts that Broseley had left. After a few months the little, rented townhouse had had to go and they had moved back to the manor Francis's parents owned. Francis's temper, always uncertain, had become vicious in his disappointment. He joined his mother in railing at his wife for her ill-bred, rapacious nature in tricking him into marriage. Lady St Auby repeatedly bemoaned the marriage to all and sundry and Francis spent more and more time gambling and drinking. And, one night, he had become involved in a quarrel over loaded dice, had been too drunk to fight and had fallen and hit his head on a stone hearth. And that was that.

Once again, Lady St Auby regained Annabella's attention by digging her in the ribs. This time she was almost beside herself with excitement.

'Look, Annabella! Oh, Millicent!' She grabbed Mrs Eddington-Buck's arm. 'I declare, it's Mundell! And the Earl and Countess of Kilgaren! At a country assembly! How thrilling!' A shadow crossed her face as a horrid thought struck her. 'What if the Viscount does not remember us? Oh, if he cuts us, I shall die of embarrassment, positively die!'

Annabella watched the Viscount's party enter the Assembly Rooms. No wonder there was such a crush tonight if word had gone round the neighbourhood that he was to be present! Once, long ago, she remembered, she had fancied herself in love with Viscount Mundell, for he was exceptionally handsome in a rather hawkish way and, as one of the County's premier landowners, was imbued with an irresistible attraction that would still have applied had he been as ugly as sin. Tonight he was with a small party, four ladies and three other gentlemen, all graciously acknowledging the greetings of Sir Thomas Oakston as he excitedly bowed them into the room. A flutter of awareness went through the assembled ranks as ladies preened themselves and turned to show their figures and profiles to advantage. Excited whispers tried in vain to elicit the identity of the other gentlemen. Dagger glances were cast at the ladies who had the good fortune to be part of the Viscount's company.

'Let me see! Let me see!' Mrs Eddington-Buck craned her neck to look over the heads of the crowd, and trod heavily on Annabella's foot in the process. 'La, how elegant they are!' She cast a spiteful, sideways glance at Annabella. 'One can always tell *true* quality, Lady St Auby!'

Annabella smiled stiffly. Her mother-in-law and her friends never ceased to remind her that Bertram Broseley had been a Cit, a rich merchant who could never aspire to county society. His early marriage to the daughter of an Earl could be conveniently forgotten, for his wife had died giving birth to Annabella and he had never again attempted to marry above his sta-

tion. It was a thorn in Lady St Auby's side that Annabella was so well-connected, with a grandmother
who was the Dowager Countess of Stansfield, and a
sister, the Incomparable Alicia, now a Marchioness.
But Annabella was estranged from her family. Had
she been close to her sister, Lady St Auby would no
doubt have boasted of the connection. As it was, she
used the rift to point out to Annabella that her family
had cast her off as beneath their notice.

Annabella swallowed hard. Over the past few intolerable months, she had been thinking more and
more of her sister and their estrangement. Probably
the very desperation of her situation in the St Auby
household made her long for a happier alternative.
Seven years her senior, Alicia had always seemed remote, for their father had fought hard to keep them
apart. If only she could think of some way of approaching Alicia, of healing the breach... But she had
given her sister good reason to dislike her, and it was
not so easy to undo that now.

'They are coming over! Viscount Mundell has noticed us! Oh, Millicent—' Lady St Auby was almost
incoherent with joy. She planted her considerable
bulk firmly in the path of the unsuspecting peer. 'My
Lord! An honour! And a pleasure to see you again,
is it not, Frederick?'

Sir Frederick St Auby, who had much in common
with his late son, dragged his gaze away from the
contemplation of a luscious blonde beauty and
grunted. 'Servant, Mundell.'

The Viscount had not the first idea as to the identity
of the large lady accosting him, but he nevertheless
had manners equal to the occasion. His bored grey

eyes moved from Lady St Auby to her spouse with indifference. 'How do you do, ma'am? Sir... I hope I find you well?' His gaze drifted past them and sharpened on Annabella. 'Mrs St Auby!' A note of genuine sincerity entered his voice. 'How do you do, ma'am? I had been hoping to see you here. I had the pleasure of speaking to your sister, Lady Mullineaux, recently. I was glad to see that both she and your new nephew are well.'

For a moment Annabella stood quite still, unsure if he was really addressing her. She was so used to slights and snubs that she could scarce believe that this deity was actually speaking to her. Then, as he waited, she realised with amazement that he was indeed awaiting a reply. Annabella smiled a little awkwardly. She was aware of nothing but surprise that Mundell had even recognised her. Though they had met on a couple of occasions in the distant past, she had made no impression on him and now she knew that only her resemblance to Alicia had helped him identify her. Although no one had ever suggested that she was an incomparable beauty, both she and Alicia had the heart-shaped faces, high cheekbones and determined chin that were the defining features of the look inherited from their grandmother. And now that Annabella had lost so much weight in the time following Francis's death, the fat that had threatened to blur her features had receded to leave her almost angular. Her hair was golden where Alicia's was auburn, and her eyes were a lighter green, and somehow she had just missed the startling beauty possessed by her sister, whilst remaining a very pretty girl.

Lady St Auby was looking furious that the Viscount's attention had been diverted to Annabella.

'La, sir,' she said, archly, 'do not speak to Annabella of Lady Mullineaux! My daughter-in-law and her sister do not see eye to eye and have not met for an age! Why, Annabella has not even been invited to visit for little Thomas's christening—'

But Annabella was not about to allow Lady St Auby to broadcast her disagreement with her sister to the assembled crowd. She had seen the faint, supercilious hint of boredom touch Mundell's handsome features at the threatened rehearsal of a tedious family quarrel, and she hurried in, with scant courtesy, 'I hope to see my sister and her family soon, my lord. It is a pleasure to hear of them going on so well.'

Mundell gave her a slight smile and made to move on, for plenty were clamouring for his attention. Annabella knew he had thought her both gauche and uninteresting, and it rankled. But any town bronze, or at least the semi-sophistication she had once achieved, had been knocked out of her by the constant criticism of her late husband, and the carping of her mother-in-law. She had never really been given the chance to sparkle.

Lady St Auby was made of sterner stuff, however. She was not about to let a Viscount out of her sights so easily. 'And your companions, sir? Will you make us known to them…?'

Fortunately for the Viscount's companions, most were in fact engaged in conversation elsewhere. The Earl and Countess of Kilgaren were still chatting with Sir Thomas Oakston, and the other ladies in the group were speaking to each other in a rather exclusive manner which suggested that they were above mingling with the *hoi polloi*. There was a pause. Annabella knew Mundell was about to snub her mother-in-law, and steeled herself.

The Viscount said with weary courtesy, 'Lady St Auby, may I present my brother-in-law, Lord Wallace? And a great friend of mine, Sir William Weston...'

Annabella, who had been admiring the elegant *ton*-nishness of Lady Kilgaren's dress, looked up, a little startled, as a shadow fell across her. Sir William Weston was bowing to her with formality. The name had meant nothing to her and she had not really been attending. Now, belatedly bestowing her attention on him, Annabella initially considered the gentleman to be nothing out of the ordinary. He was of more than average height, it was true, with a broadness of shoulder which somehow suggested strength and durability. But that was hardly a romantic attribute. Annabella, who had had little experience of true romance in her life, had always fondly imagined that her heroes would be dark and handsome, like the characters in the Minerva Press Gothics. Sir William was not particularly dark. His face was unremarkable except for a healthy tan which suggested that he had spent a long time in far hotter climes, and his thick, brown hair was bleached fair at the ends. Apart from that...

Annabella paused in her assessment as he looked directly into her eyes. Her heart skipped a beat and she caught her breath, uncertain quite what had disturbed her. Sir William's eyes, she discovered, were a rather fascinating blue, the colour of summer seas, at once sleepy and alert as they held hers for a long moment. Almost unconsciously, she started her appraisal again. Now that she was giving due consideration, she suddenly observed that Sir William Weston moved with a fluid grace that was oddly attractive when taken with his powerful physique. His face had integrity and character, and his smile was like his eyes, sleepy and disordering to the senses, hinting at all kinds of possibilities beneath the surface... Annabella felt herself blush to the roots of her hair as those very eyes scanned her face and appeared to read her mind.

'Mrs St Auby...' Sir William was smiling slightly, taking her hand in his. 'I have heard much about you. It has long been my wish to make your acquaintance.'

Lady St Auby cleared her throat noisily, bustling forward between them before Annabella could respond to this. 'A friend of Viscount Mundell!' she gushed. 'An honour, dear sir, an honour! And are you a landowner, like his lordship?' She might as well have asked his income, Annabella thought, closing her eyes in momentary despair. Her motives could not have been more transparent.

Sir William appeared unperturbed by this ill-concealed curiosity. 'Alas, no, ma'am! My estate is small. I am only a humble sailor.'

Lady St Auby's nose turned up as though the idea had reminded her of the smell of rotting fish. Unlike Annabella, she did not see the look of faintly ironic amusement which crossed Viscount Mundell's face at his friend's words. The music was starting up, but not quickly enough to cover Mrs Eddington-Buck's comments about *parvenus* who hung on the coat-tails of the nobility. Sir William's amiable smile did not wa-

ver, but his blue gaze moved from one to the other
with thoughtful consideration. Annabella's blush
deepened. He had said that he had heard of her, and
she could easily imagine what had been said. 'The
mercenary daughter of a jumped-up Cit' had been one
of the more complimentary descriptions she had heard
applied to herself, and here was Lady St Auby con-
firming just such an impression with her own behaviour!

'I am promised for this dance,' Sir William said
easily, interrupting Annabella's thoughts, 'but may I
hope to see you again later, Mrs St Auby? Please
excuse me—'

And he was gone, leaving Annabella once again
feeling oddly disturbed. She shook her head slightly
to dispel the fanciful illusion. She had not been in
society much, but she had met some personable men,
many of them a great deal more conventionally handsome than Sir William Weston. But somehow none
of them had his air of authority leavened with such
good humour, and she found that powerfully attractive...

'...the lady in blue is Mundell's elder sister, Lady
Wallace,' Mrs Eddington-Buck was saying, her feath-
ered head-dress waggling with excitement. 'And the
lady in pink gauze is Mundell's other sister, the un-
married one. And the other lady is a Miss Hurst, of
the Hampshire Hursts, you know. There—' she
pointed across the room '—dancing with that odd
man, Sir William Weston.'

Annabella fanned herself vigorously, for the heat
in the room was growing. No one had asked her to
dance and she could only be grateful, for it would

inevitably rouse Lady St Auby's ire. It was a very
long time since she had attempted the country dances
which were so popular, for Francis had usually been
too drunk to be steady on his feet when they attended
such gatherings, and he preferred the cardroom anyway. Mrs Eddington-Buck and Lady St Auby had
moved on to discuss the dresses of the ladies in Mundell's party, and were full of extravagant praise. Annabella privately thought that Miss Mundell's rose
gauze was far too *outré* for a country assembly, and
Miss Hurst looked a cold and haughty beauty. Once
again, her gaze was peculiarly drawn to the tall figure
of Miss Hurst's partner.

'Shameless hussy!' Lady St Auby had followed her
gaze with malevolent eyes. 'Already casting out lures
to another man, and my poor, dead son scarcely cold
in his grave!'

It was not an auspicious moment for the first gentleman of the evening to approach Annabella for a
dance, and her heart sank when she saw who he was.
Glittering in his scarlet regimentals, and with a smile
easy and charming, Captain George Jeffries had managed to come upon her quite unawares. He gave Lady
St Auby a punctilious bow, acknowledged with a grin
the thin line of disapproval in which her mouth was
set, and pulled Annabella into the dance with a pro-
prietary hand she found almost intolerable.

'You must be in a fit of the dismals this evening,
my love,' he observed with cheerful informality, 'for
you have barely spoken a word all night. There!' He
gave her a grin he fondly imagined to be attractive.
'You should be flattered that I have given away the
fact that I have been watching you the whole time!'

'I did not see you come in, sir,' Annabella replied repressively. She had no heart for idle flirtation, especially not with Jeffries. Once, perhaps, she had found him attractive. But that had been at a time when she was particularly lonely and vulnerable, and he had been quick to take advantage of the fact. Unfortunately, he was not now to be dismissed very easily.

'No, indeed!' Jeffries was eyeing her with objectionable familiarity. 'You were too busy fluttering your eyelashes at a Viscount to notice a mere half-pay officer!' He leant closer and she could feel his breath on her face. 'But you should not be so dismissive of my worth, my love! How much longer—?'

'Kindly stand back, sir!' Annabella said smartly, embarrassed by the licence he was taking and aware that several of the nearer couples sought to eavesdrop on their conversation. 'And refrain from addressing me in that intimate whisper!'

Jeffries recoiled as though he had been slapped. The figure of the dance separated them momentarily, but when he rejoined her he immediately took up the theme again.

'Then where and when may I address you?' The boyish charm had been replaced by a sulky, mulish expression all too reminiscent of Francis when he was in a bad mood. Annabella's heart sank. She knew that she had encouraged Jeffries's attentions during the long and boring months of incarceration at Hazeldean that had followed Francis's death. His admiration had been balm to her after Francis's black moods and Lady St Auby's constant fault-finding. Perhaps she had even allowed him more liberty than had been

wise, but she had never intended that it should lead
to more... And now that was what Jeffries was wanting, and the thought filled her with revulsion. She had
to make it plain to him now.

'You may not, sir!' She saw him frown and added
coldly, 'Your attentions are not welcome!'

At her words, Jeffries terminated his attentions in
the most abrupt way possible. It was not perhaps the
most desirable manner in which to draw attention at
a ball, Annabella thought, to be left standing alone as
one's dance partner stormed off the floor. Other couples were circulating about her, and while she hesitated, unable to disentangle herself and in grave danger of ruining the entire set, a strong hand plucked
her from out of the other dancers' paths, and swept
her to the side of the room.

'Forgive me my precipitate action, ma'am,' Sir
William Weston said, above her head. 'I was afraid
that there might be an accident if I left you there!'

Strong arms had closed about her, steadying her,
drawing her so close for a moment that she could hear
the beat of his heart, feel it against her cheek as it
rested briefly against the crisp shirt. She felt a sudden,
astounding sense of recognition and almost closed her
eyes in relief. Then she was put very gently back on
to her feet and Sir William stepped back, impeccably
proper.

'My apologies, once again, madam.' He sketched
a bow. 'I hope I have not hurt you.'

It was extraordinary, Annabella thought, completely bewildered, her feelings still in confusion. His
lightest touch had caused an earthquake of sensation
within her. She was not sure if she liked the feeling.

She was even more uncertain of whether she could deal with it.

She took a steadying breath. 'Your actions were most timely, sir. I must thank you!' She looked up into those vivid, blue eyes and felt again the impact of his character.

Sir William's sleepy gaze dwelt on her thoughtfully, seeing she knew not what. She was aware that the faded mauve dress only served to accentuate the pallor of her face and that her hair, although a pretty honey fair, was escaping its hasty coiffure, for Lady St Auby had taken all the maid's time and Annabella had had to secure the pins herself. Yet he seemed to find no fault, and returned her smile with warmth.

'I imagine I witnessed you divesting yourself of an admirer there, Mrs St Auby,' he observed coolly. 'How very ruthless you must have been for the young man to react so! And now that I am here in his place, how may I serve you?'

Annabella had never thought of George Jeffries as a young man until that moment, but there was something in Weston's tone which made her see him suddenly as a foolish youth, for all his posturing in his pretty uniform. And in comparison with this man... Well, there was no comparison. Whilst she struggled to understand the precise nature of the difference, she realised that Lady St Auby was gesticulating at her across the floor. Annabella's heart sank. Her mother-in-law was watching her like a gaoler and she did not wish for another scene. 'Perhaps you might escort me back to Lady St Auby,' she said, a little regretfully, and saw Sir William grin down at her.

'Must I? The old dragon bullies you, yet you are

eager to return to her side?' He gave her a whimsical smile. 'It seems most odd!'

Annabella tried unsuccessfully to repress her own smile. She was discovering that there were worse fates than to enjoy a mild flirtation with a man who was as attractive as the enigmatic Sir William. It had been a very long time since any man had flirted with her—except, of course, the unappealing Captain Jeffries…

'Lady St Auby can be of uncertain temperament—' she began guardedly, only to be stopped by his laughter.

'Upon my word, ma'am, that is the most astounding piece of understatement I have ever heard! You must be a veritable paragon to describe her in such terms!'

Now it was Annabella's turn to laugh. 'Oh, no, sir, that is too unkind! Her ladyship does her best with a daughter-in-law she never sought, who is left penniless to her charity! It is not easy for her!'

Sir William grimaced. 'You are all charity yourself, Mrs St Auby! But I see that Lady Bountiful is approaching us, so I may find out for myself if your words are true!'

'Oh, no!' Over his shoulder, Annabella could see the stout figure of her mother-in-law advancing on them purposefully. She wanted no interruption. Sir William's dancing blue eyes saw her dismay and he laughed aloud.

'Never fear, I will protect you! It will seem best if we are conversing on some innocuous topic,' he added in a swift undertone. 'Yes, my ship was stationed in the East Indies for two years, ma'am…' he had raised his voice for the benefit of the approaching matron '…and the weather is indeed too hot for the British temperament! Ah, Lady St Auby—' He turned swiftly. 'Your servant, ma'am! I was just telling your charming daughter-in-law how much preferable the west of England is to hotter climes!'

Lady St Auby was in a quandary. She had no wish to offend any friend of Viscount Mundell, even though it meant missing the opportunity to rail at Annabella for flirting with another man. She forced out a chilly smile.

'Indeed, sir! I should hope so too! Nothing *abroad*—' she invested the word with heavy scorn '—can stand comparison! The French are intemperate, the Russians uncivilised—although I did hear that the Czar is a charming man—and as for the Indies…' Lady St Auby paused and took a deep breath. 'Barbarous! But I believe you said you are a naval man? That would account for your sojourn in such a place, I suppose!' Her tone implied that Sir William's service in His Majesty's fleet was nothing to be proud of and her sharp gaze appraised him for signs that the wind and weather had coarsened his appearance. Sir William smiled back, not one whit discomposed.

'Just so, ma'am! I served during the recent American Wars, but am returned home now that the conflict is over.'

Lady St Auby sniffed. She was not conversant with Anglo-American diplomatic relations, but she knew a race of ungrateful upstarts when she heard of them. 'Those jumped-up Yankees! I trust our own fleet put them properly in their place, sir!'

'Indeed not, ma'am!' Sir William's smile was rueful. He looked as though he was enjoying himself immensely, Annabella thought. 'It grieves me to relate that the fledgling American navy has ships far faster than anything in His Majesty's service!'

'The *Constitution* is one of theirs, is it not?' Annabella said, suddenly. 'I read that it is a faster build of frigate than those in our own navy.' She saw Sir William's quizzical gaze upon her and flushed a little. 'I read about it in *The Times*,' she added apologetically, 'after the *Guerrière* was sunk by the Americans.'

'Most unsuitable,' Lady St Auby said frostily.

'Most commendable, ma'am,' Sir William said, blandly. 'An informed mind can never be anything but laudable.'

Lady St Auby glared at him.

'I see trouble for Britain from those big frigates from across the sea,' Sir William continued softly. Lady St Auby snorted again, glad to have the opportunity to take him to task.

'You are most unpatriotic, sir!' she declared. 'One imagines that our dear, dead Lord Nelson might have more faith in his own navy than you appear to do!'

There was a pregnant pause.

'It was Lord Nelson himself who said those words, ma'am,' Sir William said, gently. Annabella giggled, quite unable to help herself.

It was perhaps fortunate that Viscount Mundell chose that moment to come upon them, for Lady St Auby was flushing as red as a turkeycock.

'Boring the ladies with your naval tales, Will?' Mundell asked, in his lazy drawl.

Sir William grinned. 'As you see, Hugo! It is a bad habit of seafarers!'

'Then I shall feel no compunction in taking Mrs St Auby away to dance,' Mundell returned, with a smile for Annabella. 'Will you do me the honour, ma'am?'

And Annabella found herself swept into the set with a sudden conviction that life was taking a most unexpected turn.

Once Annabella was over her initial surprise, she found dancing with the Viscount to be an entirely pleasant experience, for he was so exceptionally good that he made the whole process seem quite effortless. She soon discovered that her dance steps, though rusty, came back to her easily enough and she acquitted herself well.

'Bravo, ma'am!' Mundell said at the end, when Annabella's cheeks were pink and her eyes bright with the exertion. 'You see how good it can be for you to escape from that monster of a mother-in-law!' He ignored Annabella's half-hearted protest, taking her arm and steering her through the crowd to a quiet corner. 'We had no idea that we should find you so in need of rescue!'

'We, sir?' Annabella said, confused.

'Why, yes, my friends and I!' Mundell smiled down at her. 'Will Weston is a particular friend of your brother-in-law, James Mullineaux, you know, and when Lady Mullineaux heard that we were all to be staying at Mundell for a while, she asked that we see how you were going on! I understand that the two of you have not met for a time?' Mundell raised an eyebrow. 'She asked us especially to seek you out.' He saw her astonishment and added kindly, 'Lord and

Lady Mullineaux would have been of the party were it not for the fact that they had no wish to be parted from Thomas and he is a little young to travel! But I know your sister is anxious to see you again!'

Annabella put her hand up to a head that was suddenly spinning. It seemed extraordinary that her own thoughts about seeing Alicia again should be echoed so soon and in a totally unexpected way. And it was even more amazing that her sister, who had no good reason to think of her with anything but dislike, should apparently be willing to give her another chance. Yet surely the Viscount could not be mistaken. She looked up at Mundell, a mixture of hope and disbelief in her eyes.

'Are you certain, sir? It seems most unlikely, if you will forgive me. Alicia and I...' She struggled, not wishing to go into the complicated details.

Mundell smiled again and Annabella was astounded by such unlooked-for kindness from such a man. 'Well, of course it is a matter for you to resolve with your sister, but I assure you that she is most concerned for the two of you to be friends!'

Annabella was struggling to assimilate all that she had so suddenly learned. Hope—real hope—had unexpectedly been put into her hands, and as she hesitated over it, Lady St Auby's voice rang out across the Assembly Rooms with bell-like clarity.

'...and of course, the Countess of Kilgaren is a *great* friend of Annabella's sister,' she was saying to a dowager in purple, 'and James Mullineaux and Mundell move in the same set, so it is not surprising that he should take her up...'

'Dear me,' Mundell said, with a slight shudder,

'what an overbearing woman! But I cut Will out just now for a dance with you,' he added, smiling a little mockingly at her, 'and at last I see him coming to redress the situation! Will!' He hailed his friend. 'It is unlike you to let me steal a march! I thought you were supposed to be a sound strategist!'

Sir William gave his boyish grin. 'I was engaging the enemy,' he said, with a nod in the direction of Lady St Auby. 'But I won out in the end, Hugo, for this next is the waltz, is it not? You will grant me this dance, Mrs St Auby?'

Annabella was beginning to enjoy herself a great deal. Far from lacking excitement, the ball was proving to be the event of the Taunton social calendar! Not only was she buoyed up with the hope of seeing Alicia again, but she now had the inestimable pleasure of the two most attractive men in the room vying for her attention. 'You do not take my acquiescence for granted, I hope, sir?' she asked, with just a hint of challenge.

Sir William's sleepy blue eyes widened slightly. 'Upon my word, no, ma'am! It would be a foolish thing to underestimate one's quarry! But on the other hand...' his arm was already about her waist and he had somehow drawn her into the waltz '...it is equally foolish to risk opposition! Forgive me for my lack of grace,' Sir William finished with mock apology. 'I am but a simple sailor, after all!'

Annabella cast him a look from under her lashes. 'Oh, no, sir, you are too hard on yourself! Scarcely *simple*, I feel!' And she heard him laugh in response.

Circling the floor in Sir William's arms was so exhilarating a feeling that Annabella was obliged to keep her gaze modestly lowered in order to prevent him from reading her mind. Just the proximity of his body made her feel quite light-headed and out of control. Francis had never inspired any feelings which could compare with this delightful but disturbing excitement.

'When did you start to read *The Times*, ma'am?' Sir William enquired, after one revolution of the floor.

Annabella almost jumped at the question. 'Oh!' She gathered her wits. 'Your pardon, sir, I was woolgathering! My father used to take all the papers. I read them avidly, perhaps because I travelled so little myself, and I knew his ships went all over the world, so I used to imagine them sailing to all the places I read about.'

'Yes, indeed, I came across some of Broseley's ships when I was stationed in the Indies,' Sir William said, and suddenly there was a certain grimness in his tone. Annabella felt herself blushing.

'I know...' She hesitated, constraint in her voice. 'He trafficked in slaves and arms and other unpalatable goods...he was not a pleasant man.'

'I imagine it must have been difficult for you...' Sir William's voice had softened as he looked down at her. Green eyes met blue for a moment. Annabella found herself on the verge of confiding. There was something about him that engendered a sense of kinship—that dangerous recognition again—and she knew it could be her undoing. After all, this man was a complete stranger. She knew nothing of him at all. She lowered her gaze.

'Much of the time, my father was from home, sir. I scarce knew him well. Then I married...' She shrugged a little uncomfortably, moving on quickly. 'Though we still lived in the same vicinity, I saw even less of him then. And, of course, he died some two years ago.'

'Broseley was expected to leave some considerable fortune, was he not?' Weston said thoughtfully. 'It might have…eased…your current situation, ma'am.'

Again there was that insidious feeling of understanding, a closeness that was drawing Annabella towards disclosure. She had never had a confidant and the temptation was enormous. But it was too dangerous to allow herself to rely on Sir William. She steeled herself against him.

'When my father died it would have been pleasant to be rich, I suppose, but not on the profits of such an ill-made fortune! But tell me a little of your own plans,' she changed the subject with determination. 'How will you spend your time now that you are home from the sea?'

Weston accepted this change of direction with easy grace, but not without giving her a searching look from those very blue eyes.

'Oh, I intend to settle in the countryside,' he said, with a smile, 'and become a farmer. It sounds mundane, I know, but the delights of the capital hold little interest for me. I fear I ran through all the pleasures of the Town in my salad days!'

'But do you feel you will be able to settle in one place for long?' Annabella asked, genuinely interested. 'After all, you have spent much time in travelling and must surely find the confines of one place a little restrictive?'

Sir William looked thoughtful. 'I cannot deny that

I shall always love the sea,' he said slowly, 'but I have my yacht if I take a fancy to go sailing again! Not so grand as the *Endeavour*, perhaps, but enough! And a man can tire of having no settled home!'

Annabella registered the reference to the yacht with some surprise. There was nothing in Sir William's attire to suggest a man of great consequence, and despite his title, she had assumed that he had earned a living from the navy rather than entering it by choice over necessity. But now that she considered him further, the signs were there. The black and white of his evening dress was almost austere, but nevertheless cut by a master. A diamond tiepin nestled in the snowy folds of his cravat, and there was a heavy gold signet ring on his right hand. Annabella suddenly felt self-conscious in her old clothes. How could she be mingling with this exotic crowd, with Weston, Mundell, and their friends? She was a provincial miss with no money and no town polish. She forgot her new-found confidence and shrank.

A slight frown entered Sir William's eyes as he sensed her withdrawal. 'Whatever can I have said, ma'am, to so disturb you? I can only apologise—'

Annabella shook her head slightly, confused by both his perception and her own reaction to him. It should not have mattered that she was so far beneath his interest, but yet it did. She was in terrible danger of allowing herself to believe she could enter this world of title and privilege and escape from the existence that Lady St Auby had made unbearable for her. But suppose she tried—and failed? If Alicia had no real interest in ending their estrangement, if Mundell had only been kind and would forget her the next day, if Will Weston was only amusing himself… Her fragile composure was suddenly at breaking point.

The music was ending and she was about to ask Sir William to escort her back to the St Aubys, when Lady Kilgaren came up to them. Annabella's heart sank even further. Caroline Kilgaren was reputed to be Alicia's closest friend, and if anyone would know the sordid details of the breach between the two sisters, it would be she.

'William, I have not had the chance to meet Mrs St Auby yet!' Lady Kilgaren had a warm smile for Annabella and a beguiling look for Sir William. She was tiny, small and fair as a pocket goddess, and Annabella could not see how anyone could resist her. 'Be a kind fellow and bring us both a glass of lemonade! Please!' She saw his lips twitch and added, 'And don't hurry back!'

Sir William bowed with exaggerated deference and strolled off towards the refreshment room, stopping for a word with Viscount Mundell on the way. Caroline turned back to Annabella, her blue eyes sparkling.

'Forgive me for interfering in that ill-bred way! The truth is that I wanted to meet you and I was afraid that you would be snapped up again by Lady St Auby before I had the chance! But now I see she is enjoying a coze with that evil old gossip Millicent Eddington-Buck, so we have a little time! Will you join me?' She gestured towards two rout chairs stationed in an alcove to their left.

Annabella gave in. There was something about Caroline Kilgaren which suggested that resistance was pointless, for she was both decisive and direct.

Caroline's shrewd blue eyes were appraising Annabella thoroughly, and she was suddenly very nervous.

'Forgive me for staring,' Caroline said frankly, with another of her warm smiles. 'In truth, you are very like your sister! The gentlemen have already noticed it!'

Annabella blushed. 'Oh, ma'am, if I had a quarter of Alicia's style!'

'It's only clothes,' Caroline said practically. 'You have the basis of the rest already, and town polish can always be acquired! But you looked quite apprehensive when I came up, poor child,' she added consolingly, making Annabella feel about seventeen. 'I only wanted to tell you that Mundell told me he had mentioned Alicia to you, and it is quite true that she wishes to see you again above all things!' She touched Annabella's hand briefly. 'I know that the two of you parted on bad terms, but Alicia has always thought that there must be more to the case than she knew.'

Lady Kilgaren watched shrewdly as the colour came into Annabella's face and fled as swiftly. The Annabella St Auby she had met and of whom both Will Weston and Hugo Mundell had spoken that evening was a far cry from the avaricious and ill-bred girl who had so alienated Alicia Mullineaux. So Alicia had guessed correctly when she had thought that there was much more to the tale than the simple explanation that Annabella had grown up in Bertram Broseley's own image.

'I should tell you, ma'am—' Annabella drew breath to explain.

'No.' Caroline put up a hand. 'If you wish to confide in me I should be honoured, but you need tell me nothing you do not want! Take a little time; think about it. I only wished you to know that Alicia is quite anxious to see you—indeed, she will be writing to you soon! There now—' she had seen Annabella's eyes fill with tears '—there is no need to be sad!'

'You are all kindness, ma'am,' Annabella said, brushing the tears away before anyone had time to see them. 'If you only knew how much I have wanted to make contact with my sister—'

'We will accomplish it!' Caroline said, with a smile. 'Now—'

'Caro!' Marcus Kilgaren was standing before them with two glasses of lemonade. 'Will gave me these for you, though I doubt you really wanted them!' He bowed to Annabella, a twinkle in his eye. 'How do you do, Mrs St Auby? Sir William was about to come to rescue you, but I fear he is too much in awe of Caroline to dare!'

'Stuff and nonsense!' Caroline said, getting to her feet. 'Will Weston has vanquished greater enemies than I!'

'But none more determined, my love,' Marcus said cheerfully. 'Come and dance with me, and let the poor fellow take your place here. He is languishing across the room and quite cast down!'

It was impossible to imagine Sir William in the manner Marcus described, Annabella thought, and sure enough, when she turned to scan the ballroom she saw him dancing with Charlotte Mundell. It was enough to prompt a prickle of jealousy for which Annabella took herself severely to task. She had only met Sir William that evening, after all, and hardly had a right to feel resentful if he paid attention to another woman. She herself was hardly without admirers, anyway, for as Marcus took Caroline off to dance the cotillion, Viscount Mundell took Caroline's seat and chatted to Annabella about this and that in a manner as entertaining as it was inconsequential.

'I fear I must oust you again, Hugo,' Sir William said some ten minutes later, coming upon them as Annabella was laughing at some anecdote Mundell was telling her about Sir Frederick St Auby's exploits on the hunting field. 'Miss Hurst assures me that she is promised to you for this dance, and she is unlikely to forgive you if you slight her!'

Mundell gave his friend a measuring look, but Weston was completely impassive. He got to his feet with every evidence of reluctance.

'I do not believe you for a moment, William,' Mundell said evenly. 'Your motives are transparent! However, I will humour you this once! Your servant, Mrs St Auby!'

He got up and Sir William took his seat with alacrity. Annabella considered him thoughtfully, wondering how she could ever have dismissed him as ordinary. Beneath that air of careless indolence was an assurance and determination which were quite formidable. He was quite out of her league and she should not tangle with him. But then, Mundell's set were all a danger to her in their way. The glittering, privileged world of the aristocracy was not for her and though they might appear to see her as a new diversion, she should not depend on being part of their circle. The misery that would be occasioned when they dropped her and she was forced to retreat to her circumscribed life would be quite intolerable.

'You look quite severe, Mrs St Auby,' Sir William observed lazily. 'Can it be that you are a secret puritan? Are you dismissing us all as a group of wastrels out for our own pleasure?'

Annabella smiled. 'I am sure that I derive enjoyment from a ball as much as most,' she allowed, 'but look over there, sir— why, it is well nigh disgraceful!'

Sir William followed her gaze to where no less than four hopeful young ladies had cornered Viscount Mundell and were fluttering their lashes and their fans at him, pouting prettily, hanging on his every word. Further down the room, Sir Thomas Oakston was busy flattering Miss Mundell, whilst his wife complimented Miss Hurst on her toilette.

'It is the way of the world,' Sir William said laconically. 'Everyone wishes to befriend the wealthy!'

'So you are as much a cynic as I, sir!' Annabella was still laughing as he pulled her to her feet.

'Come and dance with me, Mrs St Auby,' Sir William said, by way of reply. 'I need you to protect me from these predatory women!'

Annabella could hardly deny that she took pleasure in dancing with him. It would have been strange indeed for her to have emerged from the seclusion of the St Auby's manor to be swept up into the excitement of Mundell's orbit without enjoying it. And Sir William's evident pleasure in her company was heady as a draught of wine. She floated through the dance, which was the last of the evening, and thanked him somewhat incoherently at the end.

'It has been a pleasure, Mrs St Auby.' Sir William smiled down into her eyes. 'May I call on you tomorrow?' The words were conventional but there was something in his expression which made her shiver a little, in an entirely pleasurable way.

'If you wish, sir...'

'Thank you.' His smile was devastating, she thought weakly. He bowed and kissed her hand, and left Annabella feeling as shaken as when they had first met.

Once in the privacy of the carriage on the homeward journey, Lady St Auby was vitriolic.

'Scheming, conniving, *wicked* girl! You think that Mundell and his friends will take you up? You are deluding yourself, my girl! They'll be laughing at you now for a country dowd! And telling your precious sister what a frump you are!'

Lady St Auby knew how to wound. Withdrawing once more into herself, Annabella concluded that it was indeed unlikely that Sir William Weston was doing anything other than amusing himself at her expense. She would do best to forget the evening and her brief enjoyment, forget the heady delight of waltzing in his arms, for he would most certainly not call upon her on the morrow and to rely upon him doing so would only leave her more disappointed in the end.

Chapter Two

'There's a gentleman to see you, ma'am.' The slovenly maid, whom Lady St Auby employed because they were too poor to have a butler, looked at Annabella with some curiosity. Mrs Francis had never had an admirer like this before—there had been Captain Jeffries, of course, but everyone knew he was no gentleman, and not averse to pinching the maids' bottoms when the mistress's back was turned as well! But this gentleman was Quality and no mistake.

Annabella pricked her finger on her needle and almost spilt a drop of blood on her embroidery. It would have made little difference had she spoilt it, for her skill was small and the uneven petals of the rose she had just completed were too poor to be displayed. Needlework was not one of her talents. She put the embroidery frame to one side and got to her feet.

So he had come after all! In the cold light of day, she had become even more convinced that Sir William had only been trifling with her, for what interest could he possibly have in furthering their acquaintance? The glittering excitement of the previous night seemed like a flimsy dream that would fade if she tried to grasp it. Yet here he was. Unless—perhaps it was only Jeffries, anxious to press her further, certain she would succumb… She turned to question the maid on the gentleman's identity, but the girl had already gone back downstairs.

Annabella ran to check her appearance in the mirror and gave a silent sigh. The dress of ruby red looked black in the dark little rooms of the St Auby townhouse, and even Annabella could see the patches where the material had faded and worn. Today she had tied her hair up in a long plait, despairing of ever being able to achieve the simple elegance of the modes she saw in the old copies of *The Fashions of London and Paris*, which were passed on by one of Lady St Auby's friends. Still, she had kept him waiting long enough. Her heart beating faster, Annabella made her way down the narrow stair.

Sir William Weston was waiting in the drawing-room, his height making him appear to dominate the poky, low-ceilinged chamber. Today he was wearing a coat of navy blue superfine which appeared almost stark in its simplicity, but again, it had the simple refinement of a master's cut. He wore buff pantaloons and Hessians, both of which were elegant without being dandified, and his white cravat was once again arranged in complicated folds. He looked, Annabella thought dazedly, rather too disturbingly attractive. And when he smiled at her…

He crossed the room in two strides and took her hand in his. 'Mrs St Auby! What a pleasure to see you again, ma'am! I hope that last evening has not tired you too much?'

'Thank you, sir, I am quite well,' Annabella said, smiling a little at the thought that she might not be robust enough to survive a ball. No doubt the young ladies Sir William knew would be exhausted with the effort. But then, they could stay in bed until midday and would not be required to be up at first light to scour the scullery...

'Then I wondered if you would care to join me for a drive in the country? It is a perfect day for it and my curricle is outside. We could stop for tea at Mundell Hall on the way back.'

It sounded a tempting plan, and Annabella soon found herself donning her pelisse and going out to the curricle. Even had it not been Sir William who was inviting her, the simple pleasure of escaping from the dark house would have been enough.

She paused to admire the matched bays which Sir William had in his team, for they were prime horse-flesh and suggested that he was a notable whip. The curricle, with its elegantly expensive lines, was creating quite a stir. Annabella noticed with interest that Sir William had chosen not to bring a groom and that a street urchin was eagerly holding the horses' reins for love rather than the coin Sir William now flicked to him as they set off.

'You are clearly knowledgeable about horses, ma'am,' Sir William commented when they had negotiated the busy streets of the town and were tooling along in the open country. 'Do you ride?'

'Oh, I used to!' As soon as she was out in the open air and feeling the warm sun and cooling breeze, Annabella remembered with a pang of nostalgia how she had enjoyed her rides about her father's estate. 'I rode a great deal before my marriage,' she said, 'and Sir Frederick used to keep a fine stable before the expense became prohibitive. I must confess that it is a luxury I miss!'

Sir William smiled at her enthusiasm. 'Perhaps we could go riding next time,' he said pleasantly, and the words echoed in Annabella's head: *Next time...*

So he planned to seek her out again, did he? A delicious little smile curved her lips at the thought. Having her company sought by so attractive a man was a new experience for her and one which was entirely delightful. She watched his hands, skilful on the reins, and repressed a little shiver.

'Did you enjoy the ball last night?' Sir William enquired neutrally, after a slight pause.

'Well, yes...I suppose so...' Annabella's reply sounded less certain than she had intended, and he gave her a quizzical look.

'You do not sound very sure, ma'am! Are dances and assemblies not to your taste? But surely I remember you saying that you liked them...'

'Oh, no, I enjoy them very much!' Annabella laughed. 'Not that I have been to so very many, sir! I only hesitated because I do not believe that Lady St Auby found the evening agreeable, which makes matters a little difficult...' She sighed, remembering Lady St Auby's vicious diatribe on the way home. She had managed to convince Annabella not only that Mundell and his set were laughing at her expense, but also that Alicia had never had any real intention of ending their estrangement.

'I realised last night how difficult it must be for you in such a household,' Sir William observed thoughtfully. 'Have you not considered the possibility of living elsewhere, ma'am?'

It was a rather impertinent question from a mere acquaintance, Annabella thought, but then he was a very direct man. She hesitated, conscious that almost anything she said about her current situation, her marriage, her father or her relationship with Alicia would lead her into difficult waters. She was unsure how far she could prevaricate with Sir William Weston—he seemed very determined.

'I have considered it,' she said carefully, 'but there are difficulties. It is no secret that my father left me very little money and my husband none at all. And I have no wish to impose on my sister, who, I am sure you are aware, sir, has reason to dislike me!' She gave him a defiant look. 'I have been thinking lately that the only solution is for me to earn a living!'

'Perhaps you have considered becoming a governess?' Sir William murmured, his voice completely bland. Annabella gave him a quick look, but could not tell if he was laughing at her. His gaze was fixed on the road and there was not even a telltale hint of a smile about that firm mouth. She looked away hastily.

'I have thought of it, but reluctantly discounted the idea, sir.'

'Oh, dear, why was that?'

Now she was sure that he was making fun of her. 'I am not bookish enough!' she snapped. 'I could hardly expect to be paid to teach a child those learned facts that I had not seen fit to acquire myself!'

Sir William's lips twitched. 'Was your education neglected then, Mrs St Auby?'

'No, sir, by good fortune I had a number of excellent governesses.' Annabella strove to be fair. 'It was my own attitude that was at fault. I had no patience with my teachers and what they tried to instil in me. So…'

'So, no governess post,' Sir William finished for her, one dark brow raised. 'A pity, but it would not have served. You are too young and,' he added under his breath, 'devilishly pretty besides!'

Annabella was startled. 'I beg your pardon, sir!'

Sir William grinned at her. 'I was merely pointing out that your relative youth and your appearance made it an unsuitable occupation for you! There will always be impressionable sons—or even fathers!— who would try to lead you astray!'

Annabella blushed. She hurried on to try to cover her confusion. 'But then I hit on a plan, sir!'

'Your resourcefulness is most impressive, ma'am,' Sir William commented, bland once more. Annabella shot him a darkling look.

'You are funning me, I know, sir, but I am quite in earnest! I intend to set up a circulating library!'

The horses swerved slightly as Sir William inadvertently pulled the rein, a terrible solecism for such an accomplished whip. 'You amaze me, ma'am,' he said politely. 'How do you propose to do such a thing?'

'Well, I have heard that Mr Lane, the proprietor of the Minerva Press, will set anyone up in a circulating library who wishes it,' Annabella said artlessly. 'And he is so very rich that I believe there must be a living in it! At the library in Castle Street they charge a subscription of a whole guinea to borrow the best books,' she added thoughtfully, 'but I have never been able to afford that!'

'As a business venture it would seem to have certain merits,' Sir William agreed. 'But where will you establish your library, Mrs St Auby? A seaside town or fashionable watering place might be the best. I suppose your father did not leave you any property that might be of use?'

Annabella shook her head. 'He left plenty of property, but all is sold to pay his debts,' she admitted. 'Why, the lawyers are still trying to disentangle his affairs! But I have no hope that there will be anything suitable. That is the only flaw in my plan.'

'Hmm, a pity.' Sir William had slowed the horses as they sped through a picturesque village. 'It seemed an excellent plan in all other particulars. But there are alternatives, of course! You might marry again, perhaps?'

'I doubt that, sir.' Annabella sounded subdued. They were back on dangerous ground.

Sir William allowed the curricle to slow down, and half turned towards her. 'You seem very certain, ma'am! How is it possible to tell what the future holds?'

'It is not, of course,' Annabella allowed, permitting herself to meet those perceptive blue eyes for a brief moment. 'But I do not think…'

'Perhaps,' Sir William said thoughtfully, 'when one has been married happily once, it is difficult to imagine such good fortune occurring again.'

'I imagine that might be so.' The sun went behind

a cloud. Annabella shivered. 'And the reverse might also be true.'

'You mean that having been married unhappily, one might not wish to risk such a situation again?' Sir William pursued. 'Yet your sister, having been so unfortunate in the past, has now found true happiness as a result of being prepared to take that risk.'

'I am very glad that Alicia is happy now,' Annabella said sincerely, swallowing a lump in her throat and looking fixedly at the horizon.

'Yes, having been estranged from James for so long, and enduring that appalling scandal of her forced marriage, she deserves her current good fortune.' Sir William took his eyes off the road to consider Annabella's averted face thoughtfully.

'And you, Mrs St Auby, were you more fortunate than your sister in your dealings with your father? Did he not have an arranged match designed for you too?'

Annabella was taken by surprise. She had a sudden, vivid flash of memory—her father, bright red with rage, storming at her when she had refused to marry the man he had chosen for her. She had had Alicia's example to learn from, after all, and had been determined not to succumb. But though Bertram Broseley had not succeeded in marrying her off, he had managed to poison her life anyway. She pressed her hands together, suddenly distressed.

'Must we speak of such matters, sir? The circumstances surrounding my marriage cannot be of any interest to you, I am sure—'

'On the contrary, ma'am,' Sir William's tone was inflexible. 'It interests me considerably! What happens to one sister can, after all, repeat itself with another! And I have the strangest feeling that your apparent love match with Francis St Auby was no such thing!'

Annabella gasped. His effrontery in speaking of such matters was beyond anything she had experienced or knew how to deal with. No mere acquaintance should speak so, and certainly no gentleman should broach such a topic, particularly when she had shown her own disinclination to discuss the matter!

'Upon my word, sir,' she gasped, 'you are most persistent! And you presume too much! Your comments are impertinent in the extreme! Kindly stop this curricle and take me back now!' She looked around and realised that she had not the first idea where they were, for she had been quite engrossed in their conversation.

The flat country of the Somerset Levels stretched around them as far as the eye could see. Verdant green fields lined with thick hedgerows and edged with water-filled dykes stretched into the distance, empty of habitation. Her half-formed idea of stepping down and marching off in high dudgeon died a death. It would be impractical. She would look foolish. Worse, she would be lost. She looked across at Sir William, who was obeying her instruction and was bringing the curricle to a halt in the middle of the road. He did not look in the least abashed.

'My friends are always telling me that I have no decorum,' he said regretfully. 'It is a great trial to me!'

Annabella did not believe him. 'A great trial to everyone else, rather!' she snapped. 'I wonder that your friends bear with you!'

The ghost of a smile touched Sir William's mouth. 'I do believe you have a temper to rival your sister's, Mrs St Auby,' he said admiringly. 'She has always had a swift way of administering a set-down!' The amusement in his sleepy gaze only served to infuriate Annabella all the more. Despite her widowed state she was very young and inexperienced, and had no idea how to handle a man like this. And she did indeed have a temper which was slow to kindle but red-hot once aroused.

'Do I take it then, sir, that you actually require a response to your impertinent and intrusive question?' she asked coldly.

'Certainly,' Sir William responded, with equal coolness. 'That is why I asked the question! I shall not take you back otherwise!'

Bright flags of colour flew in Annabella's cheeks at this effrontery.

'Very well, sir! You will have your answer! No doubt it will give you immense gratification to know that your suspicions are well founded! I married Francis St Auby to escape my father's plans for me, for he did indeed have a suitor in mind! There was a business associate of his, a man of similar stamp to Alicia's first husband, albeit a little younger and a little less fat—and no doubt likely to live longer! Everyone thought that I loved Francis, but the truth is that I bought my husband with the promise of my fortune, and I did it simply to run away from the alternative! I had too much pride to let people see that my marriage was a sham, but I lived with that truth for the whole of my married life!' She stopped,

her eyes bright with angry animation, her cheeks a
vivid, becoming pink.

There was a silence. 'It was uncivil of me to push
you so far, ma'am,' Sir William said, still watching
her intently, 'but I find I cannot regret it. Do you wish
to tell me more?'

Annabella sat staring at him. She was astonished
to find that she did indeed want to tell him more: the
truth about her marriage, her estrangement from Alicia, the indignities of her life in the St Auby household—words jostled with each other in her head, willing her to spill them out and tell him everything—
but the conventional part of her was utterly appalled
at her behaviour. One instinct was prompting her to
let the whole sorry story tumble out with the artless
confidence of a child, but the self-control she had
learned in a hard school was asking her how she could
be so foolish as to trust a complete stranger. And as
she stared at him in bafflement, she heard Sir William
swear under his breath and pick up the reins, making
to turn the horses.

'No, wait!' Annabella put a hand on his arm, suddenly desperate not to lose the opportunity of the moment.

'There is a mail coach coming, Mrs St Auby,' Sir
William said abruptly. 'I cannot leave the curricle in
the middle of the road!'

Annabella's face flamed. She shrank back into the
corner of her seat, trying to make herself as small as
possible as Sir William turned the curricle neatly and
pulled over to the side of the road as the posthorn
blared. The coach thundered past, throwing up the
choking dust in its path, and they were left in silence.

The moment for confidences was gone. Suddenly it did not seem such a beautiful day.

'I am sorry,' Annabella said hesitantly, uncertain what the apology was for, but moved to make it anyway. She saw the tense lines of Sir William's face ease a little.

'Not at all, ma'am. You have nothing with which to reproach yourself.' He smiled reassuringly and took her hand in a warm clasp, which had a far from reassuring effect. Annabella felt her pulse rate increase. 'I forgot your relative youth,' Sir William continued, 'and I am trying to go too far, too fast, which is not a mistake I make often! Now—' his tone changed '—shall we take tea at Mundell, or do you prefer to go straight back to Taunton?'

Annabella, who had not understood his comment, was tempted to go straight home to nurse her humiliation, but then found herself torn by the wish to prolong her time in Sir William's company. She frowned.

'Tea at Mundell would be very nice,' she ventured.

'Very well.' There was nothing but a brisk agreement in his voice. Annabella's fragile confidence shrivelled a little more. Oh, how could she have acted like such a little ninny? She shuddered as she remembered her ingenuous comments about starting the circulating library. How could she have imagined that such a man, with his wide and sophisticated experience of the world, would have the slightest interest in her parochial plans? And then, how could she have overreacted so when he had asked her about her marriage to Francis? She had about as much notion of how to go on as a five-year-old!

* * *

As she sat silently beside him, Sir William Weston was also thinking about his conversation with Annabella, though perhaps in terms that would have surprised her. In common with all their friends, he had heard of Alicia Mullineaux's estrangement from her sister and the widely accepted view that Annabella had more of her grasping, materialistic father in her than was at all acceptable. He had been both surprised and intrigued to find her so inexperienced and unspoilt, when he had expected to meet a brass-faced harpy, old beyond her years. He had quickly seen the miserable torment caused by Lady St Auby, and had been determined to help Annabella if he could. That his motives sprang from something other than altruism, he was prepared to admit at once, for he had no time for self-delusion. A man of action, accustomed to rapidly sum up a situation and make a decision, he had known almost immediately that he would pursue his interest in Annabella St Auby.

He glanced sideways at her averted face, her expression unreadable in the shadow cast by her bonnet's brim. She was deliberately keeping her head tilted away from him, as though embarrassed by their recent exchange. Sir William smiled to himself a little, wondering if she had any idea how desirable she looked, how that air of innocent aloofness was at once both part innocent and part alluring. He was tempted to stop and kiss her, partly to see how she would react, but mostly just for the pleasure of feeling that sweet, pink mouth beneath his own... They had reached the gates of Mundell Hall. Will Weston gave himself a mental shake and concentrated hard on the complicated business of driving the curricle through the gateway with inch-perfect precision.

When Annabella saw Viscount Mundell's guests taking tea beneath a huge tented pavilion on the green lawns, she almost regretted the impulse that had led her to agree to Sir William's suggestion. Lord and Lady Wallace were not present, but the rest of Mundell's guests of the previous night were there, and looking so privileged, so immaculately *ton*nish, that Annabella felt both drab and dusty.

'Courage, Mrs St Auby!' Sir William had taken her elbow and was giving her an encouraging smile. 'You look delightful, you are charming company and—they are really quite friendly, you know!'

Annabella smiled despite herself. Strange, she thought, that her discomfort appeared to have communicated itself almost immediately to this most enigmatic of men. Even stranger to her was the fact that he was concerned enough to wish to reassure her. Her heart lightened a little.

They crossed the lawn to join the party, and Annabella immediately saw the scornful amusement in Miss Hurst's eyes as she surveyed the worn red dress and the unsophisticated plait. Miss Hurst herself was dressed in crisp pink and white candystripe, her hair an artful creation of tangled curls. Before her on the table was a sketching pad showing a water-colour drawing of the gardens and the distant church spire. It was quite beautiful. But one gift Miss Hurst lacked was the gift of generosity, and as Annabella and Sir William reached them, she drew her chair very carefully towards Miss Mundell, effectively excluding

Annabella from the circle. It was Caroline Kilgaren who moved to make room for her at the table.

'Sir William!' Miss Hurst cooed, as though she had just seen them for the first time. 'Pray come and sit by me! We have been desolate without your company!' And she gave him a melting look through her eyelashes. Sir William seemed unmoved, but he sat down next to her all the same. So that was how the land lay, Annabella thought. A small spark of rebelliousness caught in her and began to burn.

More tea was brought and poured.

'Did you enjoy your drive?' Caroline Kilgaren enquired, with a friendly smile. 'You are very favoured, you know, for Sir William is accounted a notable whip, and seldom takes anybody up! And I imagine this countryside is beautiful to drive through—'

Before Annabella could answer, Miss Hurst had intervened, yawning ostentatiously. 'Lud, but the country is so slow! Bath and Cheltenham may be tolerable, I suppose, but Taunton! Why, did you see the clothes last night?' Her malicious brown eyes dwelt on Annabella's faded red dress again. 'I declare, some of those coats last night cannot have been fashionable since my father's day! And as for country manners, did you hear the way Sir Thomas Oakston addressed us last night? Not an ounce of finesse—'

'I'm surprised you stay in the country so long if you dislike it, Ermina,' Sir William observed, in a lazy drawl. His gaze moved from Miss Hurst to Viscount Mundell and paused thoughtfully. Miss Hurst reddened unattractively. Annabella began to wonder if Sir William had in fact told the truth when he had said that his friends found it hard to bear with him.

'Oh, Sir William, how you do tease!' Miss Hurst had decided to be arch. 'But I shall punish you later! A duel at the butts, perhaps?'

The archery butts were set some distance away across the lawn, and a bow was propped up behind Miss Hurst's chair. Another of her accomplishments, Annabella thought, with a private smile, surprised to find that the evidence of Miss Hurst's achievements was starting to amuse her rather than make her feel inadequate. Sir William picked up the sketching pad and viewed it pensively.

'This is exquisite, Charlotte,' he said to Miss Mundell. 'Should Hugo ever fall on hard times, you will be able to keep him through your artist's skill!'

Miss Mundell blushed and disclaimed whilst Miss Hurst flounced, disliking the attention of the group being distracted from her. She turned to Annabella.

'Do you have any skill with the bow, Mrs St Auby?'

Annabella shook her head slowly, her mouth full of plum cake. For a moment she was tempted to speak with her mouth full and display her deplorable country manners.

'I regret I do not, Miss Hurst!'

'A pity!' The brown eyes were sharp now. 'But perhaps you have other accomplishments? Your sister, Lady Mullineaux, plays the piano exquisitely. Do you have the same talent?'

Annabella was beginning to feel like a scientific specimen, but was determined not to let this fashion-plate intimidate her. All Miss Hurst's conversation seemed aimed at disparagement.

'I fear I do not play well,' she said solemnly, ignoring the fact that she had a very pretty singing voice and could accompany herself perfectly well. 'I have no accomplishments, Miss Hurst—I have no skill with a needle and I draw very ill.'

Miss Hurst, missing the look of covert amusement Will Weston exchanged with Marcus Kilgaren, looked scandalised. 'My dear Mrs St Auby! But then I dare say such accomplishments are not regarded in your circle! More commercial pursuits—' she put just the right hint of doubt into her tone '—must be valued higher!'

'Oh, indeed, ma'am!' Annabella was all sweetness now. 'My father taught me how to barter at an early age! And I can estimate the value of a cargo of sugar cane—' She broke off, seeing Sir William's bright gaze resting upon her thoughtfully.

'Unusual talents are so much more interesting, are they not?' Marcus Kilgaren came to Annabella's rescue. 'Why, Caro is a case in point!' He smiled across the table at his wife. 'Her father was a historian who did not hold with the notion that females should be beautiful but witless. Recognising Caroline's potential and—'

'And realising her brother Charles's lack of it,' Mundell put in dryly, to general laughter.

'He taught her himself,' Marcus finished. 'Caro now has an encyclopaedic knowledge of medieval architecture which few could match!'

'Have you visited Stogursey Church, Mrs St Auby?' Caroline Kilgaren asked, leaning forward eagerly. 'It is a very fine example of—'

Miss Hurst yawned again. 'I fear my father never instilled in me anything so fascinating,' she inter-

rupted, with a wearisome look that robbed the words
of any sincerity. 'He considered that skill in music,
needlework and drawing were the true measure of an
educated woman!' She smiled complacently. 'I am
happy to feel that I have not disappointed him!'

Annabella was startled to discover in herself a
strong temptation to empty the contents of the teapot
over Miss Hurst's perfectly coiffed head. She saw
Marcus Kilgaren turn away to hide a grin, then Mundell said coolly,

'Surely, Miss Hurst, you would include gracious
conversation and an informed mind on your list of
prerequisites?'

'Oh, the art of conversation, perhaps!' Miss Hurst
waved one white hand, as if to suggest that she had
a natural talent that required no practice. 'And an informed mind, as long as one did not have to study
too hard…such bookishness is not at all attractive!
Lud, I do not believe I have picked up a book from
one month end to the next!'

Annabella thought that she heard Caroline Kilgaren
snort with disgust. Her gaze moved on to Miss Mundell, whose head was bent over precisely the type of
embroidery that would win Miss Hurst's praise.
Where Miss Hurst was surprisingly opinionated for
her years, Miss Mundell was silent and in obvious
awe of her friend. She had said very little, apart from
a subdued greeting and her confused disclaimer over
Sir William's compliment, and appeared to be a fashionable cipher. Annabella guessed that both young
women were close to her own age, but seldom had
she felt she had less in common with her contemporaries.

Conversation around the table became general again. Caroline Kilgaren turned back to Annabella.

'Mrs St Auby,' she said in an undertone, 'since our conversation last night I have become even more concerned to help you heal the breach with Alicia. I considered writing to her at once, but wondered whether you would prefer to do so yourself? What do you think?'

Annabella leant forward impulsively. 'Oh, Lady Kilgaren, I would so like to do so! But I do not know how to explain matters to her—there's the rub! Would you…could I tell you the story, and ask you to advise me?'

Caroline smiled. 'Of course—if you truly wish it!' She stood up. 'Have you finished your tea? Then you must come for a stroll in the gardens with me. The rose borders are accounted particularly fine, and should not be missed!'

Sir William had been watching them with a particularly intent look in those deceptively calm blue eyes. Now he turned and engaged Miss Hurst in conversation at the precise moment that she was about to invite herself to join the party. Caroline slipped her arm through Annabella's, and steered her away across the lawn.

The gardens at Mundell were indeed very fine, Annabella thought, for the rich green lawns were dotted with tall, shady trees and ornamental shrubs, whilst the flower borders were a riot of colour on this summer afternoon. They chose a bench in the shade of a huge oak tree, and Caroline turned to Annabella with a smile.

'So how can I help you, my dear? How did this sad estrangement come about?'

Annabella sighed. 'I never knew Alicia very well,' she said. 'You are no doubt aware that she is seven years older than I, and when I was a child she was away at school, and then she went to London for her Season and...' her eyes dropped from Caroline's kind blue ones '...our father forced that hateful match with George Carberry! I know that she wrote to me several times after Carberry died, but our father would never let me see the letters. I believe he threw them away unanswered, or returned them. I once saw one on the hall table when one of the maids had accidentally left it lying there. I was about to open it when he snatched it from my hand and sent me away to my room. I would have written to her myself if I could, but I could not find her direction!'

'Alicia wondered if that was the case,' Caroline said calmly. 'I think she realised that that was none of your doing. But then you met again, did you not, a couple of years ago? I understood that your father indicated to Alicia that you would like a London Season under her aegis?'

'Yes, but it was not at all as Alicia might have imagined!' Annabella's anguished green eyes met Caroline's. 'I discovered that our father had used me to bring her to Greyrigg, spinning the tale about a Season as bait! In truth, what he really wanted was to entrap her in his business dealings again, or force her into a second marriage! But I swear that I did not know that until the very day of her visit!' She shook her head. 'He never confided in me, you see, barely spoke to me at all from one week to the next, if the truth be told! Oh, he thought he knew me, thought that I was like him because I kept quiet and always agreed with him on the rare occasions he did tell me a little of his plans! But I knew nothing of his designs for Alicia, I swear it!'

Caroline was frowning. 'I believe you, but—' She broke off and started again. 'Forgive me, but I think Alicia believed you were party to his plans because you seemed so at ease with him, so complaisant.' Caroline looked uncomfortable. 'The way she described your behaviour—'

'Oh, I can well imagine what she said!' But Annabella's bitterness was directed against herself, not her sister. 'I played a marvellous part, you see, Lady Kilgaren. I was so mercenary, so insincere! I modelled myself on Lady Grey, my future sister-in-law, and she is the most affected creature I know!' Despite herself she gave a little giggle. 'Oh, I was dreadful! My conversation was larded with 'la' and 'lud' and I am sure I gave my sister a complete disgust for me! It fooled our father, who knew me too little to realise it was all pretence! He just thought that I was jealous of her.'

She looked up and met Caroline's look directly. 'And so I was, in truth! Alicia is so elegant, so assured, so much as I would wish to be! But that's nothing to the purpose! All the time I was waiting for my chance to warn Alicia without alerting our father's suspicions, but it was hopeless! He would not leave me alone with her and he had already threatened that if I did not aid his plans he would punish me—' She broke off, closing her eyes briefly for a moment. 'In any event, Alicia did not need my help! But, of

course, she left Greyrigg believing me to have con-
nived at his plotting.'

There was a silence. A dove began to coo in the
branches above their heads. It was cool in the leafy
shade. 'I am so sorry,' Caroline said softly. 'It must
have been intolerably frustrating for you. And at your
wedding,' she prompted gently, 'no doubt you had
little chance to talk to her then...'

Annabella shook her head dolefully. 'Oh, no, I
could not!' This was difficult, for it entailed telling
something of her reasons for marrying Francis, and
after her outburst to Sir William she was disinclined
to discuss the painful details again.

'There are very few opportunities for real discussion at a wedding,' she said truthfully, 'particularly
one's own! Besides...' she smiled a little, remembering how James Mullineaux had made such a determined attempt to monopolise Alicia that day '...Ali-
cia had matters of her own to divert her! James was
very particular in his attentions!'

Caroline was surprised that Annabella had noticed
that, for Alicia's description of her sister's behaviour
at the wedding had not suggested that Annabella was
anything other than a self-absorbed flirt. She eyed her
more closely. As she had suspected, there was far
more to this than was at first apparent, although she
could understand Annabella's reluctance to tell her
the whole and awaken unhappy memories.

'And when Alicia came to see you after your father
had died,' Caroline said, again gently persistent, 'you
still could not tell her the truth about your relationship
with him? I realise that Alicia was deeply unhappy at
the time because she thought that she had lost James,

so that may have influenced her feelings, but she told me that…' she paused unhappily '…oh dear, this is so difficult, for I see that there must have been a grave misunderstanding here! Alicia thought that you were…that you had an interest—' It was unusual to see Caroline Kilgaren lost for words, and Annabella came to her aid.

'She thought me mercenary and vulgar, and only interested in her fortune!' she finished for her.

Caroline was so startled that she forgot to be embarrassed. 'My word! You have much of both your grandmother and Alicia in you!'

Annabella laughed. 'I do apologise if my plain speaking offends you, Lady Kilgaren, but there is no point in beating about the bush!'

But Caroline was laughing too. 'No, indeed! My dear Annabella—I may call you Annabella, may I not?—pray do not apologise! As you say, it is so much easier to sort matters out if one is frank! I was only taken aback because you sounded like old Lady Stansfield! But—' she sobered '—since a description of you as vulgar and mercenary is fair and far out, you must tell me how such a misunderstanding occurred!'

Annabella's smile faded. 'Oh, it was not so inaccurate,' she said with constraint. 'You should know, Lady Kilgaren, that Francis—my husband—married me for my money, and when my father left me virtually penniless he was not best pleased. Then Alicia came to visit us and I think he could not bear to look at her and think of all her fortune. His insulting questions about her wealth and his obvious resentment that she had so much when I had inherited so little must have given her a disgust of us both—I tried to smooth matters over, but then I only angered him.' She bit her lip. No need to tell Caroline of the unpleasant scene where Francis had threatened to beat her if she did not do as he said. 'He said that I should have a thought to secure our future so, of course, I asked Alicia a little about her plans, which made it look as though I had an eye on inheriting her money. It was all profoundly uncomfortable and I was so mortified that, when Francis died, I did not dare approach Alicia for very shame!' She shrugged her slim shoulders. 'And there it is—a sorry tale indeed!' She gave a watery smile. 'I thank you for bearing with my confessions!'

Caroline patted her hand. 'Thank you for confiding the tale in me.' Her blue eyes were very kind. 'I had no notion that your marriage was anything other than a love-match. May I be even more impertinent and ask how that came about?'

Annabella fixed her gaze on a fat bumble bee buzzing drunkenly in the rose border. Even now, it was distressing to describe the events leading up to her marriage and their painful consequences.

'My father had a suitor in mind for me, in much the same way as he had done for Alicia,' she said haltingly. 'I imagine that you, more than most, know a little of how that might be, Lady Kilgaren. I…found I could not accept his choice, so I looked around for a means of escape and Francis came to mind. I knew that he needed to marry money.' The colour had come into her cheeks and she could no longer meet Caroline's eyes. 'So I made my bargain and then pretended that it was what I had always wanted.' She shook her head. 'I was a fool. I never thought that I would live happily ever after, but I had no real notion of what marriage entailed, least of all to a man I could not respect—' She broke off.

Caroline took her hand. The knowledge of what had happened to Alicia made it easier to understand her sister's tale. 'You poor child! I had no idea! Oh, if only Alicia had known, I'm sure she would have helped you!'

Annabella's green eyes were bright with unshed tears. 'Please may we talk on other matters now, ma'am? I have no wish to succumb to a fit of the megrims!'

'Of course!' Caroline acquiesced gracefully, unwilling to press Annabella for details when she was clearly upset. 'But you asked my advice, and I can only suggest that you tell Alicia all that you have told me. She will be very sympathetic, you know, for she wants to be reconciled to you above all things!' Caroline jumped to her feet. 'Let us rejoin the rest of the party and hope for some entertaining company. One may not include Miss Hurst in that, I know, but the rest are tolerable or—' a twinkle entered her blue eyes '—more than tolerable, perhaps!'

'Miss Hurst is very beautiful, is she not?' Annabella said, a little sadly, remembering the way the haughty young woman had summoned Sir William to her side earlier.

Caroline Kilgaren smiled encouragingly. 'Oh, she has all the beauty that money can buy, certainly! But you should not repine—you are very pretty, you know, and have far more character! Miss Hurst, I am afraid, has been told from an early age that her opinions are worth more than other people's, on account of her being in possession of a fortune of eighty thousand pounds! I am a cat to say so, I know, but nevertheless it is true!'

Eighty thousand pounds sounded like a vast fortune to Annabella. She felt even more despondent. Money had a habit of attracting money, and Sir William Weston was not poor. True, he was a less eligible *parti* than a Viscount, but if Miss Hurst could not bring Mundell up to scratch, he would prove a very acceptable alternative...

Caroline's next words echoed her thoughts. 'Do not imagine that Miss Hurst dislikes you for yourself, Annabella! The truth is that she came here to catch herself a husband and is becoming annoyed by her lack of success. Mundell, her first target, is surprisingly old-fashioned and has some nice notions about being married for his title! He does not need money enough to fall for the lure. So Sir William Weston was her next thought, but—' Caroline smiled a little '—she did not know him well and understands even less what attracts him! All her overtures have met with the same bland indifference—and then, of course, you came along last night and he paid you more attention in one evening than he has given Miss Hurst in an entire fortnight! I'm afraid it has piqued her pride!'

Annabella blushed slightly at the implication that Sir William was interested in her. 'Sir William has been very kind to me,' she said guardedly, 'but I fear I cannot understand him any better than Miss Hurst does! You see,' she added naively, 'I have very little experience of the world and have never met anyone quite like him!'

'I doubt there is anyone quite like Will Weston,' Caroline said drily. 'You should know, my dear, that Will's father was very rich, but Will chose to enter the navy through inclination and rose to prominence by his own merits rather than through preferment! He has only sold out now because his estates require more attention than he felt able to give whilst away at sea so much, and I think perhaps that he is looking for a more settled life. But as a man he has a lot of attractive qualities...' she smiled at Annabella '...though I doubt you need me to tell you that! To Marcus and myself he is the best of loyal friends, and we would do a great deal for him. There now, I sound quite sentimental! But loyalty and integrity are qualities which are not always found in abundance in the superficial world of the *haut ton*!'

Annabella was not entirely sure that it was for these characteristics that Miss Hurst wished to attach Sir William's interest. There was something self-contained and a little distant about him which gave him an added mystery and must add to his attraction. And if one also considered his physical attributes... Annabella remembered the warm admiration in those bright, blue eyes and felt a little breathless. Perhaps it was not a good thing to dwell on Sir William's attractions too much. 'But surely there are plenty of titled gentlemen who would be happy to marry Miss Hurst?' she said, turning the conversation on to safer ground.

Caroline smiled with gentle malice. 'Oh, yes,' she said, with mock-sorrow, 'but she wanted a handsome one!'

They were still laughing as they crossed the lawn

and heard Miss Hurst's fluting tones holding forth once more:

'La, Sir William, I insist that you join me in a game of croquet! I shall brook no refusal, sir!'

'I fear I must decline, ma'am,' Sir William's lazy drawl was as unperturbed as ever. 'I must escort Mrs St Auby back to town shortly.'

'But can you not send her back in the carriage?' Miss Hurst made her sound like an unwanted parcel, Annabella thought. 'Surely the wretched girl—' She broke off as Caroline and Annabella came into view, and bent a false, dazzling smile on them.

'La, we were just saying that the carriage must be called to take you home, Mrs St Auby—'

'But then I insisted on the pleasure of escorting you myself, ma'am!' Sir William finished, without a flicker of expression.

Miss Hurst scowled. It was not becoming.

'You are all goodness, sir,' Annabella said politely. 'Do not let me put you to any further trouble, however! It has been a delightful afternoon and I am most grateful to have the use of Viscount Mundell's carriage—'

'Lud, yes,' Miss Hurst said, brightening, 'a carriage with a crest on! What could be more exciting for Mrs St Auby?'

This time, a smile definitely touched the corners of Sir William's firm mouth as his gaze rested on Annabella. 'I insist, ma'am,' he said, gently.

'But you must not go yet,' Marcus Kilgaren said, in his amused drawl. 'Caro has monopolised you! Come and sit by me, Mrs St Auby, and tell me what you think of Sir William's team. His cattle are accounted very fine, you know.'

It was some half-hour later that the party finally broke up. Miss Hurst bore an unresisting Viscount Mundell away to play croquet with Caroline Kilgaren, whilst Marcus offered to escort Miss Mundell on a tour of the hothouses. Caroline had pressed Annabella to stay and join in the game, but Annabella had uncharitably suspected that Miss Hurst would take the opportunity to attack her ankles with the croquet mallet. She declined the offer and Caroline kissed her impulsively on the cheek, and said that she hoped they would meet again soon. Miss Hurst, by contrast, had frowned horribly as she watched Sir William's curricle set off down the lime tree drive, and had had to be gently recalled to the game by her companions.

Chapter Three

The following day was fine and bright when Anna-bella set out with a long list of commissions for Lady St Auby in the town. Her ladyship always sent her daughter-in-law on errands, arguing that she could not spare the maids and that Annabella never earned her keep. It was one of the less onerous of the household duties laid at her door, and today she was particularly light of step and of heart.

She matched a ribbon successfully in the drapers and bought Lady St Auby several pairs of gloves, resisting the impulse to buy herself silk stockings. What use would she have for such fripperies? What she needed was thick woollen ones to keep out the creeping chill of winter at the St Aubys' Manor! She moved on to the butchers and the grocers, haggling for the cheapest cuts of meat and the damaged veg-etables, for she knew Lady St Auby would chide her for overspending and accuse her of pocketing some of the money herself. On impulse she bought herself an apple and ate it in the street, only to regret it when she turned the corner to see Mrs Eddington-Buck watching her with malevolent eyes from the other side of the street. The apple incident would no doubt be reported to Lady St Auby. Annabella sighed. Sometimes it seemed that all possibility of spontaneity had been crushed out of her life.

A knot of people were coming down the street towards her, chattering and laughing together. With a slight shock, Annabella recognised Viscount Mundell strolling along with Caroline Kilgaren on his arm, Miss Hurst and Sir William following behind and Miss Mundell bringing up the rear. The sight of Miss Hurst's smiling face upturned to Sir William's was sufficient to keep Annabella still for a moment and then prompt her to run away. It was too late, however. With a glad cry, Caroline hailed her.

'Mrs St Auby! What a delightful surprise! We had just called in Fore Street to find you from home, and here you are!'

Mundell took her hand, a broad smile on his face. 'Delighted to see you again, ma'am! A fine day, is it not! Would you care to join us?'

'Marcus is at the gunsmith's—' Caroline was saying, when Miss Hurst's whispered aside to Miss Mundell could be heard,

'She is a novelty in the same way as people will crowd about a freakshow booth…'

Annabella blushed bright red and even Caroline's voice faltered.

Sir William spoke into the embarrassed silence, his tone expressionless but his blue eyes as cold as ice. 'And will we see you at the concert tonight, Mrs St Auby?'

'I…imagine not, sir.' Annabella pulled herself together. Lady St Auby was tone deaf and detested musical soirees. 'I believe my mother-in-law has other plans for this evening.'

'A pity.' Sir William smiled warmly at her. 'But perhaps you could join us for a while now?'

Despite the temptation of his company, there was nothing Annabella wanted less at that moment. Miss Hurst's cold gaze was resting on the bulging contents of her marketing basket and to her horror Annabella could see the oxtails she had just bought lolling out of the corner of the brown paper parcel. She switched the basket to her other arm, out of sight, and gave Sir William a flustered look.

'You are kind, sir, but I must be getting home. I have a hundred and one matters to attend to! Good day!'

She scurried down the street without a backward look, conscious only of her humiliation. They must think her nothing but a socially inept fool! Oh, Miss Hurst had been unkind, but she had been gauche! Would she never learn? And now they *certainly* would not pay her any further attention!

'Mundell and his cronies have turned your head, you foolish girl!' Lady St Auby, a malignant smile on her lips and predatory gleam in her beady eyes, was standing in the stone-flagged corridor of the Taunton house, watching with no little satisfaction as Annabella scrubbed the floor. 'There, girl—no, not there, you booby—the stain is over on this side—' and Lady St Auby deliberately smeared the mud over the piece of floor which Annabella had just cleaned.

Two days had passed since Annabella had met the

Viscount and his guests in town and in that time she had heard nothing further from them. Her excitement and confidence in the future, severely dented by the encounter, had waned further as time had passed and the inescapable facts became clear. They had dropped her. She had bored them with her awkwardness and lack of sophistication. Lady St Auby, quick to see Annabella's unhappiness, had been delighted.

'It's as I would have thought,' she continued spitefully now. 'You have no graces to recommend you to the Quality. Why, they could see you for the little nobody you are! A man of Mundell's distinction is not going to want his guests imposed upon by a fortune-hunting adventuress!'

Annabella sighed, biting back the intemperate retort which rose to her lips. Once, long ago, she had answered Lady St Auby in kind when her mother-in-law had indulged in one of her vituperative attacks. The response had been swift. She had not been given any food for several days. The same thing had happened when she had refused to perform the demeaning household tasks which Lady St Auby had demanded. Whilst her mother-in-law did not resort to physical violence as her son had sometimes done, her retribution was just as difficult to bear. And now she was angry and frustrated by the attention that had been shown to Annabella. It was there in her eyes as she looked at her daughter-in-law, a savagery that was just waiting for an opportunity to explode into life.

Annabella wrung out the dirty cloth and reached for the pail of water. At the same time, Lady St Auby leant forward and calmly tipped the bucket over so the dirty dregs soaked Annabella's skirt where she knelt on the rough floor.

It was too late for Annabella to avoid the tide of filthy liquid. She leapt to her feet, feeling the water soaking through her kerseymere skirt and the apron she wore on top of it. She lost her balance, stumbling and falling. Lady St Auby cackled with laughter.

The front door opened, although nobody had rung the bell. Lady St Auby froze. All Annabella could see, from her position on the floor in the retreating suds, was a pair of highly polished topboots.

Then: 'You appear to be in some discomfort, ma'am,' Sir William Weston said, carefully expressionless. 'Allow me to help you.'

Her elbow was taken in a very firm grip. As she stumbled to her feet, her skirt dripping and sticking to her legs, Annabella could smell the faint scent of his cologne mingled with the aroma of fresh air that she had always loved. Her gaze fixed itself on his green waistcoat and stayed there. She did not dare to look up into his face. Of all the desperately undignified situations in which to be found... She discovered that she was shaking with mortification. There was no possible way to explain...

'Sir William...' Lady St Auby had at least the grace to appear a little abashed. 'How do you do, sir. We were just—'

She was silenced by one searing flash of those blue eyes. 'There is no need to say anything, madam. The facts speak for themselves. Mrs St Auby...' his cold tone softened '...I was calling to see if you would be attending the subscription ball this evening—' He broke off. Annabella had still not been able to look him in the eye. Now she did look up as his grip tightened on her hand. He was standing, head bent, studying the raw, chapped skin of her fingers where the brush had scoured it. Then he let her go abruptly.

'Will you come for a drive with me, ma'am?'

'If you can wait whilst I change, sir—' Annabella gestured clumsily towards her drenched skirt.

'Of course…'

They were well clear of the town when Sir William reined in his horses and spoke again, and when he turned to her, Annabella realised that he was still angry. There was a tight set to his mouth and a glitter in his eyes. The butterflies in her stomach fluttered again. Whatever was he going to say to her?

'Why did you not tell us—?' he began, then broke off in frustration, slamming one fist into the palm of his other gloved hand. 'Lady St Auby is unpardonable!'

Annabella fixed her gaze on the middle distance, which consisted of a very pretty millhouse, its wheel turning.

'I have known you but a couple of days, sir,' she said carefully, 'and felt disinclined to confide my domestic arrangements to a group of strangers!'

The stormy blue gaze held her own eyes. 'That is ungenerous of you, ma'am! Have we not given you every indication that we would all stand your friends?'

Annabella looked away unhappily. 'Indeed, sir, but…' She turned back to him and said in a rush, 'Your very friendship is the goad which makes Lady St Auby worse! She cannot bear that Mundell's set recognise me when she has always been below his notice! It has always been a thorn in her flesh that I am Alicia's sister and the Countess of Stansfield's granddaughter. Before you all arrived in Taunton it did not matter, but now...'

Sir William's eyes had narrowed with concentration and now he nodded slowly. 'I see. Then you do not pretend that what I witnessed this morning was an accident?'

'I collect you mean with the pail of water?' Annabella was a truthful girl and just now it was making her uncomfortable. 'No, I cannot pretend... Oh, she means no real harm—'

'No harm!' The words exploded from Sir William with all the wrath he would have preferred to visit upon Lady St Auby's head. It was extraordinary, Annabella thought, that the placid exterior she had seen at the ball could conceal such a depth of feeling. She managed a watery smile.

'No, truly, sir... She is unkind and malicious, but she does me no real harm!'

'No,' Sir William said through his teeth, 'she simply makes you scrub her floors and no doubt a hundred other menial tasks besides!'

'Well, I am the poor relation—'

'Will you stop being so humble!'

They sat staring at each other. Then Sir William seemed to shake himself out of his bad temper. He gave her a slight smile.

'I beg your pardon, ma'am. I have been most uncivil to you.' He gave the horses the office to move off again. 'We must—' He stopped and started again. 'If I could arrange for you to stay at Mundell until you go to visit Alicia, would you be prepared to accept the invitation?'

It sounded like heaven to Annabella, but it also sounded dangerous. 'You have more faith in my sister's forgiveness than I dare have, sir,' she said, trying to speak lightly. 'If Alicia and I are unable to bury our differences—'

'Then we must make other arrangements.' Sir William sounded his usual cool, composed self once again. 'You cannot continue living in that household!'

'How very high-handed you sound, sir!' Annabella marvelled sweetly, and saw some expression flare in his eyes before it was replaced by reluctant amusement.

'Well?' he challenged her. 'If you wish to martyr yourself by staying there, pray do not let me interfere!'

To her amazement, Annabella found herself on the verge of giggling. How extraordinary! To be sunk in misery one minute, yet to feel this dizzy excitement the next! She cast a look at Sir William under her lashes. His stern expression had relaxed slightly; a smile still lingered around that firm mouth.

'It would be delightful to stay at Mundell,' Annabella capitulated, dismissing the fleeting thought of Miss Hurst, who would be far from delighted.

'Thank you. Are there any other dark secrets that it would be useful for me to know before I make the arrangements?' Sir William's quizzical blue gaze rested on her thoughtfully, before returning to the road.

'I think not.' Annabella spoke demurely. 'You have already provoked me into divulging far more about

my marriage than was seemly, and now you know the
sordid truth of my existence with the St Aubys. That
only leaves my quarrel with Alicia, and I imagine that
she will have told you enough of that!'

Sir William shook his head slowly. 'Your sister is
remarkably loyal to you, Mrs St Auby! Oh, I believe
that she told Caroline Kilgaren the whole of it, but
the rest of us only know that there has been some sort
of dispute between you. It would be a pity if it could
not be resolved, for I imagine the two of you would
get on famously. Now…' he sighed '…I suppose I
must take you back to that old harridan, but if you
can be prepared for a remove to Mundell tomorrow,
I will come to fetch you.'

He dropped her at the door of the house in Fore
Street with a reminder about the subscription ball that
evening. A couple of hours later, a pair of exquisitely
made evening gloves were delivered to the house. Annabella looked at her sore fingers and smiled.

Lady St Auby was nervous. Previously she had not
cared how Taunton society viewed her treatment of
Annabella, for the girl had no one to champion her
cause. Now, unexpectedly, she had acquired powerful
protection, and that had changed the whole case. She
made no demur when Annabella raised the subject of
the ball and even sent her own maid along to help
Annabella with her toilette. Pleading a sick headache
to excuse herself, Lady St Auby told her daughter-in-
law that Sir Thomas and Lady Oakston were only too
happy to ask her to join their party for the evening.
Annabella could not wonder at it.

There was a little awkwardness to begin with. Sir

Thomas had never acknowledged Bertram Broseley as an acquaintance, and had paid scant attention to his daughter even when Francis had been alive. Now, Annabella's elevation to Mundell's social sphere suddenly made her a worthwhile connection, but Sir Thomas did at least have the manners to feel the delicacy of the situation. Fortunately the Oakstons had a very lively and unaffected son, Julius, and an equally vivacious daughter Eleanor, who was just out. Annabella, happy in her new-found friends and excited at the prospect of seeing Will Weston again, was prepared to be generous.

This time, the heads turned as she came into the ballroom, and it was a new and entirely enjoyable experience. In a determined effort to look her best, Annabella had dug an old dress of purple taffeta out of a chest, had stripped it of all frills and furbelows, had sponged it down and made it look quite acceptable. It had originally been made for her before her marriage, and the effect had been far too sophisticated for a young girl. Now it was eminently suited to a widow, albeit one of only twenty-one. Joan, Lady St Auby's maid, had cleverly turned one of the frills into a matching headband, and had arranged Annabella's honeyed curls to tumble in barely restrained profusion about her heart-shaped face. Her green eyes glowed with pleasure and for the first time she thought she might be almost beautiful.

The party from Mundell had yet to arrive, but Annabella danced with Julius Oakston and several other young men who eagerly solicited her hand, and chatted to Eleanor, who was anxious to tell her about her recent visit to the spa at Bath. There was also other, less congenial company about. When Annabella went out on to the balcony for some fresh air, she was cornered by George Jeffries.

'The divine Annabella! Too far above my touch now, are you not, my love!' He swayed a little, and Annabella realised with apprehension that he was already drunk. Although they were within easy call of the ballroom, it would be embarrassing in the extreme to have to summon help. Beyond the billowing curtains, she could see dancing couples circling the floor. They could have been several thousand miles away for all the help it gave her. She could smell the wine on Jeffries's breath as he came closer, put up a hand to paw her arm. His grey eyes were narrowed with the intentness of the very inebriated. He was having enough difficulty just standing up.

'Go home, sir,' Annabella said wearily. 'You are drunk and I have no wish for your company.'

'S'what I'm saying…' Jeffries caught her arm as he lurched forwards, forcing his face close to hers. 'No time for your old friends now! Out with the old and in with the new! But do they know the things I could tell them, eh? Things Francis let slip…' The cunning expression on his thin face made Annabella feel sick.

'Francis was forever talking in his cups, just as you are now, sir,' she said coldly.

'S'true I'm a little foxed…' Jeffries tried to smile engagingly. 'Fra-Francis told me all about the time he—'

'I am persuaded that the lady does not wish to hear your squalid gossip, sir!' Sir William Weston, looking awesomely authoritative in his immaculate evening

attire, had stepped out on to the balcony and had had
the presence of mind to pull the curtain to behind him.
His contemptuous gaze raked Jeffries, who had stag-
gered backwards with an oath.

'Weston!'

'You have the advantage of me, sir,' Sir William
said silkily. 'I shall not, however, press for an introduction! Now, take yourself off!'

He watched without comment as Jeffries, still
swearing under his breath, slipped back into the ballroom and disappeared from view. 'Foolish young
puppy,' he said without emotion, turning back to Annabella. 'I hope that he did not upset you, Mrs St
Auby?'

'Oh, no.' Annabella was feeling rather foolish. First
he had found her with Lady St Auby tipping dirty
water over her, and now he had had to rescue her
from the undignified scene with Jeffries! He was
scarcely seeing her at her best!

'Then perhaps we should step inside. Your absence
from the room will be missed if you spend much more
time out here.'

'You always seem to be saving me from the consequences of my own folly, sir,' Annabella said, as
he held the curtain aside for her to re-enter the ballroom and took her arm to guide her around the set of
dancers that was just forming.

'How so?' Weston slanted a look at her. 'You can
hardly blame yourself for the discourtesy of others,
Mrs St Auby, be they your mother-in-law or that foolish young cub! But perhaps…' a questioning note entered his voice '…you feel you have something with

which to reproach yourself over the unfortunate Captain Jeffries?'

Annabella laughed. 'I am not at all sure that you should quiz me on such a matter, sir!'

'Why? Because you have something to hide?'

'No, indeed!' Annabella looked indignant. 'I only meant that such a direct question invites a snub!'

'Ah—' a smile curled Weston's mouth '—and you have just administered one, ma'am!'

'Well, you are a most persistent man! But to answer your question, the only thing I have to reproach myself for is a certain lack of judgement, I believe! I made a mistake in choosing to marry where I did, and also in allowing Jeffries to befriend me afterwards.' Annabella put her head on one side thoughtfully. 'He was the one who sought to take advantage of my loneliness, and not for kindly motives!'

'No, I can well imagine!' Weston suppressed a smile and allowed his gaze to travel over her consideringly. What an odd mixture this girl was, half solemnity and half naïveté! It seemed to him that she was not so much lacking in judgement but lacking anyone to advise her, and that she had always been so. It gave him a strange pang to think of her so friendless in a hostile world. Her situation had been an unenviable one! But now, perhaps… He felt a sudden determination that she would not be so isolated again.

'I see that Lady St Auby is not here tonight,' he observed, as they reached the door of the refreshment room and Miss Hurst could be seen glaring at them across the rim of her glass of lemonade.

'No, she had a sudden headache.' Annabella allowed herself a smile. 'She is afraid of you, sir, and of what will be said about her in the neighbourhood!'

Sir William sighed. 'I do not seem to be making friends for myself here in Somerset! And now I see I shall have to share your company, for Mundell is coming this way!' He pressed a kiss on her hand. 'You will dance with me later, perhaps?' As green eyes met blue, Annabella knew she was unlikely to refuse his request. She watched him go off to dance with Miss Mundell, then turned her attention to the Viscount. Miss Hurst was, rather improbably, dancing with Captain Jeffries. Annabella noticed this with a vague feeling of surprise, and almost immediately forgot about it. Later, she was to remember the incident and wish she had paid more attention.

It was the beginning of a golden few weeks for Annabella. The Mundell Hall house party swept her up into its activities and entertainments, and she felt as though she had unexpectedly stumbled into an extraordinary dream. There were outings and picnics, evening parties and entertainments. Under Caroline Kilgaren's benevolent patronage, Annabella found herself overcoming her initial lack of confidence, until she was even able to deal with Ermina Hurst with equanimity. And throughout it all there was Sir William Weston, attentive, concerned, it seemed, only for Annabella's enjoyment, to which he of course contributed in no small measure.

Miss Hurst had not been pleased with the addition to their party. At first Annabella had assumed this was because of Sir William's attentions, but after a little while, and with a sense of surprise, she realised that

Miss Hurst's antagonism was wider than that. She genuinely saw Annabella's beauty as a real challenge to her own supremacy, and although she could assert breeding and fortune, it was still irksome to her to have so pretty a rival. And, as is often the case with such things, the knowledge gave Annabella's green eyes an extra sparkle, and her complexion an extra glow, which led Miss Hurst to fume all the more.

The second day after the ball had dawned clear and sunny, and Mundell had announced casually at breakfast that he proposed to join the villagers in making up a cricket team to challenge the famous Gentlemen of Taunton to a match. Marcus Kilgaren and Will Weston readily agreed to participate, and Caroline, her blue eyes sparkling, proposed that the ladies should take a picnic along and support the contestants. Miss Hurst's expression mirrored shocked disapproval.

'Lud, a village cricket match!' She saw Mundell's quizzical gaze and added hastily, 'I am sure I do not dispute the privilege of gentlemen to mix with the common folk in such games, but I cannot believe my mama would approve of me attending!'

Caroline shrugged, doing little to conceal her irritation. 'As you wish, Ermina! Mrs St Auby and I shall get along very well if you and Charlotte do not care to join us!'

Surprisingly, Miss Mundell now spoke, blushing a little. 'For my part I should enjoy the fresh air,' she said, a little defiantly. 'Cricket is a very gentlemanly and sportsmanlike game, dearest Ermina. I am sure your mama could find no fault!'

'Upon my word!' Miss Hurst stared at her friend,

amazed Miss Mundell should speak out. Annabella also looked at her with renewed interest. She had dismissed Miss Mundell as a shy mouse in the shadow of her opinionated friend, but now she realised that some powerful feeling must be prompting the girl to speak thus. Charlotte Mundell's face was flushed and her eyes bright, and for once she looked almost pretty. She was very like her brother in appearance, but whilst the hawkish features and piercing grey eyes were handsome in a man, they were not very appealing in a woman. Yet now, Charlotte was animated, with a curious expression of excitement tinged with apprehension, almost as though, Annabella thought shrewdly, she were in love…

'Well!' Miss Hurst said crossly. 'If you *insist* upon going, Charlotte, I suppose I must join you! Though why you should wish to watch so tediously dull a game, I cannot imagine—'

Sir William Weston rustled the pages of *The Times* loudly and Annabella caught the tail-end of an ironic smile he exchanged with Marcus Kilgaren. Yes, clearly there was something going on here which might well become more plain during the course of the day.

The match was being held on the village green, and Caroline, Annabella and the other ladies arranged themselves comfortably under the spreading branches of a huge oak, in dappled sun and shade. It was a shame, Annabella thought, that Miss Hurst had insisted on accompanying them. She complained about everything. There were twigs and insects dropping off the tree and her flimsy parasol could do nothing to

ward them off, more insects had crept into her sand-
wiches, the seats were uncomfortable and the rules of
the game unintelligible.

Annabella secretly found the match rather entertaining. The Gentlemen players, in their white top
hats with black bands, were far more elegantly attired
than the motley selection of villagers who were, nevertheless, determined to win against their illustrious
opponents. The village side were batting, Mundell
and the local blacksmith building up a creditable
score of runs. Across the pitch, Annabella could see
money exchanging hands as bets were taken on the
outcome of the match. There was also some heavy
drinking, but the day was hot and the thirst of the
players in particular was acute. As the beer was
downed, the support became more voluble and the
language unbridled. Miss Hurst looked pained at being exposed to such crass company.

Mundell eventually fell to a fast ball that hit his
middle stump so cleanly it knocked it out of the
ground. He walked off to a sympathetic round of applause and his place was taken by a tall young man,
loose-knit and ambling with a kind of gawkiness
which was rather attractive. Miss Hurst, who had been
in the middle of a peevish complaint about the slowness of the roads in the westcountry, broke off in the
middle of her sentence, staring hard.

'Good God, surely that cannot be John Dedicoat!
At a village cricket match?'

Annabella hid a smile. She was reminded of Lady
St Auby's astonishment that Mundell should have
chosen to patronise a country assembly. She had no
idea who the newcomer was, but now she observed

that Miss Mundell had sat up a little straighter and that her pale complexion was once again a becoming rose, her grey eyes brilliant. Miss Hurst, by comparison, was both unobservant and completely self-centred.

'Well!' She was preening herself with a satisfied smirk. 'Perhaps he is here because he knew I should attend! You must have seen, dear Lady Kilgaren, how Lord Dedicoat singled me out last night!'

Caroline's expression was hidden by the lid of the picnic hamper as she rummaged inside for something she had apparently mislaid. Her voice was muffled and Annabella wondered whether she had mistaken the note of amusement she thought she had detected.

'I am persuaded that Lord Dedicoat is here because he enjoys the game of cricket, Ermina, although…' Caroline shot Miss Mundell's rapt face a quick glance '…he *may* have another motive for attending!'

Miss Hurst smirked again. 'I knew it! Does he not cut a handsome figure! This is very pleasant entertainment!'

There at least, Annabella thought, Miss Mundell could be in full agreement with her friend, for the girl's eyes never left the tall figure at the crease. And Lord Dedicoat played with flair and grace until a wickedly spinning ball caught him off guard and he was out. He took his dismissal with the same good-natured ease that had characterised his innings and was succeeded by the village doctor.

'Lud, these vulgar people!' Miss Hurst said, with a sudden return to peevishness. 'Drinking and gambling on the village green! Why—' She stopped abruptly and blushed bright red. John Dedicoat, accompanied by Will Weston, had come upon them suddenly, both men looking rather dashing in their cricket whites. At close quarters, Lord Dedicoat was indeed a pleasing young man, but Annabella had eyes only for Sir William, whose athletic physique was peculiarly suited to the elegance of his attire.

Both men were carrying tankards of beer, Annabella noticed, and stifled a giggle as she caught Caroline's eye. Miss Hurst was unlikely to continue her diatribe now.

'I had a monkey wagered on John reaching fifty before he was out,' Sir William said cheerfully, sitting on the grass at Annabella's feet, and giving her a grin which suggested that he had also heard Miss Hurst's last utterance. He took a deep draught of ale.

'This local brew is very good, isn't it, John? I'm glad to see the villagers entering so wholeheartedly into the spirit of the occasion!'

Miss Hurst glared at him. Now that she had all but given up on the prospect of attaching Sir William, she felt quite comfortable in treating him with disapproval. Besides, there was metal more attractive in Lord Dedicoat who was equally handsome and had a title into the bargain.

'Do tell me a little about the game, my lord,' she gushed unbecomingly. 'Those men standing about over there—what is their purpose?'

John Dedicoat began to explain the fielders' positions to Miss Hurst whilst simultaneously watching Miss Mundell. Will Weston leant back on one elbow so that his head was on a level with Annabella's knee. She resisted the surprisingly strong impulse to touch his ruffled brown hair.

'Are you enjoying the game, Mrs St Auby?' Weston asked softly, looking up at her with those brilliant blue eyes.

'Yes, sir, I thank you.' Annabella smiled. 'I have absolutely no understanding of the rules, but that has not marred my enjoyment!'

'I could explain them if you like,' Weston offered, taking a bite out of a cucumber sandwich with his strong white teeth. He looked at Miss Hurst, who was insisting that Dedicoat give a running commentary of every ball bowled, and smiled.

'Pray do not put yourself to the trouble, sir!' Annabella said, following his gaze and scorning to behave in so foolish a fashion as Ermina Hurst. She spoke with gentle malice. 'I have no need of such guidance!'

Weston shook his head in mock sorrow. 'Spurning my offer, Mrs St Auby? You are very hard on a fellow's self-esteem! Can it be that you do not wish for my company?' There was a teasing light in his eyes, a challenge that Annabella rose to.

She was enjoying their sparring and he knew it too. There was an edge to the encounter that the presence of the others did nothing to diminish, an attraction that was instant and mutual. And dangerous.

'For shame, sir, that you need to fish for compliments from your friends!' Annabella spoke lightly, and caught her breath as he touched her hand fleetingly, almost accidentally.

'Is that then how you see yourself, Mrs St Auby?' Weston asked, dropping his voice even lower. 'As a friend of mine?'

Annabella tore her gaze away from his compelling one. 'Friendship is to be prized, sir…'

'Oh, as to that, I agree with you.' Weston selected another sandwich from the hamper. 'True friends are indeed to be valued. But from you, Mrs St Auby, I might ask for something more…'

'Just at the moment,' Annabella said tartly, 'your *friends*—' she emphasised the word '—are asking something of you, sir! I believe it is your turn with the bat! Pray try to concentrate on the game!' And, well pleased with herself for not succumbing to his flirtation, she watched Sir William lope away to take up his stance at the wicket.

Miss Hurst had exhausted the topic of field placings and Lord Dedicoat had, with some relief, moved away a little to converse in a low tone with Miss Mundell. And for the first time, Miss Hurst was watching her friend with a less than amicable expression, her brown eyes narrowed thoughtfully as she saw Dedicoat smile at Charlotte. A moment later, a shriek rent the air.

'A beetle! Oh, Good God, a beetle has just dropped from that tree on to my lap!' Miss Hurst leapt to her feet clutching Lord Dedicoat's arm and leaning heavily against him. Caroline shook her head in exasperation.

'Really, Ermina! It will do you no harm!'

'Oh! Oh!' Miss Hurst was drooping artistically. She allowed Lord Dedicoat to lead her gently towards his own seat with soothing words and much careful support. The beetle, Annabella observed, was nowhere to be seen. She watched, a small smile curving her lips, as Miss Hurst lowered herself slowly on to Lord Dedicoat's seat with small gasps of distress and shock. Poor Charlotte Mundell was quite disregarded. Annabella leant forward. She had seen a bee, drunk with pollen, lurch onto the cushion beneath Miss Hurst's descending bottom. Annabella sighed and sat back again. She did not say a word.

Chapter Four

It was later the same evening that they were sitting in the Blue Saloon after dinner, with Viscount Mundell and his sister engaging the Kilgarens at cards and Sir William and Annabella listening to Miss Hurst, who was exhibiting her proficiency at the piano.

Miss Hurst's recovery from the bee sting had been remarkable. Since the injury was to a part of her anatomy that precluded discussion, she had decided to bravely ignore the incident and soldier on with only the slightest wince whenever she sat down.

As Miss Hurst played, Annabella was covertly studying Sir William's profile. His blue eyes were distant, as though he were dwelling on matters far beyond the lamplit room and the music. The sweep of his lashes cast a shadow against the hard line of his cheek, and in repose that handsome mouth looked uncompromising, almost harsh. Though relaxed in his chair, there was something almost watchful in his stillness.

Annabella frowned slightly. What was it that caused this tension in him? She doubted that he was

such a musical purist that Miss Hurst's rendition of
Bach could offend him, although whilst technically
brilliant the performance certainly lacked feeling…
Suddenly, Annabella felt a hollow feeling in the pit
of her stomach, a conviction that she scarcely knew
Sir William, and understood him even less. The passage of time in his company had given her only a
superficial knowledge of his interests and dislikes, for
the conversations that one could hold in a group were
inevitably very general, or hampered by the presence
of its other members. Annabella frowned again. She
had to admit to herself that she most ardently wished
to have a better understanding of Sir William Weston.

The music rippled around her, and Annabella
shifted slightly, trying to find a better position on the
gilt sofa, which was no doubt most fashionable but
made no concessions to comfort. Her wriggling disturbed Sir William from his reverie and he turned his
head and looked directly into Annabella's eyes, and
again she experienced that small tremor of shock
which made it impossible for her to be indifferent to
him. Worse, he then smiled, that slow, heart-shaking
smile of his, and she was utterly lost.

'Mrs St Auby!' The music had stopped and Miss
Hurst's voice was sharp. 'Did you not attend me? I
asked if you would care to play now?' There was an
equally sharp look in her dark eyes, for she had not
forgotten Annabella's claim to play very ill. 'I am
sure,' she added patronisingly, 'that we can find
something suited to you!' She rifled through the
sheets of music on top of the piano. 'Scarlatti? No,
too difficult, perhaps…'

Annabella tore her gaze away from the compelling

blue heat of Sir William's, and took Miss Hurst's place at the pianoforte.

'Thank you,' she murmured, 'I shall sing, I think.'

'As you please.' Miss Hurst shrugged, moving across to Sir William's side with an ostentatious swing of the hips matched by the sway of the ostrich feathers in her hair. She seated herself and arranged her skirts, looking expectant. A minute later, she had started to chat to Sir William in an undertone, much to Annabella's annoyance.

After a few bars, Miss Hurst had fallen into chagrined silence, aware that her companion's attention had wandered. The card-players paused in their hand to listen. Annabella had not chosen a classical piece, but an old Scottish love song, 'The Wild White Swan', and sang with a depth and pathos that could not help but touch the listener. The melodic cadences fell gently, sorrowfully on the ear. And as the last notes died away there was a breathless hush before everyone broke into spontaneous applause and cries for more. This time Annabella picked a saucy little song calculated to shock a little, but the purity of her exceptionally fine voice somehow robbed it of anything but innocent naughtiness. The smiles were broad as she ended.

Finally, she was prevailed upon to sing a duet with Sir William, who turned out to have a fine tenor voice, rich and a little mocking in tone, and then she begged a rest and took her glass of lemonade out on to the terrace. Dusk was falling, casting its shadows across the sentinel cypresses and turning the formal gardens into a cool and mysterious place. Annabella leant her elbows on the parapet and looked across to the pleasure lake.

'You have been exceptionally reticent about your musical talent.' Sir William Weston, the same mocking tone evident in his voice as there had been in his singing, had followed her out and came to lean on the stone parapet beside her. 'I have seldom heard such a fine voice.'

Annabella smiled. 'Thank you, sir. I'll allow that on the occasion I was quizzed on the subject I saw no need to make my questioner free with the information! But,' she added seriously, 'you should not criticise in others a trait which serves you well!'

'You mean to imply that I give little of myself away?' It was becoming too dark to see his face, but Annabella thought that he was smiling slightly. 'Well, in the main I'll concede the truth of that! But I have no sinister motive, I assure you! It is simply that on board ship, living in each other's pockets, one becomes accustomed to keeping one's own counsel in order to avoid unnecessary disputes. It is a habit which has served me well on occasions such as this houseparty, which requires much the same approach!'

Annabella laughed despite herself. 'Surely you exaggerate, sir! I have been among you a few days only, but I see no sign of disputation!'

'You would be surprised, Mrs St Auby,' Sir William murmured. 'Why, only yesterday there was a heated debate between Miss Hurst and Miss Mundell over which had most recently used Miss Hurst's silver thimble, and Lord Kilgaren was called upon to arbitrate! I kept quite out of the matter, I assure you!'

'You are absurd, sir!' Annabella smiled. 'I suspect

that you really keep your silence just to appear more mysterious!'

'Acquit me!' Sir William said, humorously. 'Though,' he added with sincerity, 'I should be flattered to think that you would wish to learn more of me, Mrs St Auby. On what may I enlighten you?'

'Oh...' Annabella turned away to look out across the darkening garden. She essayed a light tone. 'Simple things only, sir! Of your family, your home...'

'Well...' Sir William spoke easily '...my father died a few years ago when I was away at sea, and my mother a year later. I have two elder sisters and I had a younger brother, who married the daughter of a Charleston plantation owner and lived abroad. He died last year.' He brushed aside her words of condolence as though it still hurt him to speak of it. 'And as for my home...' Sir William's voice changed, took on a deeper quality. 'There is a house on the Berkshire Downs, just north of the little village of Lambourn... In the winter the wind whistles down from the chalk hills and across the wide valley below with the snow on its edge, but in the summer the countryside drowses in a verdant, green peace. There is an ancient track which cuts its way across the hills, bone dry in the sun, and butterflies drift through the poppy fields.' His voice changed, became brisk. 'But it is a long time since I have been there. Are you cold, Mrs St Auby?'

Annabella had shivered suddenly as a stray breath of wind touched the back of her neck and trickled down her spine. She was aware of a vague feeling of disquiet, but she knew not why. She allowed Sir William to take her arm and steer her back into the lighted room, where the card-players had just concluded their game.

Caroline Kilgaren came across to sit by Annabella as Sir William moved away and was almost immediately pounced on by Miss Hurst, who demanded his opinion on a letter she had just received from her mother:

'For it says, dear Sir William, that Lady Frankland has inherited an estate of fifty thousand pounds from her uncle, Mr Cobbett, and yet I positively thought that she was cousin only to the Cobbetts, and surely the Drysdales are his closer relations…'

Caroline smiled ruefully as Miss Hurst bore Sir William away to a corner of the room to continue the discussion. 'Now my dear, there is a matter I wanted to broach with you. It is about the ball on Friday.' She hesitated. 'Tell me to mind my own business if you wish, but I could not help wondering… I have a dress, you see, a very pretty confection in silver and gold, which would be just the thing for you if you do not have something you prefer to wear.' She considered Annabella thoughtfully and smiled. 'We may have to add a flounce, for you are somewhat taller than I, but that should not be beyond the skill of Ellie, my maid. She is a most talented sempstress.'

Annabella could have hugged her for her tact and kindness. The ball had been on her mind, for although Miss Mundell had referred to it as a small gathering for friends, Annabella had the feeling that the small gathering could be both exclusive and very smart, a far cry from the Taunton assemblies. She had wanted desperately to go, but had almost cried off through a lack of appropriate clothing. But now, perhaps, that problem might be solved.

'You are very kind to me, ma'am,' she said, gratefully. 'I do not mind admitting that I was wondering how I might go on.'

'Come upstairs now,' Caroline urged her, 'and you may try it on. I'll call Ellie, my maid, and she can help us with any adjustments.'

Lord and Lady Kilgaren were occupying a well-appointed suite of rooms in the east wing of Mundell Hall, with charming views over the flower gardens and the deer park beyond. Caroline went across to the wardrobe, which seemed to Annabella's dazzled eye to be absolutely packed with dresses of all styles and materials. With a cry of triumph, she pulled out something from the back.

'Here it is! Now, what do you think?'

Annabella thought she was imagining things. The dreamy, ethereal creation draped over Caroline's arm could surely not be intended for her! When she tried it on, its softly flowing lines seemed to caress her body in the most seductive way, and she stood back in amazement to consider her reflection in the long mirror. The low bodice was cunningly cut to cross over in a V shape rather than the less sophisticated square or round necklines she was accustomed to, and she looked impossibly slender and elegant. Behind her in the glass, she could see both Caroline and the maid smiling.

'Perfect!' Caroline declared. 'It lacks length, of course, but with a ruffle of silver taffeta, Ellie...' the maid nodded in silent agreement '...if the dressmakers of Taunton can run to that...' She swooped on a

bandbox at the back of the wardrobe, 'And here is
the silver circlet which is intended to match.' She
placed it on Annabella's honey-coloured curls and
stood back to admire. 'Oh, my dear, you will look
divine!' Then, as Annabella remained silent, she said
anxiously, 'What is the matter? Do you not care for
it?'

Annabella shook her head slowly, a lump in her
throat. 'It is the most beautiful thing… I cannot believe that I am really going to wear it!'

Caroline smiled, reassured, and Ellie, her mouth
full of pins, instructed Annabella to turn around
slowly so that she could see the rest of the fit. A tweak
here and a tuck there, and the maid nodded her satisfaction.

'You will be the belle of the ball, my dear,' Caroline predicted, 'and I'll warrant Sir William will
think so too!'

Annabella smiled, still dazzled by the subtle, shifting patterns of silver and gold. Her eyes were like
stars as she turned before the mirror. 'Oh, do you
really think so, ma'am?' She sounded quite wistful
and very young. To Caroline she looked suddenly so
like her sister that she too felt a lump in her throat.

'If Sir William tells you of something—' she began, stopped then started again. 'You must never
think that Sir William is interested in you other than
for yourself, my dear.'

Annabella's wide, uncomprehending green eyes
turned on her in puzzlement.

'I do so hope that you are right in thinking he likes
me, ma'am.'

Caroline gave up. It was not her story to tell, any-

way, and she had already told Will Weston in the
most forcible tones possible that the sooner he told
Annabella the truth, the better. Will had argued that
he had wanted the chance for them to get to know
each other properly first, before this matter interfered
to muddy the waters. Caroline thought he was a fool,
but knew she could not sway him. She sighed. There
was such a clear, innocent light in Annabella's eyes
as she stood, rapt in wonder at her own appearance,
that Caroline hoped she would never suffer disillu-
sionment. Like Will Weston before her, she contem-
plated the curious mix of characteristics that was Annabella St Auby. Sometimes so collected, so
sophisticated, and at others so young and lacking in
confidence. And she was, after all, only twenty-one,
with no one to show her how to go on or help her
form sound judgement. Caroline thought it was extraordinary that she had turned out as well as she had.

When Annabella came down the stair at Mundell
Hall on the night of the ball, she was delighted to see
that William Weston, who was waiting with Marcus
Kilgaren, actually stopped talking when he saw her.
There was uncomplicated admiration blazing in his
blue eyes and a more complex, and far more exciting,
emotion which set Annabella's pulse racing. As Weston moved forward to take her hand, Marcus Kilgaren
crossed to Caroline's side.

'You seem to have played the fairy godmother
rather successfully, my love,' he murmured to his
wife, with a grin. 'Little Mrs St Auby looks quite
ravishing tonight. Certainly, Will looks as though he
would like to ravish her!'

Caroline dug him reprovingly in the ribs. 'Marcus! She's a sweet girl, and she deserves to enjoy herself. But—' a tiny frown marred her brow '—Will still hasn't told her about Larkswood! I worry that if she finds out some other way, it may all go wrong...'

Marcus's shrewd blue eyes scanned her face. 'You really have taken her under your wing, haven't you, Caro? But there's nothing we can do. Will must sort it out for himself.'

Caroline looked across to where the two heads were bent close together as Sir William scrawled his initials on Annabella's dance card. She sighed. 'I know... But Annabella is only twenty-one and I know she has been unfortunate before, even though she has not confided the whole to me. It would be most unlucky if something was to spoil her current happiness.'

Nothing was further from Annabella's mind. She felt truly beautiful in the gold and silver dress, and the admiring glances cast her way were a delicious contrast to the pitying looks usually reserved for her at such events when she was obliged to turn out in her old, outmoded gowns. Then there was the warmth of Sir William's hand beneath her elbow as he guided her into the first dance. Her dance card was already filling up, her company sought by plenty of eligible young men. It was promising to be a delightful evening.

'You look quite captivating tonight, Mrs St Auby,' Sir William observed, as he led her into the dance. 'I might wish not to have to share your company with all these other gentlemen!'

Annabella smiled, a little flirtatiously. It was an

evening made for romance and the experience was most enjoyable. She cast him a look from under her lashes.

'Are you always so direct, sir?'

'No…' Sir William's smile broadened '…generally I am only so outspoken when I want something a great deal!'

The movement of the dance fortunately separated them at that moment and gave Annabella the opportunity to compose herself.

'I cannot believe that you speak to all young ladies like that, sir,' she said severely when they came together again. 'They would likely slap your face or faint dead away!'

'I never give them the chance,' Sir William said laconically.

'Oh, indeed?'

'No, for I have never addressed myself thus to a young lady. As a type they bore me!'

Annabella choked back a laugh. 'Upon my word, sir, you are very severe! To condemn all my contemporaries thus—leaving aside the doubt it cast upon my own status in your eyes! Which do you dispute? That I am young, or that I am a lady?'

Sir William's gaze considered her enchanting face. 'Ah, now you are trying to trap me, ma'am, and it is too bad of you! You must know that I consider you to be indisputably a lady!'

'Punish you, rather, for your dismissive view of my sex!' Annabella considered him thoughtfully. 'Do you really have such a low opinion of us, Sir William?'

'Why, not in the least! But I would never generalise.' Sir William turned her expertly. 'My interest usually lies in people as individuals and at the moment—' his smile was mocking '—one individual in particular!'

Annabella's euphoria lasted until just before supper, when she happened to find herself in the ladies' room at the same time as Miss Hurst, who was pinning up a torn flounce. Miss Hurst watched, her brown eyes bright, as Annabella tweaked a curl back inside the silver circlet.

'La, what a charming dress!' she said with gracious condescension. 'Lady Kilgaren is the kindest creature in the world, always taking care of waifs and strays! And Sir William…' here Miss Hurst paused, her brown eyes brimful of malicious laughter '…well, he is the kindest creature too, except when he wants something—when he has a *particular* reason for acting the gallant!' She gave a little trill of laughter. 'But I expect he has told you *all* about that by now, Mrs St Auby!' And she gathered up the skirts of her dress in one hand and, laughing still, went out of the door.

Annabella stood quite still before the mirror, her comb forgotten in one hand as Miss Hurst's words began to do their poisonous work. A particular reason, Miss Hurst had said. But what could be Sir William's reason for acting the gallant with her? She had no money, and he had no need to hunt a fortune anyway. Certainly he was a friend of Alicia and James Mullineaux, but then all of Viscount Mundell's set had been kind to her because of that connection. Her heart missed a beat. Surely Miss Hurst did not mean to imply that Sir William was interested in setting her up as his mistress? Though he had perhaps been more explicit in his attentions than a more conventional man, there had been nothing disrespectful in his attitude, no indication that he intended to offer her *carte blanche*.

There had been such a spiteful look on Miss Hurst's face…but then, Annabella reasoned, Ermina Hurst had never liked her… She gave up and tried to forget about it. She was certainly not going to please Miss Hurst by asking her to explain her meaning.

Some of the enjoyment seemed to have gone out of the evening. The light from the chandeliers was not so sparkling and bright now and the animated chatter of Mundell's guests seemed to wash over Annabella rather than involve her. Nor was her heart in the dancing any more, and when the next set of country dances ended she excused herself to her partner and slipped into a cool alcove behind a pillar and sat down in the shadows. Whatever had Miss Hurst meant…?

'Mrs St Auby…' When Sir William's voice spoke in her ear, she jumped a mile.

'Oh, Sir William! You startled me, sir! I was not attending…'

Those searching blue eyes scanned her face thoughtfully. 'No, indeed, I can see you were thinking of something else entirely, ma'am. A penny for your thoughts?'

Annabella shifted uncomfortably. 'They are not worth it, sir!'

Sir William raised one dark brow. 'No? Then perhaps you will tell me why you are hiding yourself away behind a pillar? I met a most disconsolate fellow on my way here. Apparently you were supposed to be his partner for the boulanger, but he could not find you. But...' Sir William shrugged and sat down beside her '...his loss is my gain, after all!'

Annabella's answering smile felt stiff and insincere. Oh, why could she not put Miss Hurst's malicious remarks from her mind? And Sir William was not unaware of her discomfiture, for his gaze had not wavered and he was studying her face with relentless intensity.

'You look as though you need a pleasant diversion to take your mind away from these melancholy thoughts,' he observed after a moment. 'Would you care to come for a sail on the lake with me?'

'On the lake? In the dark?' Annabella's green eyes widened to their furthest extent at this audacious plan, distracted as he had intended her to be.

'In the moonlight,' Sir William amended. 'There is a full moon tonight. This is one of those moments, Mrs St Auby, when I find that I miss the soothing influence of the sea. A sail on Mundell's artificial lake is a poor substitute, I know, but it must suffice!'

Annabella smiled in spite of herself. 'That is definitely the sort of invitation I should refuse, sir!'

'Indeed it is...' Sir William also had a smile lurking in his eyes '...and it is the sort of invitation I should not be offering. However...'

'That would be delightful, sir,' Annabella said with a small, demure smile.

It was indeed a very clear night. The moon glittered on the water and cast their shadows across the lawn. The turf was springy and already wet with dew, but the air was warm. Sir William took Annabella's hand as they crossed the lawns to reach the jetty and the small rowing-boat that was tied up there.

'Not a sail, to be precise, but a row,' Sir William said. 'Well, Mrs St Auby? You should think carefully now, for you cannot change your mind once out in the middle of the lake!'

Annabella cast him a sideways look. 'No, sir? Can I not trust you to bring me safely back again?'

There was a split second of tension. 'Let us hope so,' Sir William said, cryptically, holding out his hand again to help her step into the boat.

The splash of the oars in the water seemed magnified in that still night, but the sounds of music and laughter floating from the windows of the terrace ballroom masked all other noises. Annabella glanced around, a little fearful of being seen, for she could still only half-believe that she had had the temerity to do this. But the shadowed gardens were empty of movement and in a few moments she sat back in the boat, relaxing. The cushioned seats were very comfortable, and she trailed her hand in the cool water, looking up at the stars shining in their cold, lonely splendour.

Neither of them spoke. Sir William had the habit of silence, and Annabella was too wrapped up in the enchanted beauty of the night. Somewhere at the back of her mind a quiet voice was counselling that this was no fairytale and that she should be very careful of what she did, but she did not wish to regard it. This seemed pure romance and she knew she was tumbling head over heels in love with Sir William Weston. It was so agreeable an experience that she had no inclination to put a stop to it with common sense.

Sir William rested on the oars and smiled at her in

the darkness. 'We are almost at the island. Would you care to step ashore?'

This time Annabella hesitated for fully five seconds. 'I think perhaps…yes, that would be very pleasant.'

The island was tiny, with a small decorative summerhouse in the middle, surrounded by neatly trimmed lawns and flowering shrubs. On hot summer days it was the scene of picnics by the water, but now its shuttered windows had a secretive look. The boat grated on the shingle and Sir William leapt ashore, securing the rope to an overhanging branch. He turned back to help Annabella, taking her hand in a firm grip as she stepped from the swaying boat onto the shore.

'It's very beautiful, isn't it?' she said, a little wistfully, for there was something magical about the night which seemed quite unreal. The moonlight shimmered on the black lake as the slight breeze stirred .the water. The cypress trees stood clear against the sky and the air was filled with the scent of flowers. And then, like the snake in paradise, Miss Hurst's words slid into Annabella's mind again, poisoning the night. She shivered.

'What is it?' Sir William spoke from close at hand. 'Something is troubling you, is it not, Annabella? You would do far better to tell me what is wrong.'

Annabella drew in her breath at his use of her name, but there was something about the intimate darkness that encouraged confidences. She took a deep breath.

'Sir William, I must ask you—' She stopped. Oh, how difficult this was! What could she say?

'Yes? Ask me what?' His voice was cool, dispassionate, giving no indication of his feelings. It chilled her, but she was suddenly determined to continue.

'For what reason have you sought me out, sir?' The words had tumbled out and Annabella felt her whole body burn with mortification. How could she have asked so naïve a question? She wished she had never started this.

'I take it that you mean to ask what prompted me to seek your company when we first met,' Sir William said, still with the same detachment. Annabella could not see his expression, for his head was bent, his hands deep in his pockets.

'Yes.' Her voice had shrunk as her embarrassment had grown. 'I thought perhaps that it was for my sister's sake...'

Sir William shifted slightly. 'I cannot deny that it was my friendship with James and Alicia which first brought you to my attention, Annabella.'

'I see.' Annabella's voice was now a tiny thread of sound. So he had only tolerated her company for friendship's sake. And no doubt Caroline Kilgaren's kindness had sprung from the same source... Annabella's fragile confidence wavered. The cold charity of it made her feel like crying. 'It is as I had supposed, sir. No doubt you are all acting from the same obligation to my sister—'

Sir William moved surprisingly quickly, taking hold of her upper arms and turning her so that the moonlight fell full upon her face. He gave her a little shake. 'Just a moment, Annabella! You do us all a disservice by that assumption! Yes, Mundell and all our friends initially sought you out because of your connection with Alicia, but do you think we would have done any more than merely acknowledge your acquaintance if we had not liked you for yourself?' His hands slid down to her wrists, but he did not let her go. 'As for me,' he said, an undertone of amusement in his voice, 'I like you all too well, and it is damnably difficult for me! It was foolish in the extreme of me to bring you out here when I have been avoiding just such a situation for days! I gave in to a reckless impulse tonight, and should have known better!'

Annabella freed herself and moved away slightly, her silver dress gleaming in the light. Her heart was suddenly beating light and fast. His touch had awoken in her something which could not be dismissed easily, a hunger that invaded her senses. 'I do not understand you, sir,' she said coolly, knowing full well that she lied.

'I think that you do.' Sir William sounded exasperated, though whether with her or with himself, Annabella could not tell. 'It was most imprudent for us to court scandal by stepping apart alone. For all your widowed state you are still young and inexperienced, and I would not care to risk your reputation or damage that innocence—' He made a sudden, violent movement away from her. 'Devil take it, Annabella, you understand what I mean...'

Annabella hesitated. Half of her was begging her to retreat from this hazardous conversation whilst the other half, the dangerous half she scarcely understood, wanted her to push him as far as she could. She shivered a little in the cool air, but more from the peculiar excitement that gripped her than from the cold. Sir

William was standing half-turned away from her and she put her hand tentatively on his arm.

'We had better go back now.' Sir William's tone was uncompromising, but Annabella could feel the tension in him, taut as a spring. And she had to know…

'You flatter me with your protestations that you have sought my company for pleasure, sir,' she said lightly. 'Do you not, then, wish to know my opinion of you, in return? Or are you so confident of your own attractions that you need no reassurance?'

Sir William smiled then, but it was not a comfortable smile. Annabella had the distinct impression that she had bitten off more than she could chew, but she was filled with a wilful determination to see if she was right. She looked across the lake, where the lights of the ballroom glittered amongst the dark trees, and she spoke very deliberately.

'I thought when I met you that you were an interesting man, a man who held some…small…appeal to me. And I wondered whether I would find you more or less interesting were you to kiss me?'

It was, after all, exactly what she had asked for, and it proved conclusively to Annabella that she was well out of her depth in provoking a man like Sir William Weston. The kiss was shocking and frightening in its explicit demand. His hands were mercilessly hard as they held her against the tense lines of his own body, his mouth hungry as it plundered the softness of hers. Annabella pushed hard against his chest to free herself. In some things she was indeed the innocent he had suggested. Francis had never shown her any tenderness in their brief marriage, being concerned only for his own selfish satisfaction, but here she sensed emotions and needs far more complex, in both herself and in Sir William, and she was suddenly afraid of them. And when he let her go straight away, she was also disappointed and confused.

'Is your curiosity satisfied now, Mrs St Auby?' Sir William asked with scrupulous politeness, 'or are there some points on which I can offer further clarification? You need only say the word!'

She could not see his expression in the darkness, but there was something so cold in his tone that Annabella shrank, transformed from the provocative sophisticate she had pretended to be into the inexperienced girl who realised the extent of her wilful mistake. How could she have behaved so? To have encouraged him, flirted with him so outrageously, so immodestly, then withdrawn in maidenly haste and disarray like a startled virgin when he had taken her in his arms. Impossible to explain to him that she had never felt any affection for her husband and never received any in return, that he had never held her with love and that her feelings were as unawakened as any new debutante... And now, no doubt, Sir William would think her just a cheap flirt, the sort who would encourage George Jeffries, or indeed any man, because she was bored, but was not prepared to deliver on those promises...a shallow tease...

'Forgive me, sir,' she said, in a voice so stifled with mortification that it was scarcely hers. 'I have behaved very foolishly...I am not always so flighty and superficial...' She swallowed a sob. So much for her

pretty dreams of romance in the moonlight! Could it
have been any more embarrassing?

She had to take his hand to allow him to help her
back into the boat, and she held out her own so gingerly that she heard him catch his breath with irritation. Every moment that prolonged this interlude was
impossibly humiliating. Then he took her hand in his,
and, extraordinarily, everything changed. There was
a moment when they both stood quite still, then she
found she was in his arms again, held wordlessly
against him. Once again, as on that first evening at
the assembly, her head was resting against his chest
and she could feel the strong beat of his heart against
her cheek, the warmth of his body close to hers. But
this time he did not let her go. It was the first time
Annabella had ever been held with love and the same
sense of recognition and peace flowed through her as
on that first evening. How long they stood there she
did not know. An eternity could have passed, but she
would not have cared, for she was truly happy. Then
she felt him brush the hair back from her face and
kiss her gently.

'There is no need to be afraid,' he said a little huskily. 'It need not be like you knew before.'

Annabella raised her head to look up at him. The
moonlight cast deep shadows. 'How did you know?'
she said, a little uncertainly.

'It seemed the logical explanation.' Sir William
loosened his grip a little so that he could look at her
properly. 'You were married to a man you did not
love or respect, a man I have heard described—in no
doubt more complimentary terms than he deserves—
as a boorish cad. I do not imagine he showed you any

consideration, not least in the physical demands he made upon you. But it is not always that way…' he touched her cheek lightly, sliding his hand into her hair '…let me show you.'

This time he was extraordinarily patient and gentle. His lips touched first one corner of her mouth then the other, before returning to it fully with the lightest of tantalising kisses. Annabella felt some of the tension within her begin to uncoil. His lips drifted along her jawbone to her throat, causing delicious shivers to touch her spine. Suddenly her skin felt incredibly sensitive, just waiting for his touch. Involuntarily, her lips parted, and his mouth returned to hers with the same teasing, frustrating lightness. Annabella's senses were beginning to burn. She forgot all about Francis and his selfish demands, forgot her fears and nervousness, her foolish provocation. She slid her arms around Will's neck and brought his head down to hers.

'Kiss me properly,' she whispered, and heard the amusement behind his soft words.

'Whatever you wish, Annabella…'

Then it was like her imaginings. Warm and tender, yet somehow indescribably exciting as he led her step by step towards some mysterious conclusion. Her blood was racing through her veins, the smell and taste of him filling her senses. The world receded as she became lost in the pleasure of his embrace. Dizzy, melting with longing, she pressed against him with total abandonment.

Then Will raised his mouth from hers and said, in a voice that was a mixture of amusement, regret and something else she could not identify, 'I still think I should take you back now, Annabella. In fact, I should say the need to do so has become even more pressing...' But she knew that he was smiling, and only smiled in return as she snuggled closer to him, turning her face against his chest, for she knew that somehow everything was all right.

'Whatever have you been doing, Will?' Marcus Kilgaren's voice was full of resigned humour. 'You have been away the best part of an hour, and Annabella St Auby looks almost incandescent with happiness. You may tell me to go to the devil if you wish,' he added pleasantly, 'but I thought to point out that if I had noticed, so had others.' He nodded significantly in the direction of Miss Hurst, who was whispering urgently to Miss Mundell. The two of them were standing, somewhat inappropriately, in front of a statue of the Three Graces. 'But perhaps I am to wish oyou happy?'

Will grinned. 'Not yet, but soon, perhaps...'

'Then you have not told her about Larkswood?' Marcus persisted. 'I only ask, because, again, there are those kind friends who may do the telling for you.'

Will's grin faded. 'Surely you do not think—?'

'Miss Hurst has not taken her implied rejection well,' Marcus said obliquely. 'She may feel it necessary to impart the truth to Annabella as one good friend to another... Evidently Annabella knows nothing of her inheritance?' he added quizzically.

Will shook his head slowly. He took a glass from a passing flunkey and drank deep. 'She told me a little while ago that the lawyers were still trying to sort out

Bertram Broseley's business affairs. I had hoped to be able to negotiate an agreement with them, without involving Annabella.'

Marcus was shaking his head. 'But she will find out, Will. Someone will tell her—'

'Very well.' Will put his glass down with a decisive click. 'I had wanted to get to know Annabella properly, to make sure she understood my reasons for wanting Larkswood, but I know you are right. I must go away in a couple of days,' he added, 'but after that I will tell her…' And he strolled back to Annabella's side as though drawn by a magnet.

Marcus watched him go, watched Annabella's face upturned to his, her eyes bright with happiness, and sighed. 'Let us hope,' he said under his breath, 'that you are not too late, my friend.'

Chapter Five

Annabella woke the next day to bright sunshine and warm happiness that made her smile even before she was fully awake. Mundell Hall was very quiet, for most of the Viscount's guests would not be rising so unfashionably early, but Annabella felt full of energy despite the lateness of the ball the previous night. She slipped out of bed, dressed swiftly in another of the gowns which Caroline Kilgaren had pressed on her, and sped downstairs for some fresh air. An impassive footman informed her that Lord Mundell was out walking his dogs, but that the rest of the party was still abed. Annabella thanked him prettily and ran down the steps into the garden.

Her steps took her, by accident or unconscious design, towards the ornamental lake which was glittering in the early morning light. A number of waterfowl preened and swam on its glassy waters; on the island in the centre, the windows of the pretty little summerhouse reflected the rays of the rising sun. It was very quiet. Impossible to believe, Annabella thought dreamily, that the scene between herself and Sir William Weston had really happened. Perhaps she had imagined it all, a dream conjured by the romance of the night and her own wishful thinking... She was still staring at the view, remembering the night before, when a voice called her name from near at hand. Turning quickly, she saw with a rush of disappointment that it was Viscount Mundell and not Sir William Weston who had accosted her. Mundell, his pack of King Charles Spaniels pressing at his heels, came up to her with a broad smile.

'Good morning, Mrs St Auby! A beautiful day, is it not? You must have plenty of stamina to be up so early after the ball! I imagine most of my guests will not appear until mid-afternoon!'

Annabella smiled at him. 'The sunshine beckoned me out, my lord, and it is too fine to be abed! I was just admiring your lake. You have a fine selection of waterfowl!'

Mundell, who was in his way quite an ornithologist, started to point out to her the different breeds, including the rare Cinnamon Teal which he had had specially imported from South America. 'Of course, it is difficult to prevent the ornamentals interbreeding with the native ducks who are attracted to the water here,' Mundell was saying, then realised from Annabella's glassy expression that birds were perhaps not really a point of interest to her. He smiled slightly. 'But I am boring on about the estate as I often do! I spend comparatively little time here, you see, and each time I return I discover afresh what draws me to the country...' They started walking along the edge of the lake, discussing the rival merits of town and country life, until they reached the point where the ha-ha divided the formal garden from the deer park, and Mundell bade her farewell, saying that he would give the dogs a run in the park.

As Annabella turned back towards the house, an amused voice from near at hand said, 'At last! I was afraid that he would never go!' And Sir William Weston stepped out of the shelter of the beech hedge directly on to the path in front of her.

'Sir William!' Annabella was annoyed to discover that her voice came out rather squeakily, with a combination of shock at seeing him so suddenly, and residual embarrassment over remembering their encounter in the clear light of day. Last night had been an enchanted evening, but now the sun was bright and showing all too clearly the vexatious blush in her cheeks. She looked at him a little accusingly.

'Have you been skulking in the bushes for long, sir?'

'I have. I thought that Hugo would never leave you alone!' Will looked completely unrepentant. The early morning breeze had ruffled his brown hair, and he put up a hand to smooth its disorder. He was dressed very casually in an old hunting jacket and breeches, a cravat tied carelessly about his neck, but the ensemble still had a distinction which was hard to define but immediately obvious. Annabella, running a mental eye over her own toilette, was glad that she had made the effort to wear the pretty straw-coloured dress and matching cloak, but she had little idea how appealing she looked with the breeze tugging at the tendrils of honey-fair hair and accentuating the pink of her cheeks and brightness of those green eyes.

'Come into the rose arbour,' Will said abruptly. 'There is something I wish to say to you.'

A little apprehensively, Annabella followed him through the archway, out of the sight of prying eyes, and into the heady-scented shadows of the walled garden. The sun had not yet warmed the old walls, and she shivered a little within the cloak from a combination of anticipation and cold. What was it that he wished to say to her? She looked up into his face, and discovered that it appeared Will Weston did not wish to talk after all. His arm went around her waist and he drew her deeper into the shadows. Mindful of her reaction the previous night, he kissed her very gently, waiting until he felt some of the tension leave her and her body become pliant against his own. Encouraged, he deepened the kiss a little, leading her by skilful stages to the point where he could tell her innocent but heartfelt response to him was sliding over the edge into genuine desire. So far he had given little thought to his own pleasure, but suddenly his awareness changed. The seductive softness of her in his arms awoke a need in him that almost pushed him beyond all restraint. He teetered on the edge, within a hair's-breadth of abandoning caution and crushing her to him. Then there was the sound of steps on the gravel beyond the archway, and Miss Hurst's tones could be heard addressing a nameless companion.

'Of course, whatever they say, the family is bad *ton*. How could it be otherwise when the father was that disgusting nabob Broseley, the elder sister married some degenerate septuagenarian for his money, and the younger one set her cap at Francis St Auby in that shameless way? Why, do you know, I heard the most *delicious* piece of gossip from Lady Oakston last night. Apparently Annabella Broseley was in the habit of making illicit trysts with Francis in the woods. This was well before the wedding, and they say he was not the first…' Her voice faded away.

Will straightened and let Annabella go gently, watching with regret as the intrusion of reality caused the colour to leave her stricken face and the bright light fade from her eyes. He captured both her hands and held on to them.

'You have nothing to reproach yourself with, Annabella,' he said gently, 'neither now nor in the past. Miss Hurst has a vicious tongue, and at the moment her disappointment leads her to exercise it on you. I beg you not to regard it.'

'Who was she with?' Annabella whispered.

'I do not know. Miss Mundell, perhaps, for no one else would bear her ill-bred prating!' There was real violence in Will's tone. He saw how upset she was and added gently, 'As I say, do not regard her, Annabella. She is bitter with disappointment.'

Annabella nodded slowly. To have returned to reality with such an unpleasant shock had somehow spoilt the sweetness of what had happened before. Spoilt it, but not put it from her mind altogether. She had never felt like that before. It had been a little frightening, but at the same time entirely pleasurable and it had left her wanting more…

'Don't look at me like that, Annabella, or I will forget my good resolutions,' Will said a little roughly. 'There really was something that I wished to say to you. I have to go away for a few days.' He saw her face fall and added, 'I have business with my lawyer in London, or I would never go away at such a time. Will you stay at Mundell until I return, so that I know that you are safe here?'

Annabella shook her head again. The memory of Miss Hurst's spite was still in her mind and she would have been quite happy never to have to see her again. To spend several days in her company, without the protective presence of Will Weston, was not to be considered. Even Lady St Auby was a preferable option.

'No,' she said slowly, 'I will go back to Taunton, I think. I was intending to return today, and I find I do not wish to stay here in such company.'

Will tightened his grip on her hands. 'Very well, I shall not seek to dissuade you. But there is something most particular I wish to say to you, Annabella. I doubt we shall have the opportunity to speak privately again until I return from London, but when I do, do I have your permission to call in Fore Street to see you?'

Annabella caught her breath. She could not misunderstand him. He intended to make a proposal in form. Even as she smiled her acquiescence, and felt his lips brush her cheek in the tenderest of kisses, her heart cried out for him to speak here and now. But he was silent, and in a moment he pressed another kiss on her hand, tucking it through his arm.

'We must go back to the house now.' He scanned her face and his expression softened. 'Can you try to look as though our attention has been concentrated on nothing more exciting than the roses? At the moment there is a certain air of distraction about you which, whilst completely charming, will certainly put ideas into the heads of the more observant of Mundell's guests!'

Inevitably Annabella blushed all the more at this, and equally inevitably Will found himself obliged to kiss her again as a result. It was a long, delicious, passionate time later that they finally managed to disentangle themselves. Annabella's hair had completely escaped its pins and her cloak had become snagged on the thorns when Will had precipitately pushed it from her shoulders so that his mouth could trace the delicate line of her jaw and throat. Her lips felt swollen and beestung with kissing and her eyes were bright with unsatisfied desire. Nor did Will look any less shaken than she. He took several deliberate steps away from her.

'Enough of this! I'm not made of stone, sweetheart! We really must seek the safety of the house!'

He took her arm again, and this time they wended their way slowly through the maze of garden paths to the house. It was unfortunate that Miss Hurst was just crossing the marble hall as they came up the steps, for she paused and her sharp gaze took in every aspect of their appearance.

'Lud, Mrs St Auby, you look as though you have been pulled through the hedge backwards! Why, there are twigs in your hair!' Her gaze moved to Sir William's inscrutable face, and whatever she saw there made the words wither on her lips. 'Well,' she said, with playful lightness, turning back to the easier prey, 'you must be sharp set after such a morning's activity, Mrs St Auby, though from all I hear, it is not new to you! Breakfast is being served in the dining-room, I believe! You must have worked up quite an appetite!'

And with a trill of laughter at Annabella's furious, mortified face, she set off up the stairs.

'So, has the navy stolen your affections away from the militia, my dear?' Mrs Eddington-Buck asked, her bright brown shrew's eyes darting maliciously. Lady St Auby drew a sharp breath before Annabella even had time to think of an answer.

'It's a scandal, Millicent! First she has young Jeffries paying court and then she goes jaunting about the country with that ramshackle Sir William Weston! But—' she gave a thin smile '—it's all of a piece! Her mother was another such, by all accounts, forever throwing out lures to any man who would take her! Why, how do you suppose she ended up with that Cit, Broseley? Do you know, I heard—'

Annabella rose and quietly left the room. She had become reasonably inured to criticisms of her own conduct, but unjustified attacks on the mother she had never known had the power to hurt her more deeply. Lady Julia Broseley had been a gentle girl, shy and unsure of her own worth, momentarily dazzled by Bertram Broseley's golden good looks and supreme self-confidence. He had married her for her family connections, and when her parents had disowned her for the runaway match, had treated her with the crushing contempt he had for all commodities that no longer held any use for him. Poor, sad Julia had provided him with two daughters, and died as quietly as she had lived, when Annabella was only a few days old.

Annabella went up to her tiny bedroom, the only place where she could escape Lady St Auby's sharp tongue, and sat by the small window, trying to read. After the airy simplicity of the rooms at Mundell, the St Aubys' poky old house felt particularly claustrophobic, especially as her mother-in-law had picked up immediately on her happiness with the curious awareness that unhappy people have for the joy of others. She had chipped away at Annabella with the same bitter comments as before, and though she could not touch her daughter-in-law's inner contentment, she soon had Annabella wondering whether the veiled malice of Miss Hurst might have been easier to bear.

It was only two days since she had left Mundell Hall, and yet it seemed much longer. Annabella sighed. She found she could not concentrate, for her mother-in-law's mention of George Jeffries had brought back the extraordinary conversation she had had with him the previous day.

She had hardly been expecting to see Jeffries at all, for their quarrel several weeks previously had seemed final, and her head was full of Sir William Weston. They had been riding on the afternoon of the previous day, up on the Quantock Hills in the bright summer's day, and it was the last in a series of happy memories which remained with Annabella from the time they had spent together. She had been vaguely surprised when Jeffries was announced, but too secure and wrapped up in her new-found love to spare much thought for why he was there.

He had strolled into the drawing-room as though their disagreement had scarcely occurred. He had brought with him a bunch of gaudy red roses, well past their best bloom and with the petals about to drop, and had laid them carelessly on the table as he had come in.

'Annabella, my love!' He took her hand and pressed a damp kiss on it, looking at her languishingly. 'You are in excellent looks today! All this fraternisation with Mundell and his set must be good for you! It is the talk of the town!'

Annabella felt the irritation rising in her at this odious familiarity of his. Worse, the drawing-room door was ajar, and she could see her mother-in-law's flushed red face in the opening as she eavesdropped shamelessly, and the maid grinning in the hallway behind her.

'I scarce expected to see you again, sir!' she said coldly. 'The last time we met, your departure suggested that you would be taking your compliments elsewhere in future!' Too late, she realised that he had interpreted this as jealousy on her part, for he was grinning complacently. He had a round, impudent face with pale grey eyes that somehow always managed to appear over-familiar, and now he was admiring her figure in a way she found frankly insolent. She sat down hastily, and Jeffries took a chair opposite, continuing his ogling. Annabella itched to slap his face.

'You must forgive me,' he said, with an obvious assumption that she would. 'I was disappointed by your reticence on the occasion of the ball, but I understand that you feel you must observe the conventions of mourning a little longer.'

Annabella felt her temper rising. 'My reticence did not stem from hypocritical conventionality, sir,' she said, frigidly. 'I infinitely regret that you find it difficult to believe that I have no interest in your attentions!'

'Ah, the respectable widow!' Jeffries's tone was still easy, but Annabella saw a flash of anger in his eyes. 'Say no more, my love—we shall not quarrel again over this! But remember—' his lips tightened into a humourless smile '—your distinction by Mundell and his set may be short-lived. They may drop you as quickly as they have taken you up, and then my attentions may not be so unwelcome!'

Sighing, Annabella wondered how obtuse, or just plain conceited, a man could be, and also how rude she was going to have to be to get rid of him. She raised an eyebrow. 'Was that all you had to say to me, sir? If so—'

'No, there was another matter.' Jeffries was still smiling, and there was an unpleasant edge to it. 'I came to warn you.'

'To warn me?' Annabella was so surprised that she forgot to be angry. 'About what, pray?' She watched him sit back, very much at his ease, and her mystification grew.

'About Sir William Weston.' Jeffries's grey eyes slid away from hers. 'He is not…a man to be trusted.'

All Annabella's bad temper returned with a rush. 'And what can you know of the case, sir?' she asked scathingly. 'I was not aware that the gentleman was known to you!'

'I had not met him before that night at the ball,' Jeffries admitted, 'but he was known to me by reputation.' He shifted a little in his seat, still avoiding her gaze. 'And that reputation is not a sweet one, Annabella. I speak only out of concern for you.'

'Very fine of you, sir,' Annabella snapped. 'I scarce consider you to be the man to criticise another's apparently unsavoury reputation!'

Jeffries had the gall to look more sorrowful than angry. 'I did not mean to imply that he had a penchant for women,' he said apologetically, 'although there were tales—'

'I thank you, I do not wish to hear them!'

'No, indeed,' Jeffries murmured, with an unctuous smile, 'I should not sully your ears. But this is more serious, Annabella.' There was something in his tone which caught her attention. Her anger died a little. Could this really be as serious as he implied? She did not want to hear this, and yet...

'What do you mean?' she asked slowly.

'I mean treason,' Jeffries said, in the same ingratiating tones as before. There was a silence. On the mantelpiece the clock ticked loudly.

'I think that you must be quite mad, sir,' Annabella said faintly. 'Treason? Whoever could think such a thing?'

'I wish I was.' Jeffries was determined to finish. 'There was talk when I was serving under General Ross out in the United States. Weston was the captain of a frigate which was involved in the naval battle for Lake Champlain in '14. When he came under fire, they say he retreated and ran instead of coming to the aid of a fellow ship... There was talk of dereliction of duty, but no charges were ever brought, for as you know, Weston has friends in high places. I had already heard some tales of him falling in with privateers when he was in the Indies, for how do you think he made his fortune? But again, no charges were brought…I thought you should know…'

Annabella found that she was full of wild, unreasoning rage. Her thoughts were spinning in a kaleidoscope of colour and images. Chief amongst them was the memory of Sir William's face. How could this man, who had not one ounce of Will's integrity or courage, come here to make such outrageous accusations…? She stood up. 'I thank you for coming to spread your wicked, unfounded gossip, sir,' she said, her voice shaking with suppressed rage. 'You will oblige me by leaving the house immediately. I want to hear no more of this poisonous tale. If no charges were ever laid against Sir William, it ill behoves you to raise such slanderous defamation again! Upon my word, this rings with spite and malice, nothing more! Good day, sir!'

Jeffries stood up too. There was an ugly look on his face, blurring the good-natured features into a sneer of malevolence. 'Oh, it suits your purposes to disregard my words, madam, for I know you have high hopes of Weston! Well, he will never marry you, for what are you, after all? The destitute daughter of a disgraced merchant, whose own family want nothing to do with her! Weston is after bigger fish and don't give a toss for you!' He marched to the door and flung it open, sending Lady St Auby flying. Annabella felt sickened. She had temporarily forgotten her mother-in-law, with her habit of listening in to every conversation within the house. Now it could be guaranteed that the whole of Taunton society would hear the shocking tale, much embroidered, and before teatime. Lady St Auby's features were a compound of delight at the insults Jeffries had heaped upon Annabella, and unholy glee at being in possession of such a prime piece of gossip. As the front door slammed behind the Captain, Annabella caught her mother-in-law's arm in a grip that made the older woman wince.

'I had forgot your vulgar habit of eavesdropping, madam! If this story goes the rounds I shall have no hesitation in laying it at your door!' She gave Lady St Auby's arm a shake. 'Further, I shall advise Sir William to sue you for slander! He is a rich man and can well bear the expense—which you can not, can you, madam? Now, for once in your life, make a decision based on sense rather than gratification!'

Lady St Auby recoiled from the fury she saw in Annabella's eyes, but her daughter-in-law had already dropped her arm, privately shocked at the violence of her own emotions. She had known that she was falling in love with Sir William, had revelled in the romance and the pleasure of his attentions, had been looking forward to the declaration that she knew to expect when he returned. But first there had been Miss Hurst's spiteful insinuations, then Lady St Auby's sniping, and now Jeffries's vicious slander. Was everyone determined to spoil her happiness? And how intolerable for Sir William that men such as George Jeffries should go around repeating their poisonous tales simply to cause trouble, and that women such as Lady St Auby would batten on them! Jeffries should be careful, Annabella thought, that Sir William did not call him out. But then, what did one do about such unpleasant gossip? Should it be given consequence by acknowledging and responding to it?

Remembering the incident, Annabella threw her book aside in vexation and looked out of the dusty window on to Fore Street. She would have to speak of the matter with Caroline Kilgaren, whom she had arranged to meet for a shopping trip the following day.

Caroline would reassure her that it was all a hum and not worth a moment's thought. And soon Will would be back, and it could all be forgotten. With a little sigh, Annabella picked up her book again and forced herself to concentrate on the page. At least it helped to pass the time.

A wet morning greeted her when she rose next day, with skies of an unrelieved grey to match her mood. It was still early when the knocker went and the maid brought in a bouquet of roses from the gardens at Mundell, the dew of morning still fresh upon the velvety petals. Unlike Jeffries's tribute, these roses were still tight buds with a heady scent that promised the richness that was to come, and the card that accompanied them was written in Sir William Weston's hand, telling her not to forget, and that he would see her soon. Annabella smiled a little dreamily as she put the roses into water, and hummed as she went about her tasks for the rest of the morning. The impact of Jeffries's cruel words was receding, and she knew it would not be long until Sir William returned. Lady St Auby's malice slid off her without touching, deflected by a love she was sure must be reciprocated.

The town was busy when she went out to the market. Since the incident with the pail of water, Lady St Auby had given her only the lightest of household tasks, and Annabella was quite amenable to doing the marketing. She had an eye for good produce and the stallholders liked her friendliness. Where the maids tended to return with old vegetables about to rot, either because they wished to buy cheap and keep the change, or because the vendors fleeced them, Annabella usually found a bargain. But this morning the experience was far from pleasant.

Small knots of women stood about, baskets over their arms, their eyes sharp as Annabella walked by. The whispering started behind her back: comments about Sir William Weston's sudden departure from Mundell Hall, allusions to the gossip Annabella had heard, speculation that he had dropped her. All of it was murmured in an undertone, the speakers looking hastily away when she turned to challenge them. She had seldom had so uncomfortable a trip out. So it seemed Lady St Auby had been unable to hold her tongue, or else Jeffries had been dropping his venom into other ears as well as hers… Annabella hurried back to confront her mother-in-law, only to be thwarted by finding her out on a visit to Mrs Eddington-Buck.

It was almost midday when the sharp rat-a-tat of the knocker startled her again. Annabella was so sunk in despondency that she scarcely wondered who it was. There was the sound of voices in the passage, and then the drawing-room door opened.

'My dear Mrs St Auby! How do you do, ma'am?' With a slight shock, Annabella recognised the stooping gentleman in the doorway as her father's lawyer, Mr Buckle. She had not seen him since the time, immediately after her father's death, when he had had the unfortunate task of telling her that Broseley's estate had nearly all been swallowed up by debt. He tipped the rain from his hat and handed it to the maid, gratefully accepting Annabella's offer of a cup of tea.

'An inclement day,' he observed, divesting himself of his coat and fussily laying it out to dry, 'but not a day of ill tidings, I am glad to say!' He beamed at Annabella over his half-moon spectacles. 'I have good news for you, young lady! Very good news indeed!'

Annabella got up and closed the door. There could be nothing untoward about an interview alone with her father's man of business, and she was damned if she was going to share the news of any good fortune with her mother-in-law's servants.

Mr Buckle was unpacking his case, shuffling papers self-importantly. 'We have finally wound up your father's business affairs,' he said a little pompously, 'and I am pleased to tell you that there is a residue from the estate—a very small residue given the significance of your father's fortune at one time— but, nevertheless, enough to give you a modest income.'

Annabella's gaze had wandered back to the tiny unfurling buds of the red roses, glowing softly on the corner table. She dragged her attention back. 'But that is excellent news, Mr Buckle! Is it...' she was almost afraid to ask the question '...is it enough to live on?'

Mr Buckle primmed his lips. 'A moderate sum only, but with proper investment...yes, I should think that, if you are careful, it could be enough.'

Enough to help me escape from this house at least,

Annabella thought, and found her attention almost imperceptibly drifting back to Sir William Weston again. Perhaps she need not worry about continuing much longer in the St Aubys' household… But this could only make it easier for her, for she would feel that it was less of an unequal match if she had some money of her own… Scolding herself for letting her mind wander to Sir William yet again, she realised that the door had opened to allow the maid in with a steaming cup of tea, and that Lady St Auby was lurking expectantly in the corridor. The door closed quietly and Annabella realised that Mr Buckle was still speaking.

'…all the property has been sold to cover the debts,' the lawyer was saying, 'but there is one estate left. Well,' he corrected himself, 'perhaps estate is not the right word, for the property is small, but thirty acres, with a farm and a modest house…'

Modest was evidently one of Mr Buckle's favourite words, Annabella reflected. And it suited his own moderate and respectable demeanour. It had always been a surprise to her that Bertram Broseley had chosen such a demonstrably honest lawyer, but then perhaps that was precisely why he *had* chosen him.

'There is a problem, however,' Mr Buckle was saying, suddenly fixing Annabella with a severe look as though the obstacle was her own making. 'The title to the property is in dispute.'

'In dispute?' Annabella was confused. 'Do you mean that the house is not really mine?'

Mr Buckle made a deprecating movement. 'No indeed, my dear Mrs St. Auby! The property is yours, inherited from your father who, in turn…erm…

bought it from the late owner some five or six years ago. What is apparently in dispute is the manner in which—' he cleared his throat discreetly '—your father purchased the estate.'

'Extortion?' Annabella asked politely. 'Blackmail? The possibilities are endless...'

Mr Buckle looked scandalised, as he always did when someone suggested that Broseley's business methods had been less than scrupulous. 'Mrs St Auby! No, indeed, nothing of the kind! The house was offered as repayment for some gambling debt— a wager between your father and the owner, which he later regretted. But the deal was sound, if a little...' he cleared his throat '...a little unorthodox, shall we say? Your father,' Mr Buckle added, nodding sagely, 'always preferred property to money in these circumstances. It's value always increased handsomely and made him a splendid profit!'

Annabella sighed. Mr Buckle sighed too, but for a different reason.

'But now the owner's son is threatening to take the case to court, claiming that the arrangement was illegal. He evidently feels very strongly about the manner in which his father lost that particular piece of his heritage! He is not a poor man, but I believe he wants the property back for family and sentimental reasons.' Mr Buckle frowned. 'I have to say that he has been somewhat intemperate in his demand to settle the issue.'

The faintest scent of roses drifted across the room to Annabella, and at the same moment the faintest shadow touched her heart, the smallest of suspicions...

'Where is the house?' she asked, her throat suddenly dry.

Mr Buckle shuffled the papers again. 'In Berkshire, I believe...'

'...a house on the Berkshire Downs, just north of the little village of Lambourn...'

'...the late owner was a Sir Charles Weston...'

'...my father died a few years ago... But it is a long time since I have been there...'

Annabella could hear the echo of her own voice: 'For what reason have you sought me out, sir?'

The blinding tears came into her eyes, blurring the outline of the beautiful red roses. Through her numb despair, she remembered that she had suspected that Sir William Weston had had a reason for pursuing their acquaintance. He had soothed her doubts, made her fall in love with him, pretended that he cared for her too. How ironic that Miss Hurst had been correct all the time, that Sir William's charm was a means to an end, a means of regaining his patrimony one way or the other... Mr Buckle carried on speaking for some time, but Annabella had no idea what he said.

'I understand how you feel, my dear,' Caroline Kilgaren said, her piquant face creased with anxiety and distress, 'but will you not wait a little? This hasty departure surely cannot aid matters. And I am persuaded that Sir William would wish to explain the situation to you himself—'

She broke off. Long experience of Annabella's sister Alicia had taught her when she was wasting her breath, and in the past few weeks she had realised that Annabella was more like her sister than anyone had ever realised.

Annabella was very pale, sitting tense and upright in the chair opposite Caroline's. Her eyes burned with fury and her expression was set. 'I do not wish to hear any of Sir William's excuses, ma'am.'

The wind hurled another flurry of rain against the parlour window.

Caroline sighed, abandoning that particular tack. 'And I was so hoping that Alicia would send a letter soon, and invite you to stay with her! That would have solved all your problems! You did write to her, did you not?'

Annabella nodded slowly, regretting the impulse that had prompted her to set pen to paper and contact her sister. 'I did, but I do beg you, ma'am, not to tell her of this. Sir William's friends should not be embarrassed by a division of loyalties! I have no wish to cause trouble for my sister, nor indeed for you, ma'am.' Her hard tone softened a little. 'You have shown me nothing but kindness, and I do thank you for it! But my mind is made up. I travel on the morrow.'

Caroline gave a graceful shrug. 'I can see that there is no dissuading you! The house is fit for habitation, I take it?'

'Oh, yes!' Annabella lied brightly, trying to dismiss the memory of Mr Buckle's horrified face as he had begged her to allow him at least to have the house cleaned for her. He had been deeply disapproving when she had expressed her intention of travelling to Larkswood immediately. Realising that something had upset Annabella, but not understanding the cause, he had entreated her to be reasonable and had evidently thought her a half-wit to go to a place that had not been inhabited for three years. His protestations had fallen on deaf ears, however. In the space of a few minutes, Annabella had become so determined to claim her inheritance from under Will Weston's nose that she would stop at nothing.

Will Weston... First, he had made it impossible for her to continue living under the St Aubys' roof by showing her another, far more desirable existence. She had fallen into the very trap she had wanted to avoid, the trap of thinking that the life led by Will and his friends was for her, that she could become a part of it. Worse, she had allowed herself to fall in love with romance and with him equally, and now the romance had gone but her painful love for him remained, twisted out of all recognition. She could not bear it, but it seemed she must...

'And you have a companion to accompany you?' Caroline pursued, recalling Annabella to the present, to the musty room and the claustrophobic life she was trapped in. 'It would not be the done thing at all for you to live at Larkswood alone!'

'Have no fear on that score!' Annabella had already chosen the only maid in the St Auby household who was not slovenly and sullen. Whether she would pass muster as a companion was another matter entirely, but she would have to do, for there was no one else.

Caroline still looked dubious. She got to her feet and picked her reticule up from the table. 'Then I can only wish you good luck. But, Annabella—' she gave her an impulsive hug '—if you ever need anything at all, please let me know! I do not like matters to end this way!'

Annabella blinked back the tears. 'It is far better—'

'Will was only ever interested in you for yourself,' Caroline said abruptly, to cover her own emotion. She could not bear the heartbreaking, stricken face of the girl before her. It was so clear that Annabella St Auby was hopelessly in love with Will Weston, and that love made her feelings of anger and betrayal all the more intense. And Caroline was a loyal friend who could not bear to see two people she cared for make such a mull of so promising a situation. 'Will would never have married you just for Larkswood,' she said, trying again when Annabella's stony silence was her only reply.

'Oh, I am persuaded of that,' Annabella said, with bitter anguish. 'He would never wish to tie himself to an unloved wife for the sake of so small a property, not when he is so rich!'

'Then why cannot you believe that he cares for you?' Caroline asked, perplexed.

Annabella shrugged angrily. 'Because he did not tell me about Larkswood in the first place! Because he did not tell me the truth, did not trust me! Perhaps he thought to make me fall in love with him so that he could persuade me to sell Larkswood back to him at less than its value, hoping that I, poor fool, would be so besotted that I only wished to please him! Perhaps he was just trifling with me as a small revenge against the family which cheated his father out of a pretty property! I do not know, since he did not see fit to tell me the truth!' Her voice fell again. 'He did not trust me,' she repeated.

Caroline shook her head, aware that it was pointless to persist. Annabella's sense of betrayal was too
raw, too new, for her to listen to reasoned argument.
'I shall not say goodbye, for I am sure we shall meet
again,' Caroline said slowly, devoutly hoping it
would be true. 'Farewell then, Annabella, and good
luck!' And she went out, tripping over Lady St Auby
in the doorway and giving her so searing a glare that
the older woman positively shrank away.

The carriage took Caroline swiftly back to Mundell
Hall, her shopping trip forgotten. She was greeted
with the news that the men were out shooting, and
she had no taste for the company of Miss Mundell
and Miss Hurst. She hurried to the study, paused
briefly as she remembered Annabella begging her not
to tell anyone about the dispute with Will, then called
for pen and ink and settled down at the escritoire to
write a hasty note to her oldest and dearest friend,
Alicia Mullineaux.

Annabella's sense of misery and disillusion had
grown with the passage of time. Too inexperienced
and too in love to be able to achieve even a degree
of equanimity over Will Weston's behaviour, she had
dwelt on his betrayal until she was quite sure that she
hated him. It angered her that her mind seemed incapable of blocking him out, surprising her at the
most inappropriate moments with the image of him,
or a memory of some time they had spent together.
When she dreamed one night that she was in the rose
arbour at Mundell with him again, she awoke confused and tearful, feeling betrayed all over again.

To add to her woes, her impulsive decision to move

in to Larkswood had proved to be nothing short of disaster. On the day after Mr Buckle's visit, she and the maid, Susan, had left Taunton at first light for the long and arduous journey into Oxfordshire. The coach had lurched and jolted its way along the roads until they both ached in every joint. Annabella had just enough money to pay their fare on the stage as far as Faringdon, and from there a kindly carter had taken them across the wide, flat valley towards Lambourn. The carter had dropped them by the gate of Larkswood just as the sun was sinking behind the hills, those sweeping chalk hills which Sir William Weston had described so memorably that time on the terrace at Mundell. They had been tired and dusty from the journey, the last part of it jarring over rough tracks behind the labouring horse. As the carter set off again up the steep track, a silence descended that seemed as old as time. The evening sky was bright blue, and the setting sun gilded the rosy sarsen stone of the house with a warm glow. A tabby cat was sitting in the deserted courtyard, its golden eyes watching them unblinkingly. And then a rat had dashed across the yard and into an outhouse, the cat had raced after it, and Susan had screamed and flung herself into the arms of a young man who had just come through the field gate to see what was going on.

It had turned out to be a useful introduction. The young man, Owen Linton, was the tenant farmer at Lark Farm, and Susan was a very pretty girl, and soon the besotted young man was at their beck and call for such matters as mending doors and hammering down loose floorboards. But despite that, they were fighting a losing battle.

Annabella sighed to herself, thinking of all that needed to be done. Larkswood was a neat and charming house, standing foursquare a little back from the track which linked Lambourn with the road east to Oxford. It had four bedrooms, a dining-room and a well-appointed drawing-room which looked out over the gardens and the orchard. Between the house and the farm was the cobbled courtyard, and at one end was all that remained of 'The Old House', as Owen Linton put it, a small medieval manor which had once stood on the spot and was now reduced to a couple of rooms and a pile of stones. Not, Annabella thought, that the old house was much less habitable than the new. Three years of neglect had left their mark in damp walls, rotten carpets and curtains, and mildewed furniture. There were mice in the kitchen, despite the presence of the tabby cat, and the only water had to be drawn each day from a well in the courtyard. Paint was peeling, tiles loose, floorboards squeaky. They were five miles from the nearest village, and had no transport…

Annabella sighed again. The spar that turned the well chain was rotten and the chain itself old and rusty from disuse. She could hear the bucket splashing about below but the handle stubbornly refused to turn. She could feel herself perspiring in the morning sun, feel her headscarf slipping back as her face grew redder with her exertions. It was just another of the small irritations which now made up their everyday life.

This is all Sir William Weston's fault, Annabella thought, turning her anger once more into the iron resolve that she would keep Larkswood as her own

and never let it go. She would show him that she was
not to be charmed and brushed aside when the fancy
took him. Let him challenge her right to the house in
a court of law if he wished! She would never yield.

The sound of hoofbeats on the track distracted her
and she straightened up. Visitors were rare here, and
except for the odd cart or hay wain, few vehicles used
the track over the hills. Annabella pushed her headscarf back from her honey-coloured hair and the cobwebs on it tickled her neck. It had proved unexpectedly useful to have nothing but old clothes, for she
had no need for finery here. It could not have been
more different from the splendour of Mundell.

The horseman turned the bend in the track, can-
tered into the yard and slid out of the saddle, hitching
his reins over the fence in a gesture which suggested
that he had done the same thing a hundred times before.

'You!'

For a moment, Annabella stared in total disbelief.
The ride across the valley had ruffled Will Weston's
tawny hair, but it was the only sign of dishevellment
to compare with her own disarray. Those compelling
blue eyes were as vital as ever as they rested upon
her and he moved towards her across the cobbled yard
with the same contained grace that had always drawn
her gaze. Annabella found that the passage of four
weeks had done nothing to lessen the shock and pain
of seeing him again. She could not be indifferent to
him. She told herself that she hated him.

'Good afternoon, Annabella.' It was almost a physical pain to hear her name spoken again in that well-
remembered voice, the resonant tone, cool, consid-

ered, authoritative… She had admired him so much, she realised suddenly, and felt all the more disillusioned as a result.

And now not even the courtesy of her formal name, now that he no longer had any reason to hoodwink her! For some reason, Annabella had never imagined that Will would seek her out again, let alone here at Larkswood, which was the very cause of the dispute between them. But now that he was here, she wondered why on earth she had not thought to anticipate such a meeting, for she was indeed woefully unprepared to deal with him. Acutely aware of the cobwebs clinging to her skin, her flushed face and her stained and torn gown, she glared at him.

'You are not welcome here, Sir William! Leave my property immediately!'

Will showed no sign that he had even heard her, strolling imperturbably across the cobbles towards her. Annabella's fury locked in a tight pain in her chest.

'I want to talk to you.' Now he was standing in front of her.

'Well, I have no wish to talk to you!' Annabella raised her chin. 'Take yourself off, sir!'

Will seemed unmoved. He smiled slightly, as though she were a spoilt child. It made her blood boil even more. 'Must you be so melodramatic?' he enquired. 'I had hoped that we could go into the house and talk sensibly about this.'

Talk sensibly! It was the last thing Annabella wished to do! 'You are not listening to me, sir,' she responded furiously, her green eyes flashing. 'I do not want to speak to you. Now, go away!'

No gentleman that she had ever met, and certainly no one whose manners were as good as Sir William's, was likely to disregard her wishes in this and force his company on her. She had already turned away when Will picked her up and carried her, kicking and shrieking, into the house. Susan, who had come into the yard to find out what had happened to the pail of water, stood in open-mouthed amazement as Sir William strode past her.

'The devil you don't!' he said equably, as he put Annabella down on her feet in the drawing-room and prudently stood back out of range when she might have tried to slap him. He closed the door, then looked about him with what Annabella could only interpret as horrified surprise.

'Good God,' he said, quietly.

She could imagine what prompted his thoughts and it filled her with even greater anger. The once-delicate plaster of the ceiling was crumbling into dust and mould was growing on the walls. The floorboards had given way in one corner and the curtains were rotting where they hung. There was barely any furniture and a fusty smell filled the air.

'You cannot possibly stay here,' Sir William said, still in the same quiet tone.

'Yes, I understood that was what you came to tell me,' Annabella said nastily, suddenly afraid that she might cry. The temerity of the man in pretending to care about her was too much. 'So, do you intend to try to buy me off, sir? Or perhaps you have no wish to offer money for such a ruin of a house, and have simply come to tell me that you will take the case to

court? You are too late, sir—my lawyer has told me
as much already!'

Sir William sighed, driving his hands into his trou-
ser pockets. 'I meant only that the place is not fit for
you to live in and you will make yourself ill in the
trying. Good God, the walls are running with damp—
you will succumb to a chill within a week!'

'Your concern touches me, sir,' Annabella said,
filled with a perverse enjoyment that she appeared to
be able to be as horrible to him as she wanted without
him retaliating. 'You need pretend no longer, however! Had you had any genuine consideration for me,
you would have told me of your interest in Larkswood from the start, instead of cozening me with soft
and sweet words!'

'So now we come to it,' Will said softly. He
opened the door again, letting in the fresh air and the
sunlight. 'It is not as you imagine, Annabella. How
could I have told you? I was caught— I knew that if
I told you about Larkswood as soon as we met you
would assume that the house was my only interest in
you, or that I was trying to charm you into letting me
have it back for a minimal price...I knew that you
would not believe I was interested in you for yourself
alone!'

'Whereas now, of course,' Annabella said sarcas-
tically, 'I know just how true your sentiments really
were!'

She saw a muscle tighten in Will's jaw and felt
even happier to see that she could pierce his indifference and make him angry when he was trying so hard
to be rational. She felt almost drunk with the pleasure
of it.

'Have you now come to tell me that you have changed your mind and will not be claiming Larkswood back?' she demanded, and saw her answer at once as he turned away.

'If you would let me explain,' he said, with constraint. 'My father regretted the wager he made with Bertram Broseley by which he signed away this house. He tried to buy it back several times, I believe, but your father would have nothing to do with it. I am willing to try to prove that the wager was illegal because I need the house—'

'*You* need the house!' The hurt burst in Annabella in a huge, angry tide. 'No, sir, *I* need this house—really need it! You, who have so much, think of taking from me the only thing that really is mine! What am I to become—a pensioner of my sister and her husband, or worse, the continued object of Lady St Auby's charity?'

'I had once hoped,' Sir William said very quietly, 'that you would become my wife.'

'Oh!' The cruelty of his words touched Annabella to the quick. She felt all the breath go out of her as though she had been punched. She turned on him in blazing fury. 'There is no need to gild the lily, sir! All pretence between us is at an end! You never cared for me, and I never had any feelings for you!'

'Is that so?' Sir William had moved with surprising agility to catch hold of her and pull her into his arms, despite her struggles. Annabella could not free a hand to slap him, so she kicked his shins viciously.

'You little vixen!' Sir William still sounded amused and it infuriated her. If he had tried to kiss her, she would have bitten him. He did not do so, however, merely holding her so tightly that she could barely move. He spoke into the golden curls.

'Now, my love, I remember thinking once that honesty was one of your greatest virtues. Be honest now, and tell me that you are indifferent to me.'

'I see that you are amusing yourself at my expense as well—' Annabella said hotly, only to be interrupted.

'Amusement be damned!' There was angry vehemence in Weston's tone now behind the quietly spoken words. 'You are determined to think the worst of me, are you not, madam? What, then, if I live up to your opinion of me?'

It was unfair, Annabella thought desperately. Held close in his arms, all she could concentrate on was the treacherous persuasion of his body against hers, the feeling of attunement that was both familiar and yet intoxicatingly exciting at the same time. She looked up into his eyes, her own darkening with despair.

'You need not make your feelings any more plain, sir—'

'Oh, indeed!'

She could not fight him, nor, she found, did she have any inclination to do so. This time there were no concessions to her inexperience. He kissed her with a ruthless demand and she returned the kiss in full measure. They were so swept away that neither of them heard the carriage that rumbled up the track, or the voices in the yard and the footsteps in the hall. They did not break apart until an amused masculine voice behind them said,

'Well, William, I have found you in some extraordinary situations before now, but none so remarkable as this!'

It was a moment of some delicacy. James Mullineaux was lounging in the doorway, a whimsical smile on his face as he regarded the couple. Annabella, her heart sinking, saw that Alicia was at his shoulder, immaculately beautiful as ever in a dress of bright yellow that should have clashed horribly with her auburn hair, but of course did not. And worse, behind them, but still with an undoubtedly clear view of proceedings, stood her grandmother, the Dowager Countess of Stansfield, whom she had never previously met but whose identity was obvious. Lady Stansfield, in vivid emerald green that matched her bright green eyes, was watching Annabella with an incalculable expression.

'We had thought to invite you back to Oxenham with us, Annabella,' Alicia said to her sister, hurrying into the sudden silence, 'but perhaps, if you have settled your differences with Sir William…' Her thoughtful gaze travelled from Annabella's bright red face to Will's studiously blank one.

'I have not!' Annabella snapped. 'Sir William has made some arrogant and groundless assumptions that his suit would be welcome! Well, it is not, whatever appearances may say to the contrary!'

'It was a good try though, Will!' James Mullineaux observed with a broad smile, and Annabella glared at him, quite forgetting that she had always been in awe of her sister's devastatingly handsome husband.

'Well, then…' Alicia said, a little inadequately, as the silence again threatened to become embarrassingly long, 'would you care to stay at Oxenham for a little, Annabella, just until Larkswood is made more comfortable for you?'

Annabella caught Alicia's eye and was shaken out of her self-absorption. Preoccupied with her feelings for Will Weston, appalled that she had responded so fervently to his kiss, humiliated to have been discovered thus, she had not really thought how difficult such a meeting could be for Alicia. Now she came forward with a sudden, shy smile to kiss her.

'Oh Alicia, I am so sorry! I am really so very glad to see you again, and nothing would please me more than to spend some time with you, but only—' her gaze fell on Will and hardened again '—as long as it is understood that I do not give up my claim to Larkswood! I do not care if our father robbed, cheated or murdered his way into this property—I intend to keep it!'

Alicia hugged her, a little apprehensively. Seeing her own temper reflected in someone else was a rather nerve-racking experience. 'Of course! We can talk about it all later. For now, let us get you out of this place before the whole house comes tumbling about our ears—'

'Annabella!' The autocratic tones stopped them all in their tracks. Lady Stansfield had drawn herself up to her full—tiny— height. 'Come here, my gel.'

Annabella's heart was suddenly in her mouth. She knew of her grandmother only by repute, but had heard that the old lady was sharper than a needle and never minced her words. She dropped her a demure curtsy. Lady Stansfield's jewel-bright eyes scanned her face thoughtfully.

'Hmph! Don't seek to cozen me with your milk-and-water airs, miss! It's a bit late for that! I saw you just now, aye, and heard you too!' She took Anna-bella's chin in her hand. 'You have a great look of your mother about you, child,' she said surprisingly, 'and a Stansfield through and through, to judge by that temper!' She gave a dry cackle of laughter. 'You'll have to try harder, Sir William, to win this one's heart!'

'So it would seem, ma'am,' Sir William said ex-pressionlessly.

The bright green eyes moved on to search his face for a moment, then Lady Stansfield laughed again. 'You'll do,' she said, with a malicious smile, 'and I shall enjoy the entertainment of watching you try to prevail!'

'Grandmama,' Alicia said severely, 'we are not all here simply as a diversion for you! James, I shall take Annabella off to pack now, if you wish for a word with Will! Annabella, I think that little maid had bet-ter come with you...' And she shepherded her sister and her grandmother out of the room.

As she packed her meagre belongings for the sec-ond time in a month and instructed Susan to do the same, comforting the lovelorn girl with the thought that they would soon be back, Annabella was prey to very mixed emotions. She had no intention of letting go of Larkswood now that she had found it, nor of falling victim to Will's convincing lies for a second time. And whilst she was glad to have the chance to get to know both her sister and her grandmother bet-ter, she was aware that it could distract her from the problem of the house, and that could be dangerous. Besides, whilst neither Alicia nor James had expressed any view on her relationship with Sir William, they were both great friends of his and could therefore not be impartial… Annabella sighed. Looking out of the window, she saw James and Will emerge from the house and part with a quick word and a handshake. No, it would not do to let her defences down.

Chapter Six

Alicia Mullineaux was reading, but her mind was not on the written word, and when the door opened softly to admit her husband into the bedroom, she cast the book aside on the bedspread with little regret.

'James, I need to talk to you!'

James Mullineaux raised one black eyebrow and sat down beside her, taking her hand in his. His wife looked distractingly lovely in a diaphanous lace nightdress, but he doubted whether she would appreciate being told so at the moment, for her face was crumpled with worry in a way that made her look absurdly childlike.

'What is it, my love?' he asked gently. 'Surely you cannot be worrying about Annabella again? She is with your Grandmother in her room, chatting nineteen to the dozen, so that is one of your fears allayed, at least!'

The frown on Alicia's brow lightened for a moment. 'Yes, I must own that I had the gravest doubts that they would like each other, and yet they have taken to each other in such a way!'

'Your grandmother,' James said, toying with a curl that was lying seductively in the hollow of Alicia's collarbone, 'recognised instantly what the rest of us have only just started to realise, which is that Annabella, like you, is a Stansfield after her own heart! So, if that is not your concern, what—?'

Alicia's frown returned. 'It is just that I cannot believe Annabella is happy,' she said in a rush. 'She loves Will, but she refuses to see him, and will not listen to a word in his favour. Oh, I can see that she believes herself deceived and, indeed, it was unfortunate that he did not see fit to tell her about Larkswood before, but...'

James's lips had replaced his fingers in stroking the delicate skin of her neck, and Alicia stopped, trying to remember what she was trying to say. 'James...'

'Yes, my love?'

'About Annabella and Will...'

James raised his head slightly. 'Alicia, I love Will Weston like a brother, and I want your sister to be happy, but we must leave them to sort out their differences. And just now I could wish them in Hades...' His fingers had found the ribbons which tied the nightdress and were giving them short shrift. He slipped his hand inside the lacy bodice. Alicia gasped.

'Do you still wish to talk?' James asked teasingly, his lips brushing hers, 'or may it wait until later?'

Annabella St Auby and Will Weston were also awake, but for different reasons. Annabella had parted company with her grandmother a few minutes before, having spent an entertaining evening being regaled with stories of Lady Stansfield's experiences in *ton* society. She was feeling too restless to sleep, pacing about in the pretty yellow bedroom which Alicia had had furnished especially for her, picking up a book, casting it aside, turning to her needlework and sighing before she even attempted a stitch.

Once she was on her own these days, she found that her thoughts reverted to Will Weston in the tiresome but inescapable way that they had done for the past three weeks. When she had first come to Oxenham, he had called to see her several times and she had refused to speak to him, but in the past week he had neither written nor called. She supposed that she deserved this but, annoyingly, his absence had done nothing to keep him from her mind. Nor did Alicia or James ever mention Will to her, an omission which Annabella was beginning to consider as rather sinister.

She wondered whether they were all conspiring against her behind her back, then scolded herself for her obsession. Whatever the case, in a strange way his absence only seemed to reinforce his presence in her mind and prevent any possibility of her forgetting him.

Other young men had called at Oxenham and had been introduced to her by Alicia, who had seemed overly anxious that she should find at least one admirer in local society. Contrarily, Annabella found herself taking random dislikes to these unsuspecting fellows: they were too young, too old, too fat, too thin, too miserable, too *cheerful*... Even Richard Linley, a neighbour of her own from Lambourn, who had every grace and circumstance to recommend him, was found to be at fault simply for not being Will Weston.

And through all her bad temper, Alicia would smile tolerantly and James would look amiable and Lady Stansfield would tease her for being a fickle madam until she wanted to scream with frustration that they did not understand. But, of course, they did, which was part of the trouble.

Had Annabella but known, she was in the thoughts of the very man whom she found so difficult to dismiss. Will Weston was sitting alone in his study with nothing but a glass of malt whisky and his thoughts for company. He had been turning the wooden globe on his desk, a faint, reminiscent smile on his lips as he remembered his travels to Zanzibar and Antigua and the Cocos Islands... He had never wished to settle on land for any length of time until now, and until now he had never met a woman he had wished to marry... He took a sip of the whisky, enjoying its aromatic flavour. From the first he had been drawn to Annabella St Auby, finding both her person and her individuality deeply attractive. It was an irony that the same characteristics which had endeared her to him in the first place were now the stumbling-block in their relationship. Had she been more tractable he would have risked another attempt at an explanation, but he had no confidence that they would not end up quarrelling. So perhaps he would simply have to try to woo her once more... He smiled again. It did not sound like a hardship.

'I am not certain whether the colours of that flower border work well together,' Alicia sighed, eyeing the drift of purple and blue with disfavour. 'What do you think, Annabella? I must discuss the matter with Fisher, I suppose, and plan a new planting scheme for next year!'

Annabella jumped guiltily. Her mind had not been on Oxenham's delightful gardens, nor indeed on much that her sister had said for the past five minutes, for she had been thinking of Will Weston yet again.

During the lazy late summer days, she had gradually grown to know Alicia better and had spent much time with her grandmother, who showed all signs of doting on her newly found grandchild. Little Thomas Mullineaux, her nephew, was also an adorable distraction. Meanwhile, James had sent a team of men to lick Larkswood into shape and soon it would be fit for habitation again. Larkswood, her inheritance. She blotted from her mind the memory of Will's strained face as he had tried to tell her that he needed the house. The mingled misery and anger rose in her once more, and she was glad when Alicia spoke again and distracted her.

'Caroline writes that Ermina Hurst has gone back to London,' Alicia said, reading from a letter that had just been delivered. 'Apparently Viscount Mundell is under siege from another young lady now, a Miss Hart, who has taken Taunton by storm! Poor Hugo! I wonder how he bears it! And Caro has also met an erstwhile admirer of yours, Annabella, one George Jeffries… Oh!' She pulled a face. 'I do not think she likes him a great deal!'

'Neither did I!' Annabella said, with feeling. She pushed the memory of Jeffries's insolent face from her mind, but the mention of his name raised other recollections, which she had forgotten until then. She had been intending to ask Caroline about the dreadful slander of Sir William Weston's name, she remembered, and whether such rumours had ever surfaced before. Their quarrel had put such thoughts from her mind, but even now, believing him false in his affection for her, she could not quite also believe that his integrity was also a lie. He had seemed too fine a man, too honourable... Stop it, Annabella, she chided herself furiously, as a warmth invaded her heart, threatening to banish her anger and undo her completely.

'Alicia...' she began, intending to ask her sister about the rumours, but at that moment, Thomas chose to crawl towards the flowerbed and put a handful of soil in his mouth. In the ensuing excitement, the nursemaid swooped on her charge with cries of alarm, and Alicia took him on her knee, wiping the dirt from his face.

'I have an errand to run in Challen village,' Alicia said, when things had calmed down, 'but I wondered whether you would mind going for me, dearest Annabella? I promised Mrs Coverdale, the vicar's wife, that I would pass her some of Thomas's old baby clothes...' Her gaze fell on her baby son again, gurgling blissfully on her lap. 'But James is due back soon, and I wanted to spend some time with him and Thomas alone. Would you mind, Annabella?'

In fact, Annabella was quite glad of the trip out. The even tenor of life at Oxenham bored her at times, but only, she told herself severely, because she was so unhappy in herself. And that brought her to the only point of Alicia's request that was inconvenient, for Will Weston's home was at Challen Court, and she knew that he was staying there despite his absence from Oxenham. She told herself that she did not want to see him—and knew that she was lying.

Alicia's landaulet was very pretty and the drive to the village was accomplished with ease, Annabella having no difficulties in controlling the matched pair that drew the carriage. She had met Mrs Coverdale the previous week, and spent a pleasant half-hour chatting and admiring her newborn baby. She drove back down Challen high street, suddenly noticing that there appeared to be babies and small children everywhere, squalling in their mothers' arms on cottage doorsteps, or playing by the side of the road. A strange feeling, part-longing, part-envy, stirred in Annabella and she blinked in surprise. That was a train of thought that was even less profitable than her hopeless dreams of Sir William Weston...

She did not see him, as she had half-hoped she would. But as she drew out of the village, past the first set of cross-roads which led to Challen Court, she saw that the stage was before her, setting down its passengers at the junction with the Oxford Road. She reined in and waited until it set off again in a cloud of dust, and was about to drive on when her eye was caught by the two passengers who had descended on to the grass verge.

The first was a young woman little more than Annabella's age, and she was heavily pregnant. A large, battered portmanteaux, surely too heavy for her to carry, lay in front of her, and a child of about three clutched her hand. More babies and children, Annabella thought exasperatedly. She pulled out to pass them. At the same moment the girl called out, 'Your pardon, ma'am! Can you direct me to Challen Court, if you please?'

Annabella paused, looking more closely. The young woman was very pale and there was a sheen of sweat on her face, no surprising thing in the heat of the afternoon, but suggestive of illness rather than mere warmth. Her thin dress was sticking to her, and a sudden grimace of pain crossed her features, causing her to grip the child's hand so tightly that she started to cry. Annabella got down carefully. She took the girl's arm as she swayed.

'Challen Court is up this road, but it is almost a mile, you know, and you cannot possible walk it! It is obvious that you are very unwell!'

'It will pass in a minute,' the girl whispered. 'The jolting of the coach...' She swayed again, catching the wheel of the landaulet to steady herself and closing her eyes for a moment.

Enlightenment burst on Annabella in a flash. 'But we must get you to the house at once! Are you able to endure the short distance in the carriage? I am afraid that it is the only way...'

The girl gave her a faint, reassuring smile. 'You are very kind, ma'am. It will be some little time yet...' Her voice trailed away and she closed her eyes again briefly. She had a sweet voice, Annabella thought, momentarily distracted, with an unusual accent... A servant girl from Cornwall, perhaps, for her tones were similar to Susan's rich West Country voice. But what did she want at Challen Court?

She helped the young woman up into the seat with some difficulty, and bent to pick up the little girl and pass her up to her mother. The child wriggled on to the seat and turned to survey Annabella with the serious contemplation of children. She was a pretty little thing, fair and sturdy, and she had the most vivid blue eyes that Annabella had seen. Unmistakable eyes...Weston eyes... At the same moment, the young woman said softly, 'I know that Will can help me...he wrote to tell me to come...' and she smiled very slightly.

A cold wave of shock broke over Annabella, and she stood back. The woman, who was slumped in her seat, had not noticed anything odd, but the little girl continued to watch her with Will Weston's bright blue gaze. Annabella gave herself a shake. Later, she told herself sharply, later you can think about this. For now, you must get her to the house. But she felt cold, and her body seemed slow to act, and her fingers felt clumsy on the reins.

A mere few minutes brought them in sight of Challen Court, which was fortunate, for the young woman had turned an even pastier shade of white and had her eyes closed as spasms of pain wrenched her body. Annabella drove straight into the stable yard. Several grooms, who had been working in the tackroom, came running at the sound of the wheels, and one, brighter than the rest, sped off into the house calling for help.

A number of servants now came hurrying forward, and Annabella's eyes fell with some relief on the unmistakable figure of a housekeeper. She jumped down from the carriage and went up to the woman, grasping her arm. There was no time for long explanations.

'Please help us, ma'am! I found the young lady at

the crossroads, asking for Challen Court. I think she is about to be confined!'

The housekeeper swept one comprehensive look over the huddled figure in the carriage. 'Yes, you are right, ma'am! John, Harry, lift the young lady down. Beatrice, run inside and heat some water. Has someone gone for the master? What—'

In the confusion, no one had noticed the arrival of Sir William Weston until the girl, now standing in the yard supported by two burly footmen, looked up and a smile broke across her strained features.

'Will, oh, Will, I am so very glad to see you...' She started to cry. Annabella felt very much like following suit. This tender reunion, following on so swiftly from the shock of meeting the woman and the child, was a little too much for her. She watched as Will swept the girl up into his arms with negligent ease. Her arms went about his neck and she turned her face against his chest. The housekeeper was holding the little girl by the hand as they followed them indoors. A pang of pure jealousy wrenched at Annabella so fiercely that she almost cried aloud.

'Don't try to talk now, Amy. You are quite safe.' Annabella watched as the girl's head drooped against Will's shoulder and her eyes closed. She turned away, her throat choked with tears, determined to drive straight out of the yard without another word.

Sir William paused momentarily. 'Jem, stable Mrs St Auby's horses; Barringer, show her into the green drawing-room, if you please. I shall be with you directly, ma'am.'

Their eyes met. Annabella opened her mouth to say that she was leaving, but the words died unspoken.

There was something so compulsive in Sir William's gaze, compounded of a bright anger and even stronger demand, that made her hold her tongue. In silence, she accompanied the little party into the house and watched as Will carried the girl upstairs, before the butler's gentle voice broke into her thoughts and she followed him meekly into the drawing-room.

'Well, Annabella, what new calumnies have you imagined against me by now?'

Annabella had not heard Will enter the room, for she had been rapt in her attention to the portrait on the wall, which was of a man, presumably the luckless Sir Charles Weston, who had the same distinctive blue eyes as all his family. The contemplation of his picture had helped her to pass the long minutes since she had been left alone and also helped her not to think too much. Now she jumped and spun round.

'The lady… Will she be all right?' she asked spontaneously, then, realising that he had already spoken, said, 'I beg your pardon, what did you say, sir?'

A shadow of what might have been surprise touched Will Weston's face.

'Amy—my sister-in-law—will be fine. Mrs Jenner is with her now, and has some experience in such matters. She assures me that we do not need to send for the midwife. It will be a little time before I am presented with a new niece or nephew.'

Annabella sat down rather suddenly. 'Your sister-in-law!'

A faint smile touched Will's mouth, but left his eyes cold. With a small shock, Annabella realised that he was angry. It was a cool, contained anger rather than a wild fury, but nevertheless it was frightening. Even when she had provoked him so at Larkswood that day, he had only appeared amused with her. But now there was no amusement in him, and no kindness.

'You are so easy to read, my dear Annabella! In that split second in the yard, I had ascertained that you had seen Charlotte's blue eyes, noted—obviously—Amy's condition, thought about her asking for me…and made some rather large assumptions!'

Annabella blushed bright red. 'I did not… I was not aware…' Her voice faded away as she realised that she had no suitable excuses to hand.

Will's sardonic smile deepened. Annabella got to her feet again rather quickly. 'I really should be going now—'

'Oh, no,' Will said softly. 'Not this time!' He was standing with his back to the door, leaning his broad shoulders against the panelling and giving every indication that he was unlikely to let her out of the room. 'This time,' he added pleasantly, 'you will do me the courtesy of giving me a proper hearing.'

'But…' Annabella cast about desperately for a reason to escape '…I am expected back directly! I am already late, for we have guests tonight and I was supposed to be collecting some vegetables from the farm on my way back…' Again her voice trailed off under his pitiless gaze.

'I have already sent a messenger to Oxenham to assure your sister that all is well,' Will said calmly. 'No doubt they will make shift to provide for their guests in some other way!'

Annabella sat down for a second time. 'Oh, but—'

'I wish to explain about Larkswood.' Will drove his hands hard into his pockets. He moved across to the fireplace beneath the picture of Sir Charles, and rested one booted foot on the fender. 'But first I should tell you about Amy—' those very blue eyes met hers expressionlessly '—in order that there is no misunderstanding.'

Annabella flushed bright scarlet again. So he thought her a gossip who might damage his sister-in-law's reputation, did he? The idea that he had so low an opinion of her was a hurtful one, but then she had done little to make him think well of her. Suddenly she deeply regretted the pride and disdain that had made her refuse to listen to him when he had tried to explain about Larkswood. Her arrogance did not reflect well on her. And now he had read her reaction to Amy Weston so accurately, and was angry, not indulgent.

'You may remember that I told you at Mundell that my brother had married an American girl and lived abroad until his death last year,' Will was saying. 'He took a fever—it was a terrible tragedy. Since the death of Amy's father, Peter had run the family plantations, but when he fell ill and died she could not continue there alone. She is not strong and, of course, there was the new baby on the way. She wrote to tell me that she would sell the estate and come to make her home in England.' He shook his head. 'I counselled her to wait until after the baby was born, fearing that such a journey would be too much for her, but I never heard from her in reply.' He sighed. 'Her letter telling me of her departure for England must have been lost in the post and is probably at the bottom of the sea by now. I had no notion of her coming here until today. Now, God willing, the baby will be delivered without difficulty…'

There was a knock at the door and Barringer entered with a tea tray. 'Mrs Jenner has asked me to tell you that all goes well, sir, but that it will still be some little time,' he said, primly. 'Shall I put the tray here, sir?'

Will did not look as though he cared in the slightest about the location of the tea tray, and it was Annabella who gestured to the butler to put it down in front of her.

'Only Barringer could serve tea at a time like this,' Will murmured in exasperation.

Annabella poured a cup. 'It is the done thing for expectant fathers, unless they are on the hunting field,' she said, commiseratingly. 'No doubt your butler felt the situation also applied to expectant uncles!'

That won her the faintest flicker of a smile. Will took the proffered cup and sat down.

'You must be desperately concerned, sir,' Annabella continued. 'Surely anything else you may wish to say to me can wait until later? Larkswood is of no importance in comparison…'

Once again, that unfathomable blue gaze rested on her and Annabella, feeling discomfited, made a business of stirring her own cup of tea.

'It surprises me to hear you say so, ma'am,' Will murmured. 'But I prefer all matters to be out in the open.'

Annabella's heart sank. 'As you wish, sir.'

Will stirred his tea vaguely, still looking at her in that reflective way, then he appeared to pull himself together for, when he spoke, his voice had regained its usual incisive tone.

'You should know that I have decided to give up all claim to Larkswood.'

Annabella almost dropped her cup. He did not appear to notice. 'My brother and I grew up there and it holds many of the happiest childhood memories for me. We moved here when my father inherited Challen, but I always preferred Larkswood, modest a property as it was.' His gaze rested for a moment on the benign, fair figure in the portrait. 'I was at sea when my father wagered the house. He wrote to me that he had been unable to find a tenant because of the isolated location, and that it had been easier simply to sell the place. I was surprised, but not suspicious.' He put his empty cup down. 'To his death, I never imagined that there was anything sinister in the sale. And then Peter told me what had happened.' His gaze came back to Annabella and she almost flinched.

'It seems my father had wagered foolishly in a game of Hazard against Bertram Broseley. The house was his stake. My father regretted it and later tried to buy the property back several times, but Broseley always refused...' He made a slight gesture. 'Father was too ashamed of what had happened to tell anyone, but when he was dying he let slip to Peter what had happened. His lawyer confirmed it.'

'And you wanted Larkswood back,' Annabella whispered.

'It seemed only fair,' Will said savagely. 'I was willing to pay the gambling debt, plus a generous rate of interest. I had been lucky with the prizes I had captured at sea, very lucky. And then a distant cousin of mine died and left me a tidy fortune. This estate, which could turn a good profit once it was properly managed, was no drain on my resources. My father had been ill for some time, and his revenues had been declining, but I had little difficulty in improving matters. So you see…' he shrugged '…if it had not been for my father's misjudgement or pride, the house need never have been lost.'

It was an untimely moment for Annabella to remember George Jeffries's words, but for some reason they rose in her mind and would not be dismissed. 'I had already heard some tales of him falling in with privateers when he was in the Indies…how do you think he made his fortune?'

So there had been nothing in that particular nasty piece of gossip, she thought thankfully. Sir William's money had come by the conventional routes of success as a navy captain and inheritance. And the other charge of cowardice—

'What is it, Annabella?' Will asked sharply. 'You look as though you have seen a ghost!'

Annabella shook herself. 'It is nothing… You do not surprise me, sir, with your account of my father's dealings. He was ever one to drive a hard, if not an illegal, bargain, and he always preferred property to money for it appreciated in value.'

Sir William shrugged. 'Naturally, the deal in itself was legal, if unethical. On my return from the war, Lovell, my man of business, told me that Broseley had recently died and had been found to have debts greater than anyone might have expected. It seemed a good opportunity to take Larkswood back. But Buckle—your lawyer, I suppose—refused to negotiate, and so I was reduced to making somewhat stark threats of legal action. And then there was Amy. I thought that Larkswood would be the ideal home for her and Charlotte. Then I met you and was obliged to reconsider my position on the house, but since I hoped that you and I—' He broke off, and began again with more constraint. 'Anyway, I want you to know that I no longer wish to reclaim Larkswood. You pointed out to me, quite rightly, that without it you have nothing. I would not wish to take that from you.'

'Why did you not tell me before…about Larkswood—?' Annabella started to say, then broke off in confusion as she realised how close she was to tears. Will was right, of course; through her own ill-considered reaction to his behaviour she had lost the chance of an alternative future. She put her cup down on the table with a rather abrupt thump and got to her feet. 'Your pardon, sir. That was foolish of me. I do not require an answer to that question. I really must go…'

'Wait…' Will had also got to his feet and the movement brought him closer to Annabella than was quite comfortable.

'No, really…I must get back…the others… dinner—' She knew that she was gabbling. 'I am so very glad to understand a little of why you wanted the house…' she swallowed hard '…and even more grateful that the rumours I had heard about your fortune were unfounded—'

There was a moment of complete stillness.

'And which particular rumours would those be?' Will asked, quite without expression.

Annabella was edging towards the door when he took her arm in a grip that was not painful, but which she certainly could not have broken without effort. She knew that she had made a mistake but, preoccupied with escaping from the turbulent effects of his presence and the intensity of her own emotions, she had not been thinking about what she was saying.

'I suppose,' Will said, with the same hard, angry edge that had been in his voice earlier in the evening, 'that I should not be surprised that you had been listening to unfounded gossip about me! After all, you have interpreted all my other actions in the worst light possible!'

'That is unfair!' Stung by his words, Annabella wrenched her arm from his grip and glared up at him. 'I did not give any credence to what I heard! And I could not ask you—'

'Why not?'

'Because you had already gone—'

'Of course, I forgot.' Will's tone was savage. 'By then you assumed that I was trying to trick you over Larkswood! Was *that* the rumour you had heard, or were there other tales? Good God, what must your opinion of me have been, when all the time I was thinking—'

'You are despicable to twist my words so!' Annabella cried. 'Yes, I'll admit that Miss Hurst planted a doubt in my mind that you had some interest in me other than for myself! That was why I asked you, that night in the summerhouse…' Her voice broke. 'But you assured me that it was not so, and I believed you!'

'Then what else has been said? Good God, I had

no idea that Taunton was such a hotbed of speculation!' But there was no humour in Will's voice and he waited in stony silence for his answer.

Annabella was twisting her hands together in distress. She knew she was getting into a terrible tangle. 'Oh, this is all so stupid! I never meant—'

'You will oblige me by telling me exactly what you did mean.' There was steel in the smooth tones now.

'Very well!' Annabella's green eyes were suddenly defiant. 'A good friend warned me about you, Sir William. He said that you were not a man to be trusted! He said,' Annabella added, with unforgivable exaggeration, 'that you had made your money conspiring with pirates and that in the American Wars you forgot your duty sufficiently to abandon a fellow ship to its fate and save your own skin!'

She thought later that she had been fortunate Will had not struck her. Out of her own hurt and misery she had spoken more wildly than she had intended, but it was no excuse. She saw the stark fury in his face as he stared at her, then he turned away as though he wished to turn his back on her forever. After a moment of silence she took an impulsive step forward, touching his arm tentatively, but he shook her off as though she were contaminated.

'Stories such as those are so vile they do not warrant any explanations,' he said at length, in a low voice. 'And for you to believe them…' He shook his head slowly.

'But I did not!' Annabella was really frightened now. She had thought him so calm, so slow to anger. Little had she known! But then, she had impugned his honour and integrity with her words, and he would not forgive her that…

'This is all so foolish,' she said helplessly. 'I told you I never believed ill of you! The rumours were idle malice, prompted by jealousy, nothing more! You must believe me!'

Will shrugged indifferently. 'If you say so. I suppose it does not matter now.' He swung round and his blue gaze chilled her to the bone. 'Well, I must keep you no longer, Mrs St Auby. Pray give my best wishes to your sister and to James Mullineaux.'

He was holding the door open for her, still with that detached, cold courtesy that was somehow more frightening than any anger. Annabella hesitated, uncertain how to reach him, wanting only to banish this hostile stranger, who looked on her with such formality and dislike.

'Will…' she said beseechingly, using his name for the first time in a desperate attempt to put matters right before it was too late.

'Good evening, Mrs St Auby.'

He was not going to relent. The unshed tears bright in her eyes, Annabella raised her chin and marched out of Challen Court, praying that she would not disgrace herself by crying until she was out of sight.

The journey back to Oxenham was a nightmare for Annabella, as she could not see where she was going. The tears came in floods, blurring her vision, dripping on to her cloak and pretty muslin dress. Fortunately the horses knew their own way home, for Annabella was utterly incapable of giving them direction. She abandoned them in the stableyard and ran into the house, oblivious of the wooden-faced footmen in the hall, and cried all over Alicia's silk evening gown when her sister emerged to see what on earth was going on.

'Oh, Alicia, it was so dreadful! I am sure that he has nothing but contempt for me... I thought his sister-in-law was his mistress, and the poor woman is but recently bereaved, and he had wanted to marry me and now he has told me that he will not press his claim to Larkswood, but I wish he would...' Annabella's voice dissolved into a wail of inconsolable despair.

Alicia bore all this with fortitude and steered her sister into the library away from their dinner guests. She asked no questions, simply sitting with her arm around Annabella until the sobs had abated a little.

Annabella raised a face blotchy with tears. 'There was the poor woman standing by the side of the road in the extremes of pain and misery, and all I felt was a vicious jealousy, and it was the most *lowering* thing imaginable! And then when he came out into the courtyard and smiled on her with *such* tenderness, I wanted to scratch her eyes out! Oh, Alicia, I know I should be ashamed of myself, but I can't because I love him, you see, and it is so painful...' And her tears started afresh.

Alicia, abandoning hope of the delicious fillet of beef which would be rapidly congealing on her plate in the dining-room, hugged her sister all the harder. 'Love can be a very difficult matter,' she allowed. 'If you have never felt like this before—'

'I haven't.' Annabella wept piteously. 'I cared nothing for Francis, and I was nothing but a stupid child to imagine him as a way of freeing myself from our father. It took me very little time to realise my mistake! And then, when I met Sir William, I thought I had been given another chance, but I threw it all away…'

'Surely it cannot be so bad—'

Annabella raised drowned green eyes to meet her sister's gaze. 'There is worse!'

'Surely not!'

Annabella was determined to make a clean breast of matters. 'I called him a traitor!' she announced tragically.

Not surprisingly, Alicia was somewhat startled at this extraordinary statement. 'Go back to the beginning and tell me the whole story,' she besought Annabella. 'I cannot make head nor tail of this!' This was hardly surprising, since her sister had been crying so much as to be practically unintelligible. Annabella blew her nose, took a deep breath and related the whole of her meeting with Amy Weston once again, and the events which had followed.

'So, when Will explained about the money he had inherited, I realised that the scurrilous story I had heard about him consorting with privateers was false,' Annabella finished, 'and I said so. I was too upset to be thinking properly, Liss, or I would never have breathed a word! But then, of course, Sir William thought that I had believed the rumours about him and became unbearably stuffy! I was so angry with him for thinking the worst of me that I told him the whole tale! It was stupid and childish of me, but I was so furious!' Her voice caught on a sob. 'Oh, it was dreadful, dreadful! And now we will never be comfortable together again!'

A small frown marred Alicia's forehead. 'So there were rumours that Will had made a fortune through piracy? I have never heard such tales!'

'Oh, worse than that.' Annabella grimaced. 'At least, I suppose it's worse... Which would you say was the greater dishonour, Liss—to be accused of piracy, or cowardice in battle?'

Alicia looked as though she would have liked to put her head in her hands. 'Oh, Annabella! You didn't—'

'I know it was foolish of me...' Annabella looked away from her sister's accusing gaze, on the verge of bursting into tears again. 'You need not reproach me—I shall never forgive myself!'

Alicia bit her lip. 'Cowardice in battle?' she repeated carefully. 'Were there specific facts mentioned, or was this just another wild tale?'

Annabella made a hopeless gesture. 'I don't know! It was something to do with Lake Champlain—a few years ago—in '14, I think he said...'

'Who said?'

'Captain Jeffries...' And Annabella dissolved once more into tears.

'That troublesome man! Well, I have never heard these charges!' her sister said stoutly, 'and we all know Will Weston is too fine a man for them to be even remotely true! But you know how dangerous gossip can be. Such talk is very damaging, Annabella—'

'Oh, do not!' Annabella wept. 'I know! I never

believed it, but Will thinks I did, and now he will never speak to me again!'

Alicia thought that this was probably true and was too honest to try to comfort her sister with false promises. To impugn the reputation of a man like Will Weston was no light matter. She made a mental note to ask James if he had heard anything of such rumours, and shepherded her unresisting sister to the door.

'You had best go to bed, Annabella,' she said gently. 'Matters will seem better in the morning. Fordyce, a tray for Mrs St Auby in her room, if you please. I will rejoin my guests for dessert.'

But, in the event, all of Cook's delicacies were wasted on Annabella, for they turned to dust and ashes in her mouth.

Annabella felt no better the next day, nor the one after that. Her days at Oxenham had fallen into a pattern: riding early in the morning, visits with Alicia, visits from neighbours and friends, trips out, walks about the estate, talking to her grandmother, playing with Thomas, and helping her sister entertain the guests in the evening. There seemed to be any number of sports and entertainments devised purely for pleasure. It was not an onerous existence and was, in fact, rather a pleasant one. Alicia had summoned her own dressmaker to provide Annabella with a wardrobe of clothes, she had every material need satisfied and she had the affection of her family.

Compared to the drab routine of life with the St Aubys, it was well nigh blissful. And yet, Annabella felt that she did not have a place. James and Alicia

would never have treated her as a poor relation and
Lady Stansfield had even indicated her intention to
alter her will to include Annabella, but she had no
function to fulfil in the pattern of life at Oxenham.
And she was not sure how long this could continue.
She began to long fervently for Larkswood to be finished so that she could go back to a place that was
her own.

It was five weeks before Amy Weston made her
appearance in local society. She had been delivered
of a boy, called Peter after his late father, and both
mother and baby were thriving. Alicia had called
early to convey their welcome and best wishes but,
not surprisingly, Annabella had felt herself unequal to
another visit to Challen Court. Her misery over Sir
William was never far from her thoughts and it was
more than she could bear to see him again. She had
thought herself unhappy before, but this second misunderstanding between them, based on so foolish an
error, was almost too much to stand. Once or twice
she thought of asking James to intercede for her with
Will, but could not bear the thought of her apologies
being rejected.

When Alicia announced a few days later that she
was giving a dinner in Mrs Weston's honour, Annabella almost invented a sick headache out of pure ter-
ror, but she knew she had to face Will some time.
She managed to work herself up into a fine anticipation of the evening, but in the event it proved to be
a sad disappointment. Alicia had prudently placed
Will at quite some distance from Annabella down the

table and when she did dare to raise her gaze to meet
his, it was to notice that he scarcely even glanced in
her direction. To Annabella's besotted gaze he looked
compellingly attractive but frighteningly forbidding.
Annabella's company was monopolised by an elderly
neighbour of James and Alicia, Sir Dunstan Groat,
who was much taken with her prettiness, called her a
buxom little wench, and spent a large part of the evening ogling her.

Amy Weston made a special point of thanking Annabella for her help that day at Challen, but when the
gentlemen rejoined the ladies after dinner, Will
steered her away to more congenial company and
poor Annabella was left feeling as though she had the
plague. She was asked to sing, but the occasion reminded her too sharply of the time she had sung at
Mundell, and her voice faltered sadly on the notes.
The applause at the end was merely polite. All in all,
it was a miserable evening, and Annabella retired
early to bed, pleading a headache.

The second time they met, it was easier. Their mutual friends, the Linleys, hosted an evening party with
impromptu dancing; although Will did not ask Annabella for a dance, he did at least manage to be civil
to her and exchange a few pleasantries. Once again,
Sir Dunstan Groat monopolised her company, which
Annabella bore with as much equanimity as she
could. She still felt very miserable. The dispute over
Larkswood had been painful enough, but the misunderstanding about the gossip was so silly and could
have been avoided if only she had thought. Now it
only served to underline the permanent estrangement

between herself and Will. Annabella could visualise a series of empty social occasions, stretching into infinite time, at which they met and smiled stiffly, exchanged a few words and separated once more. It could not be worse. But, of course, it could be worse, for he could marry... Once again, she went to bed with a headache and awoke feeling unrefreshed.

As the late summer days slid into autumn, Annabella and Will were often in each other's company. In some ways, matters grew easier; in other ways, they were more difficult. Though Will never asked her to dance at any of the events they attended, Annabella found that they could at least converse pleasantly enough on superficial topics. Once, she had started to try to apologise for their misunderstanding, only to be cut off by the cold look in his eyes and harsh words of rejection. She did not try again. Then there was the torment just of seeing him, particularly when he was in company with some lady of his acquaintance. Annabella was miserably aware that envy was becoming one of her besetting sins.

On the morning following one party, when Will had paid such particular attention to a certain Miss Watts that eyebrows were raised, Annabella rose early, determined to shake off her blue devils with a ride. The day was bright, with a soft wind off the downs and the promise of an Indian summer heat when the sun got up. The mist lay wreathing the fields as Annabella and her groom set out. She was surprised to feel her spirits lifting almost immediately. The cool air stung her cheeks to rose pink and ruffled her hair. She let her feelings dictate a speed that was perhaps a little unwise, galloped across the fields and left the toiling groom on his old bay horse far behind.

When she looked back it was to see that another figure had come upon the groom, paused for a few words, then set off towards her. It was impossible to distinguish the horseman from this distance, but Annabella had a sudden and unwelcome conviction that it was Sir William Weston. She watched for a moment as he galloped towards her, setting a killing pace on the black hunter. Then she deliberately turned her horse's head and set it at the high brushwood hedge which blocked her access to the next field. They scrambled over, but only just. The horse pecked on landing and almost threw Annabella, but she managed to stay in the saddle, urging the mare onwards with a speed that almost seemed borne of panic. There was the thunder of hooves behind her and her reins were caught in an iron grip.

'A moment, Mrs St Auby!' Sir William Weston said, very politely.

Annabella swung round defiantly. 'Yes, sir?'

'This is my land, and—'

'And you would rather I did not trespass?' Annabella said sweetly. 'I beg your pardon, sir! I shall be on my way directly!'

Sir William did not scruple to hide his exasperation. 'I was about to say that there is a treacherous bog up ahead. I was concerned that your headlong flight might lead you into it unawares.' He ran a hand through his disordered tawny hair. 'Damnation, why must you be so—?' He broke off, the lines of his mouth tightening in irritation.

The hot colour flooded into Annabella's face. 'I

beg your pardon, sir,' she said with reserve. 'I thought you were about to ring a peal over me!'

'For your reckless riding?' Sir William laughed shortly. 'Well I might, Mrs St Auby! You gave the impression of someone anxious to break her neck!' He paused and looked at her consideringly. 'However, you ride magnificently. Not one in ten riders would have recovered the way you did after that jump.'

He pulled his horse alongside hers, and they continued at a more decorous pace. Annabella was surprised that he sought her company at all. Surely his behaviour previously had only served to underline to her the dislike in which he must hold her. She found that she was nervous.

'From what were you trying to escape, Mrs St Auby?' Sir William asked now, the searching blue eyes scanning her face. 'Speed such as that is usually indicative of a need to evade something unwelcome!'

Annabella jumped. Damn him, he was too astute! She could hardly say that she wanted some time on her own away from Oxenham, for that would appear too ungracious after the welcome accorded her there. As for admitting to a need to avoid her thoughts of him—well, that was impossible. She hesitated, whilst he watched her pensively.

'Such reticence, Mrs St Auby!' Sir William's smile was mocking now. 'It is not what I have come to expect from you!'

'No, sir, for you are forever trying to provoke me!' Annabella snapped. 'Let us talk of other matters, or we shall only argue! How did Mrs Weston enjoy herself last evening?'

'I believe she liked it very well,' Sir William said carelessly. 'I have not seen her this morning, but on the journey home she was forever talking of your sister's warmth and kindness, and what good company we had. I think it would please her if you felt able to call at Challen Court, Mrs St Auby. Though Amy has the children for company, I fear she must be lonely sometimes.'

'I imagine it must be horrid for her,' Annabella said sincerely, 'having lost her husband but recently, travelling alone to a foreign land and being amongst strangers! I shall be happy to visit her—if you should not mind, sir.'

'I?' Will still sounded careless. 'Not at all, Mrs St Auby!'

Annabella began to feel rather cast down. It was indubitably better to be thoroughly disliked by Sir William Weston rather than be the recipient of such indifference. At least it meant that she had some effect on him! Unseen by Annabella, Will smiled slightly.

'Of course,' he continued in the same offhand tone, 'if you are contemplating matrimony with Sir Dunstan, you may have little time to spare for Amy!'

'Marriage with Sir Dunstan!' Annabella had risen to this before she thought about it.

'Sir Dunstan Groat,' Will said, as though further clarification were required. 'He is very rich, you know, and though he has buried three wives already, you might be considering him as a potential way out of your difficulties!'

'Difficulties?' Annabella's green eyes were flashing with anger now. 'I do not understand you, sir!'

'Oh, surely...' Will sounded vague. 'You said yourself—you cannot be Alicia's pensioner forever!'

'And what business is it of yours, sir?' Annabella returned furiously. 'It may interest you to know that I have inherited a small competence from my father's estate, and have every intention of going into business!'

'The circulating library?' Will murmured. He looked so cool, so detached, so elegant in the severe style he favoured, that Annabella suddenly wanted to slap him. She forgot that she had resolved to behave with circumspection whenever she met him. He really was the most infuriating man!

'A confectioner's!' Annabella said wildly, making it up as she went along. 'Alicia has promised to invest in my enterprise!'

'Ah.' Sir William smiled pleasantly. 'Your knowledge of sugar cane will come in useful there, Mrs St Auby! How providential! And what an imagination you have, ma'am! I commend you!'

Annabella ground her teeth.

'Of course,' Will continued, as though struck by a sudden thought, 'I was forgetting that you are now rumoured to be your grandmother's heiress! That should alter your prospects considerably! But Sir Dunstan need not marry for money, though he has always wanted Larkswood land. It completes a corner of his own estate, you see! So perhaps he has an eye on your little legacy when he is paying you those lavish compliments!'

'I had not thought that you had noticed his attentions, sir!' Annabella said sweetly.

A rueful smile touched Sir William's mouth. 'Ah, you have me there, ma'am! I noticed it very well!'

There was a silence as blue eyes and green met and held for a long moment. Then Sir William raised his whip in a mocking salute, dug his heels into the hunter's sides, and galloped off across the fields without a backward glance.

Larkswood was at last ready for habitation again.

'Stuff and nonsense!' Lady Stansfield declared strongly, when she heard that Annabella intended to move there forthwith. 'You should be settled here until you marry, miss! In my day no young gel would set up home where and when she pleased! Quite unsuitable!' She settled in her armchair and fixed her younger grand-daughter with her piercing glare.

'You forget, Grandmama, that I am a widow, not some debutante,' Annabella said indulgently, for she had seen the twinkle her grandmother had been unable to banish and she refused to be bullied. 'If Alicia could do such a thing before she married James, I fail to see why it should be different for me!'

Lady Stansfield snorted. 'Oh, do you! Your sister, miss, was another such, always thinking she knew best! Aye, and a fine mess she made of matters too!'

'Now, Grandmama, that is too harsh!' Alicia caught Annabella's eye and tried not to laugh. 'Besides, Annabella will have a footman and a gardener to help her keep Larkswood in order, as well as several maids! And she will only be situated down the road. It is all most convenient!'

Lady Stansfield made a rude and dismissive noise.

'No good will come of it, you mark my words! Young gels! In my day…'

Both sisters sighed, knowing full well that they were about to be treated to another diatribe on the shortcomings of the current generation. Both also knew that Lady Stansfield had actually been accounted quite wild in her youth, in the days when eighteenth-century society had been a lot more rumbustious than at present.

'Grandmama, tell me again how you disguised yourself as a boy in order to go alone to the races,' Alicia said sweetly, to be rewarded by a scowl from Lady Stansfield.

'Pshaw! I can see your tricks, miss! To think that I should be so beset by disobedient grandchildren—'

'In your own image, Grandmama,' Annabella murmured, leaning across to tickle Thomas's tummy where he lay gurgling on the rug.

'Well, well,' Lady Stansfield said gruffly, 'if you have that henwit, Emmeline Frensham, with you, I suppose it will be accounted quite respectable! Though Emmeline is not the woman she was—not after that incident at Bathampton!'

'No,' Alicia agreed regretfully, 'Emmy's nerves have never been strong since she was abandoned at that inn the time I was abducted! But she should do very well for Annabella—she is quite excited at the prospect of a change of scene, you know, for she has lived quite retired since my marriage!'

'Should have taken Will Weston when he offered,' Lady Stansfield said suddenly, with her famed lack of tact. She ignored Annabella's blush and added astringently, 'There's a man for you! He'd have known how to keep you in order, miss!'

'Grandmama—' Alicia began, but Annabella cut in,

'In point of fact, Sir William has never asked me to marry him, ma'am!'

'Well, why not?' Lady Stansfield looked offended. 'If you'd played your cards aright, miss, you could have whistled him up! Young people today! Always fiddle-faddling around, never getting to the point! You would do better to take Will Weston as a lover—'

'Grandmama!' Annabella besought, at the same time as Alicia said,

'Not again, Grandmama! I seem to remember you offering me similar advice about James…'

'Well, then!' Lady Stansfield looked triumphant, as though Alicia had just proved her point. 'You mark my words, no good will come of this business of living alone, Annabella! No good at all!'

Chapter Seven

James Mullineaux and Will Weston, having spent the afternoon sizing up a horse which James had eventually decided not to buy, were sitting in the library at Challen Court and were talking over a glass of excellent brandy. Amy had brought Charlotte and Peter in to say goodnight to their uncle, and James had watched with indulgent amusement as the little girl had clambered on to Will's knee and planted sticky kisses on his face.

'Thinking of setting up your own nursery soon, Will?' James asked slyly, taking a chair opposite the fireplace, where the portrait of Sir Charles looked benevolently down.

Will gave him a straight look. 'I may be. I'm sure you'll be amongst the first to know, James! You've put a lot of work into Larkswood,' he added, as a logical extension to his train of thought.

James grinned, immediately perceiving what was troubling his friend. 'You can pay me back one day,' he said coolly, 'when you take possession of the house again!'

Will laughed reluctantly. 'You'll be waiting a while for your money! Your little sister-in-law has given me to understand that she won't sell to me and I doubt she'll succumb to sweeter persuasion! She don't trust me!'

'Thought the boot was on the other foot,' James said lazily. 'Annabella certainly believes you don't like her much!'

Will shifted a little uncomfortably. 'You of all people should know, James, that you can dislike someone and still find them damnably attractive!'

'None better!' James agreed cheerfully. 'So that's why you keep avoiding Annabella! Thought you just couldn't stand to spend any time with her!'

Will smiled reluctantly. 'No, you didn't, James! You know I like her too well, not too little!'

James raised his eyebrows, not denying it. 'Then why put so much effort into avoiding her? I think you're being a little unfair to Annabella, Will.' Their eyes met for a moment and he added, 'She's very unhappy, you know. I'm sure you'd agree that there was fault on both sides in your original quarrel, and as for those ridiculous rumours—well, Annabella never truly believed them!'

Will shrugged. 'Maybe not. I don't know… Devil take it, I thought those stories had all died. That's the hell of it, James—gossip is as difficult to pin down as air, but as damaging as a stab in the back, and it's never possible to trace and destroy it. When Annabella repeated the tales to me, I was so furious to hear them from her I suppose I just overreacted. If it had been anyone else I wouldn't have cared so much. But she just stood there, looking so sweet and so desirable, and repeating such debasing tales...' Will looked away, his face strained. 'I had been hoping against hope that there was still a chance for me, but there was the complication of Amy's arrival and our quarrel, and her refusal to see me—damn it, she has the pride of the devil!'

'Alicia once told me hell would freeze over before she accepted my hand in marriage,' James said cheerfully. 'It's the Stansfield temper, I'm afraid! But you don't strike me as the faint-hearted type, Will! Why don't you put your fate to the touch—if you still *want* to?'

There was silence.

'Annabella certainly seems to have healed the breach with her sister and Lady Stansfield,' Will said, turning the conversation. 'You must be pleased for Alicia's sake.'

James nodded, willing to allow the subject to change. 'Oh, Alicia's thrilled, and the old lady dotes on Annabella!' He laughed. 'And I must admit I like my little sister-in-law! I didn't really expect to, but she's not like any of us anticipated. Proud to the point of obstinacy, perhaps, and I know how it feels to be on the receiving end of that!' He shrugged. 'Milk-and-water misses are more to some men's taste, I know, but...'

Will grinned, reaching across to refill the brandy glasses. 'But there are those of us who prefer beauty and wit! Well, you may wish me luck then, James! I think you have persuaded me to try...but she'll probably tell me to go to the devil!'

The new moon was sharp and clear in a sky of black as Annabella lay in bed at Larkswood that night. She had soon discovered that living in the country on her own was a very different prospect from living as a member of the family in a large country house where there was constant company and entertainment. Although she still had visitors and, indeed, had the use of a pony and trap to convey her to civilisation, when the blue twilight of evening fell over the hills, she was, to all intents and purposes, alone. Miss Frensham, with her endless needlework, never seemed to lack occupation. Annabella, on the other hand, had already taken to reading with far greater fervour than she had previously shown, and was even contemplating gardening. She reflected ruefully that she had few friends with whom to maintain a correspondence, and she was going to need to find new resources for solitude if life at Larkswood was not to leave her lonely and dull. Still, there were always her ideas for going into business, which might bear further investigation were she to become too bored.

She found that she missed Alicia in particular over the days that had followed her move, and her grandmother to a scarcely lesser degree. As she had got to know Alicia at Oxenham, they had begun to exchange childhood memories and experiences in a way Annabella had been unable to do with anyone else. Both had been treated harshly by their father and both found solace in the other's company. From the start, Alicia had made it clear that she would not ask Annabella any difficult questions about her marriage, but Annabella needed to confide and feel that one person at least knew the entire story.

Then there was Lady Stansfield, ancient now, the relic of a previous generation, but the most marvellous raconteur of society stories from the previous century, and fiercely protective of the family she had left. She made no secret of her delight in seeing Alicia settled so well, and her desire to see Annabella suitably married before she died. When Annabella had tried to explain haltingly about her estrangement from Alicia, Lady Stansfield had cut her off with a brief gesture.

'Bertram Broseley—out-and-out bounder!' she had declared roundly. 'As for the St Auby family, nothing for them to be proud of! No need to apologise for anything that's happened, my girl!' Her green eyes were bright. 'You're a Stansfield, remember, and you're a good girl for all your contrary ways!' And she had given Annabella a hug and a kiss that had made her feel much better.

Annabella sighed now, turning over in her bed. For some reason she felt particularly restless that evening. Normally she had no difficulty sleeping, but tonight she found that Will Weston was invading her thoughts with the same relentlessness that had dogged her when first she came to Larkswood from Taunton. It was tiresome and rather depressing that she could not dismiss him. He was not for her—fate and her own pride had seen to that. Unfortunately, her emotions could not relinquish him so easily.

She slipped out of bed and sat on the window seat for a while, listening to the sounds of the night, the wind in the trees and the scuttering of little creatures in the undergrowth. Everything sounded magnified by the quiet of the house and the stillness outside. The tiny sickle moon rode high in the cold sky, and Annabella shivered. There was something curiously compelling about the shadowy night. Without conscious thought she got dressed and slipped down the stairs.

The old house cast its silhouette over the cobbles of the courtyard as Annabella slipped past. She heard Owen's cows bumping gently against each other in the barn, and the rustle of the mice in the hay. The track to Lambourn lay bright and white in the moonlight, but Annabella turned aside from the road, slipping along the field path that edged Larkswood garden. She passed the still pond that was all that was left of the old millhouse, and paused in the shelter of the hedge to consider the empty landscape. The breeze off the hills was cool and she shivered deep within her cloak. Well, a breath of fresh air should at least help her to sleep…

Without warning, there was a rustle of leaves beside her and a man stepped out directly onto the path. Annabella drew breath on a scream, but before it reached her lips, strong arms seized her from behind and a hand came down over her mouth as she was dragged backwards against a hard, male body.

'Be still and keep quiet!'

Annabella went still with shock at the sound of Will's voice. When he realised she was not about to scream he took his hand away, but only to scoop her up into his arms. Annabella had the confused impression of someone stepping past them, then Will had strode off down the path, to put her back on her feet only when they had gained the shadow of the haw-

thorn hedge. They stared at each other in the fitful
moonlight.

'What the *hell* are you doing here?'

This time, Annabella thought inconsequentially,
Will did not sound particularly angry with her, only
exasperated. She smoothed her cloak with fingers that
were still shaking a little. Her whole body was tin-
gling from the contact with his, her blood racing with
a mixture of fright and excitement.

'I might ask you the same, sir! Whatever are you
about? Do you go creeping around in the night often?'

'I asked you first,' Will said pleasantly. He took
her arm, guiding her deeper into the shadows. 'What
are you up to, Annabella?'

'I couldn't sleep,' Annabella said sulkily. 'There is
no mystery! I thought to take a breath of fresh air—'

'It is past two o'clock! Scarcely an hour for a
young lady to be out for a stroll! Not one woman in
a hundred would go out for a walk in the middle of
the night if she could not sleep! A cup of warm milk,
perhaps, a book to induce sleepiness—'

Annabella shook his hand off her arm, annoyed by
his attitude. 'A dose of laudanum?' she said crossly.
'Perhaps you would approve of that instead? I am
sorry if my behaviour offends you, but I did not expect to find the countryside so crowded! As I said,
sir, I was unable to sleep and stepped outside for a
little. I imagine my purpose is less sinister than
yours!'

Will sighed. 'I am out after a poacher, that is all.
The man you saw with me is my gamekeeper! We
had been following the fellow for several miles and
knew he had taken a hare or two, but suspected he

was after bigger game. We were about to catch him
snaring a deer when you appeared out of nowhere and
he made a run for it. A night's work wasted!'

Annabella was not about to apologise for taking a
walk on her own land. 'I suppose it does not matter
that you gave me a monstrous shock!' she complained. 'Was it really necessary to grab me like
that?'

She saw Will smile. 'Probably not, but it was rather
enjoyable! And I did deserve some recompense for
you spoiling the evening!' He heard Annabella let her
breath out on an angry sigh. 'Come, let us call a truce!
If it is any compensation, you gave me a hell of a
fright too!'

They were walking slowly up the path towards the
house.

'Your language, sir,' Annabella said primly, 'is not
that of a gentleman to a lady!'

Will sketched a mocking bow. 'Your pardon,
ma'am! But if you choose to wander about at night,
you have to deal with what you find! You should be
more careful, perhaps.'

'Perhaps so!' Annabella looked at him. There was
an undertone in his voice which suggested that she
was not, perhaps, as safe as she might have imagined.
It was a disturbing thought, and not in an entirely
unpleasurable way. Will kicked aside a fallen branch
to clear her path, and she struggled to keep a grip on
her practicality. It would do no good to allow her
susceptibility to him to distract her.

'Those are strange sentiments from a man who has
been out on the dangerous enterprise of catching a
poacher!' she said, with deliberate lightness. 'But I

shall be more careful on my next moonlight stroll, and will carry a pistol with me!'

She saw Will grin in the moonlight. 'Can you shoot?' he enquired. 'It would be an advantage!'

'Strangely enough, I can,' Annabella said demurely. 'My father considered it a useful accomplishment, which no doubt says a great deal about him! I forgot to mention that when Miss Hurst quizzed me on my achievements! Lord, it would have been worth it to see her face!'

They had reached the door of Larkswood, and Will stood back to let Annabella go inside. 'You do not intend to invite me in?' he enquired, when she made to say goodbye. This time there was no innuendo in his voice, but somehow Annabella wondered at his meaning.

'Certainly not!' she said primly. 'That would be a most unorthodox thing for a young lady to do at two of the clock!'

And she shut the door firmly in his face.

Amy Weston called the following day, bringing little Charlotte with her, but not the baby, Peter, who was still a little too young to travel. Charlotte was full of excitement over the kite her uncle had taught her to fly on Weathercock Hill nearby, and Annabella was forced to endure both Amy and Charlotte praising Will Weston extravagantly. It was not that she grudged others their good opinion of him, but just to hear his name repeated and his virtues rehearsed was difficult for her when her emotions were so deeply engaged. She was constantly afraid that she would give her feelings away.

Amy was also warm in her admiration of Larkswood, which gave Annabella a pang as she remembered that Will had intended Amy to have the house. Then, fortunately, Mrs Weston put it all right.

'It is a lovely house and a beautiful situation,' Amy said, as they sat down for tea on the lawn, 'but do you not find it rather isolated here, Mrs St Auby? I assure you, I could not live miles from anywhere, with only the farm for neighbours! Surely you must be lonely!' Her anxious brown eyes took in the empty expanse of cornfields and the sweep of the hills.

Annabella began to realise that Amy's life on the plantation must have been far more pampered and less hardy that she had imagined. She encouraged her to tell her more about it and for a while was regaled with breathless tales of Charleston society, and how happy Amy had been with Will's brother. Then Amy seemed to droop like a delicate flower and sighed.

'But, of course, that is all gone now. It is so very hard, is it not, Mrs St Auby, to lose a husband! There are times when I still feel his loss very strongly. No doubt you feel the same!'

Annabella was tempted to say that she had been very glad to lose Francis, but thought this might upset her visitor. 'I think I understand how you must feel,' she said diplomatically. 'And you have been very brave in leaving your home and coming all this way for the sake of your family! You must have been glad to receive such a welcome at Challen Court.'

'Oh, yes, Will has been all a brother could be,' Amy said enthusiastically, accepting one of the scones Miss Frensham passed her. 'He is looking for a house for us, Mrs St Auby, but I hope it will not be far distant from Challen, for I find the society here-abouts most congenial! Your sister has been all that is kind to me, and I hope…I am sure…I could make friends here…'

Annabella smiled at her reassuringly. It seemed odd that Amy Weston had the brand of courage that could take her from one continent to another, and yet was uncertain of her welcome in country society.

'I am sure of it,' she said warmly, and saw the relief reflected in Amy's eyes.

'Of course,' her new friend continued, 'when Will marries it will be even more pleasant! I do so hope I shall like his wife!'

Annabella jumped and spilt her tea. Miss Frensham tutted and patted ineffectually at her skirt with a lavender-drenched handkerchief. Down the garden, Charlotte Weston was pursuing a brightly coloured butterfly with her little net. Annabella dragged her gaze away and fixed it on Amy's pretty, undisturbed face.

'Is that event imminent, Mrs Weston?'

'Oh!' For a moment, Amy looked confused. A little colour came into her cheeks. 'Well…that is to say, I am not really certain… But,' she said brightly, 'I heard Will talking to your brother-in-law the other day and making some mention of the changes he would make at Challen when he got married. Then Lord Mullineaux made some comment that I did not catch but I heard him say that half his female relatives had been in love with Will in their time! And,' Amy added, digressing to show her partiality, 'I cannot be surprised at it, for Will is a fine man, is he not, Mrs St Auby?'

'He is very well, I suppose,' Annabella said, a little coldly. 'He is not so handsome as James, of course, but...'

'Oh, no,' Amy agreed, with a little smile, as many women had done before her, 'but then Lord Mullineaux is so prodigiously attractive, and so devoted to your sister that it makes one quite envious! But Will is a very agreeable man, and I think any girl would be fortunate to call him husband!'

Annabella could not but agree. A chill touched her at the thought of the lucky girl who would do so. Some female relative of James Mullineaux...a highly suitable alliance between two of the county's illustrious families... *Surely* Alicia would have told her about this! But perhaps not, if she knew it would upset her sister.

'Was the name of the lady mentioned?' she asked Amy, as casually as she was able. Amy wrinkled up her small nose.

'Not precisely, but I did hear Will remark later that Lord Mullineaux had said that a cousin of his was coming to stay at Oxenham, a Miss Shawcross, who I believe currently lives with his sister in Worcestershire.'

Miss Shawcross. Annabella bit viciously into her third scone and decided that she disliked the sound of her intensely. Amy, quite unaware of the trouble she had caused, regretfully refused Annabella's offer of a second cup of tea.

'I should be going back to Challen before the light fades,' she said anxiously. 'The autumn evenings close in so fast here, and I fear there may be footpads in these hills!'

Miss Frensham, who had been dozing in her chair in the warm sunshine, now woke up with a start.

'Oh, no, my dear Mrs Weston, I have not heard of any such thing! I am persuaded that Lord Mullineaux would never have let us come here if there had been the slightest chance... Oh, dear!'

Annabella, finding herself out of sorts with both her visitor and her companion, was seized by a malicious impulse.

'I believe Serena Linley's coach was stopped by a highwayman on the Lambourn road only last week,' she said sweetly and entirely untruthfully. 'She said that it was most exciting!'

Miss Frensham looked up at the hills and shivered histrionically. 'Upon my word, we continue to live in very lawless times!'

'Did the villain take anything?' Amy enquired, looking round a little nervously.

Annabella shrugged. She was already regretting the whim that had prompted her to tell such a story, for no doubt Will Weston would hear of it now and put her down as a troublemaker. Still...

'Only a kiss, I believe,' she said lightly.

Miss Frensham gave an outraged gasp but there was a definite twinkle in Amy's eyes.

'Well, that could be quite fun!' she said brightly, and left Annabella with the impression that they might, after all, become friends.

Annabella spent the next couple of days helping Susan to make butter and cheese in the Larkswood dairy. They were fairly self-sufficient, for Lark Farm kept them supplied with the items they could not grow or make for themselves and Owen Linton frequently travelled to market and would undertake a commission for his neighbours in return for a melting look from Susan's brown eyes. Annabella had found herself being drawn more and more into the household activities. She had never had the running of a household before, for her father had paid all the bills when she and Francis were first married, and after that she had always been a pensioner in someone else's home. It was strangely enjoyable to make plans with Susan, who was proving a capable manager and a staunch ally.

Even more pleasant was the prospect of a change of scene and some different company. Alicia had written to invite her sister to stay at Oxenham for a few days, with a view to going to the Faringdon Goose Fair. Annabella grasped the opportunity eagerly. Whilst she did not regret staking her claim to Larkswood, she imagined she might turn into a mad recluse if she never went into the outside world at all and had no fresh entertainment. Perhaps, she thought, churning the butter with unnecessary violence, the fortunate Miss Shawcross would be of their party...

Both Susan and Owen Linton frowned when Annabella borrowed a horse and told them she was off for a ride in the hills on her own that afternoon. Neither of them told her she should not ride alone, although Susan looked as though she would have liked to have done so. Their expressions were so reminiscent of disapproving parents that Annabella almost laughed. As she set off up the track to Lambourn she remembered Will's comments a few nights ago and reflected that most people found independent women uncomfortable. She knew that most of her acquaintance thought it odd in the extreme that she had chosen to live on her own at Larkswood, and clearly believed her to be an eccentric. Neither Alicia nor James had tried to dissuade her from living there, but Annabella sometimes wondered whether this was not because they approved but because they wanted her to realise for herself that it did not suit her. Shrugging, she encouraged the horse to a gallop across the rolling chalk down.

There were some ancient standing stones which stood close to the track on the top of the hill. Annabella stopped to consider the view, picking out Larkswood nestling in its hollow, and beyond it in the distance the villages of Challen, Oxenham and the others that dotted the flat valley floor. She dismounted, and hitched her horse's rein over a fence post whilst she looked at the ancient stones. They were not particularly impressive for many were leaning or tumbled into the field, covered with mosses and lichens, yet there was something peaceful about the spot that made Annabella sit down in the long grass with her back to one sun-warmed stone, and contemplate the scene. Before her, a field of late poppies bobbed and swayed in the light breeze like a shifting red scarf between the heads of corn. Annabella's eyes closed.

She was not sure how long she dozed for, or what had woken her, though she thought she had felt movement nearby. A skylark was twittering away up above her head and as she opened her eyes, a shadow fell across her and blotted out the sun. For a moment she was gripped by panic, but almost immediately she recognised the newcomer.

'Oh!' She struggled to sit upright. 'You startled me, sir! Whatever are you doing here?'

Will Weston straightened up from where he was leaning against a nearby stone, and viewed Annabella's prone figure with amusement mixed with appreciation. 'I would hope that I am protecting you from footpads and highwaymen,' he said dryly.

Annabella's face flamed. She scrambled to her feet. 'Oh, she told you! It was only in jest—'

'I am more concerned that you choose to go riding alone,' Will said, 'and that you then fall asleep in the middle of nowhere! You are not very wise, are you, Mrs St Auby, despite what I said to you the other night!'

Annabella raised her chin. She knew that he was right, but unfortunately it only brought out the worst in her. 'I was in no danger,' she said hotly.

'Really?' Will stepped closer. 'There may not be highwaymen in these hills any more, Mrs St Auby, but it is no sensible thing to go out alone. I wonder that you dare to live at Larkswood, to all intents and purposes remote from civilisation...'

'But you intended it as a home for Mrs Weston,' Annabella reminded him in honeyed tones, 'so you must have considered it suitable then.'

She saw a smile touch Will's mouth. 'Very true, and quite right of you to remind me! It would not have served for Amy at all. Well...' he stepped back to allow her to pass him and regain the path '...I am glad to see that you are thriving at Larkswood. I am for Lambourn, for I visit the Linleys this evening. I should be on my way.' But he did not move, and his thoughtful gaze travelled over Annabella slowly and unreadably, appearing to linger on her flushed face and bright, tumbled hair.

Annabella found herself suffering a constriction in her breathing. She tried to steady herself.

'How did you know I was here?' she asked, a little breathlessly.

'I saw you riding up the hill.' Will's voice had dropped. There was suddenly something oddly intimate about the stone circle, the heat pulsing off the ancient stones, the skylarks twittering in the bright arch of the blue sky. Annabella swallowed, her throat dry. An intense longing for the golden happiness of Mundell, before Larkswood and the rest had driven a wedge between them, took hold of her as though she was in a vice. Their eyes met and held as the tension spun out between them.

'Don't look at me like that!' Will said harshly, stepping back with such recoil that Annabella felt shocked. There was more violence in his tone than she at first understood, but then she remembered that he was an affianced man now—or as good as such. Crimson with mortification at the thought that her face had betrayed her longing for him, she turned away hastily, caught her foot in the hem of her riding habit and stumbled against one of the stones. She scored her hand painfully on its roughened surface as she tried to break her fall.

'Oh!' She stared at the red weal as it came up on her skin, the desire to cry so ridiculously out of proportion to the injury. She looked up into Will's face and from there it was suddenly an easy step into his arms, and he was kissing her with a violence that was both terrifying and tender as the tears dried on her hot cheeks, and he drew her down into the grass in the shelter of the stone circle.

Their passion rose to consume them with a force only intensified by its long denial. Will's lips were hard and bruising, but Annabella only pressed closer, revelling in their demand and the suppressed violence of his need for her, their need for each other. Her lips parted and opened beneath the pressure of his. The taste and the feel of him filled her senses. Neither of them said a word.

The urgency between them was inexpressibly exciting. Will's imperative fingers unfastened Annabella's riding habit to reveal the flimsy chemise beneath. Annabella's breasts were rising and falling rapidly with her fevered breathing, her nipples taut against the fine material. Will caught his breath, almost ripping the fabric aside so that his mouth could take one rosy tip in his mouth. Annabella gasped, her hands tracing an urgent path of their own over the hard muscles of his back, delving under his jacket and shirt to feel the delicious smoothness of his skin. All fear had gone, all thoughts of Francis and the undignified, painful act that he had inflicted on her. All she wanted now, at once, was the exquisite conclusion of such delicious pleasure.

Will's mouth had returned to hers, its explicit demand making clear that he wanted it too. Every yielding line of Annabella's body was pressed against his as he forced her back against the stone. The warmth of the sun, combined with the burning in her blood created a feeling of languorous abandonment. Then Will's grip eased abruptly and he moved away from her.

'Forgive me…I should not…'

'Oh!' Annabella was bewildered for a moment. Dazed by the intoxication of her senses, she was slow to understand that he had withdrawn from her. She opened her eyes reluctantly. The sky above her head was still bright, the sun still shone, the grass tickled her skin… And Will was supposed to be marrying a certain Miss Shawcross.

Will was propped on one elbow, watching her with those very blue eyes. And suddenly Annabella forgot about his prospective bride, for she saw that it was as it had been at Mundell, only far, far better, for his eyes were full of love and tenderness.

'Oh!' She was in his arms again, tumbled back amid the grasses, laughing and crying at the same time.

And when he said, very seriously, 'Will you marry me, Annabella?' there was never any possibility that she would answer other than yes.

Later, when they were sitting with their backs to the warm stone, Will's arm holding her possessively close to him, Annabella was able to say all the things she had wanted about Larkswood and their quarrel and how she had thought he was betrothed to someone else. Will seemed astounded.

'Betrothed to Miss Shawcross! No such thing, I assure you! Why, I haven't even seen her since she was about twelve years old! How on earth did you imagine that?'

Annabella wrinkled up her nose. 'But Amy said…' She blushed a little, and went on, 'She had heard you talking to James, and him mentioning that Miss

Shawcross was to come to Oxenham, and also James saying that half his female relatives had been in love with you at one time or another...'

She could feel Will's chest move as he laughed. 'I rather think,' he said gently, 'that Amy must have confused two separate conversations. James was referring to you. I had just implied that I intended to ask you to marry me.'

Smilingly, he pulled her to her feet and helped her to remove most of the grass seeds that appeared to have attached themselves to her crumpled clothing. Annabella's hair was tumbled in profuse disarray, but she did not care. Will himself looked scarcely less dishevelled.

'I shall have to go all the way back to Challen to change my clothes now,' he said, with a rueful smile. 'But I will take you back to Larkswood first, my love.' He brushed the hair back from her face and smiled again. 'I wish I didn't have to leave you, but I promised Richard Linley that I would see him tonight, for he travels abroad on the morrow. But we shall spend the day together tomorrow, if you would like...' Seeing the luminous delight in Annabella's green eyes, he took her hand and led her back to where the horses were patiently tethered, eating their way through a large proportion of the hedge. Will hitched both pairs of reins over his arm and led the puzzled but docile creatures behind them as he and Annabella walked slowly, hand in hand, down the hill to Larkswood.

Susan was in the courtyard, hands on hips, watching them as they wandered dreamily homewards. Her eyebrows rose as she noted Annabella's disorder, the brightness of her eyes, the curve of her lips in a tender smile.

'Susan,' Annabella began vaguely, 'Sir William and I...' She looked at Will, smiled, and forgot what she was saying.

'You may wish us happy,' Will said, a twinkle in his eyes. 'Mrs St Auby has consented to be my wife.'

Susan's smile broadened. 'Congratulations, sir, congratulations, ma'am! And about time too!' She took Annabella's unresisting arm. 'Come, ma'am! I need to do something with your appearance before you break the good news to Miss Frensham! She may appear to be henwitted, but she is neither blind nor stupid!'

After Will had kissed her goodbye, with a reminder about seeing her the next day, and ridden off down the hill towards Challen, Annabella submissively allowed Susan to take her up to her bedroom, help her change into fresh clothes, and tidy her hair. She then went to acquaint Miss Frensham with her good news, accepted her congratulations charmingly, and sat in the garden for the rest of the afternoon, doing nothing but thinking of Will. When the chill of dusk finally drove her inside, she sat in the little drawing-room and spent more time thinking about the future. Tomorrow, after Will had called, she would go to Oxenham to tell her grandmother and Alicia the news...

Finally, when the house was quiet, and there was nothing but the steady tick of the long-case clock at the bottom of the stairs, she got up to go to bed.

It was another bright moonlit night and there was

no sound except the wind in the trees outside. Annabella crossed to the hall window, still too happy and full of ideas to rest, and pulled the heavy curtain aside. She peered out. The night was suddenly dark, the full moon hidden momentarily behind scurrying clouds. Annabella shivered. Although she was beginning to love this wide landscape with its sweeping hills, there were times when there was something elemental about it, something that she could not understand. She was not a superstitious girl, but when the sun went down over the flat fields of the valley, or the moon topped the ridge of the hills behind the house, she would find herself held by a spell as old as time. But soon she would not be alone at night any more. She shivered again, but this time with remembered pleasure, not cold. She drew her shawl closer around her shoulders and picked up her candle to light her way upstairs. She had reached the first step, had her hand on the newel post, when the quiet of the night was smashed by the sound of horses being ridden hell-for-leather into the courtyard, followed by a confusion of voices and a hammering on the front door. Annabella jumped violently.

'Open in the King's name!'

A door opened upstairs and Miss Frensham's voice quavered: 'Mrs St Auby! Mrs St Auby! Whatever is happening?'

Swallowing the retort that she had not the least idea in the world, Annabella moved across to the door and started to pull back the heavy bolts. By the time she was ready to swing it open, Frank, the footman, had appeared, pulling his coat on, obviously having dressed very hastily. Miss Frensham was hovering on

the half-landing in a dressing-gown of formidable re-
spectability and an even more terrifying bedcap. Behind her the pale faces of Susan and the other maids
could be seen peering out of the shadows.

Frank opened the door and almost immediately the
hallway was full of jostling men, one of whom was
barking orders. Miss Frensham drew back with a terrified squeak.

'You two, search the house from the attics down.
Benson, go around the back. And, Jenkins—'

Annabella raised herself to her full height. 'I am
mistress here and you, sir, will not search my house
without first giving good reason why!'

The effect of her words was remarkable. Everyone
froze. Then the gentleman turned slowly to face her.

He looked young at first glance, until Annabella
weighed up the lines of age and experience on his
face and put him at closer to thirty than the one or
two-and-twenty she had first thought. Like his men,
he was dressed in a uniform she did not recognise,
for it was a sober black, very different from the scarlet
regimentals of Jeffries and his like. And he was fair,
with a youthful complexion which was turning a little
rosy at the arctic tone of Annabella's voice.

'I beg your pardon, ma'am.' He executed a stiff
bow. 'Captain Harvard, of His Majesty's Royal Navy,
at your service. I was not aware that Sir William Weston was married.'

Annabella blinked, beginning to wonder if she had
been drawn unwittingly into a farce. 'He is not, as far
as I am aware. At least not yet. But what is that to
the purpose?'

The gentleman looked at her properly for the first

time, taking in her old dress and the hair loose about her shoulders. A shade of familiarity came into his manner whilst behind him his men fidgeted, uncertain whether to follow their orders or wait for other directions. A gust of air blew in and Frank tried to shut the door, only to be restrained by one of the burly posse.

'We are looking for Sir William to arrest him,' the Captain stated, with ill-concealed impatience, 'and you would do best not to obstruct us in our duty, ma'am! I must ask you to stand aside!'

Annabella lost her temper. 'You there, unhand my servant! And you, Captain, are looking in the wrong place! I am Annabella St Auby, sister-in-law to the Marquis of Mullineaux, and this is *my* house, not Sir William's! Now, explain your business, if you please! Arrest Sir William! I never heard such arrant nonsense! Miss Frensham—' the companion quailed before the martial light in Annabella's eyes '—please accompany us to the drawing-room!'

Captain Harvard looked slightly abashed as he followed her meekly into the room she had so recently vacated, with Miss Frensham bringing up the rear, somewhat embarrassed in her night attire. Annabella closed the door behind them and fixed him with a quelling gaze.

'Well, sir?'

'It would seem that there has been some mistake,' Harvard began, reluctantly admitting to his error. 'I understood that this was Sir William Weston's house, which was why we were sure he would be making for here!'

Annabella raised an eyebrow. She remained standing and deliberately did not ask him to be seated, and it was only Miss Frensham who perched uneasily on the edge of one of the armchairs.

'I fear you are making little sense, sir,' Annabella observed coldly. 'It lacks but five minutes to midnight. Is it likely that Sir William would be abroad at this hour, particularly out here in the middle of nowhere?'

'No,' Captain Harvard said slowly, his gaze resting on her, 'it is not likely, but it is…possible.' Clearly he had not totally relinquished the idea that Annabella was Sir William's mistress, housed discreetly away from civilisation, and with her lover visiting her at this odd hour of the night. Remembering the encounter in the stone circle, Annabella thought how easily this could be true and felt the first cold touch of a censorious world on her happiness.

'However,' Harvard continued after a moment, 'the Master of Arms from Sir William's own ship recognised him just now on the road and we imagined he would be seeking shelter here.'

Annabella raised her brows with sceptical exasperation. 'I still do not understand you, sir. What of this cock-and-bull story about an arrest? Upon whose authority do you act thus?'

'On the authority of the Lords of the Admiralty,' Harvard said with a quiet satisfaction. 'Sir William Weston is accused of treason, and I am here at the behest of Admiral Cranshaw to arrest him on that precise charge.'

There was a deep silence. Annabella reached blindly behind her to grip the hard edge of the escritoire, leaning back against it for support. Her lips formed the word to repeat it, but no sound came, and it was Miss Frensham who spoke for both of them.

'Treason…' Miss Frensham whispered, white to the lips. 'Sir William! Surely not!'

Once again, despite her misery and confusion, Annabella observed a barely definable hint of satisfaction in Captain Harvard's face. It was banished as he felt her scrutiny.

'Yes, ma'am,' he said with wooden countenance. 'Sir William is called to answer certain charges that he abandoned the sea battle at Lake Champlain in '14 when he had not been given the order to cease his fire. And,' Harvard could not resist adding, with an unattractive pleasure in the words that was far from professional, 'the fact that he sought to resist arrest suggests to me that he feels his guilt most keenly. It was not the action of an officer and a gentleman!'

It occurred to Annabella, through the anguish of hearing the cruel gossip repeated as a formal charge, that Captain Harvard did not like Sir William Weston. Her protestations that it was only gossip and Sir William was surely innocent, died a death as Harvard's cold grey eyes rested on her face, weighing her reaction to his deliberately callous words.

'You look shocked, ma'am,' Harvard observed gently. 'Pray sit down. May I offer you some restorative?'

'Of course I am shocked,' Annabella snapped, disliking him all the more for his presumption in offering her comfort when he had been the cause of her distress. 'Sir William is a particular friend of the family—'

'Most distressing, ma'am,' Harvard concurred smoothly, 'especially as Sir William was wounded—'

Miss Frensham let out a small shriek, which fortunately masked Annabella's quieter, but no less heartfelt, gasp of alarm. This midnight burlesque was becoming more bizarre, more shocking, by the moment.

'Wounded?' she repeated faintly, and saw a faint look of gratification cross the Captain's face as he noted her pallor.

'Yes, ma'am, shot as he tried to escape.'

Annabella took a deep breath, determined not to show her panic. Miss Frensham had given a slight moan at the word 'shot' and was clutching the lapels of her dressing-gown together, as though she expected Captain Harvard's men to burst into the room at any moment and shoot the lot of them.

'So,' Annabella said as coolly as she was able, meeting the Captain's eyes very straight, 'let me understand you correctly, Captain. You are seeking to arrest Sir William Weston. You thought that you identified him on the road hard by here, you presumably called out to him to stop and identify himself, he declined to do so, and you shot him.'

The stark words seemed to resound in the quiet drawing-room.

'I can only repeat, ma'am,' Captain Harvard said with stilted courtesy, 'that Sir William is a wanted man whose own actions condemn his criminal behaviour.'

Annabella felt sickened. The Will Weston she knew bore no resemblance to the Captain's harsh description. And yet, how could Will, who prized integrity so highly, seek to evade capture and bring such disgrace on himself? As for the charge of treason, Annabella had never believed it true and did not do so now. And she had no intention of revealing her feelings to this hard-faced stranger who had invaded her house with such a lack of consideration. With a supreme effort, she looked him in the eye.

'I fear I cannot help your enquiries, sir. You may have rather more success looking for Sir William at his own house, Challen Court, of course. Now it is late, and you will oblige me by leaving.'

A faint tinge of colour crept back into Captain Harvard's face at her tone. He was clearly annoyed at the cool way Annabella appeared to be taking the news and he chose to ignore her instruction.

'How well do you know Sir William, ma'am?' he challenged. 'When did you last see him?'

Annabella moved towards the door. 'As I have said, Sir, Sir William is an acquaintance of my family,' she said with chilly courtesy, 'and I last saw him earlier today when he passed on his way to dinner in Lambourn.'

'You are certain,' Harvard persisted, 'that he has not been here this evening?'

Annabella raised a haughty eyebrow. 'Captain Harvard, do you think that I do not know the comings and goings of my own household? To my certain knowledge, Sir William has not called by here this evening.'

Harvard's chill grey eyes rested on her face. It was clear that he disbelieved her, even suspected her of hiding his quarry. Annabella faced him out bravely.

'I suggest you concentrate your search elsewhere,

sir. You are wasting your time here.' She opened the door and stood politely to one side to allow him egress.

'And, sir, if you have any further questions for me, you may return in daylight to ask them. It is late and I am for my bed. I bid you goodnight!'

Annabella was unsure how she preserved her calm whilst the disgruntled Captain marshalled his men and took them off into the night. By this time, the entire house was in uproar. Frank was giving a greatly exaggerated account of his involvement to the wide-eyed kitchenmaid whilst Miss Frensham was wringing her hands and showing all signs of giving way to the vapours. After a worried glance at Annabella, Susan led the companion tenderly back to her bed with murmured promises of hot milk laced with a sleeping draught. Annabella sat down nervelessly on the bottom step and put her head in her hands. She wanted to run out into the night to find Will. She wanted to hurry to Oxenham to seek help. Neither course of action would be profitable. She needed to think…

The door was still ajar, for Frank had neglected his duties to seek consolation in the kitchen and could be heard exchanging sweet nothings with the maid as she put the milk on the hob. Wearily, Annabella got to her feet and reached for the door. It swung inwards before she could touch it.

'Will you help me then, Annabella, in spite of everything you have heard tonight?' Will Weston asked softly, stepping over the threshold.

Paradoxically, Annabella found that she was angry, rather than pleased to see him. Having sustained the shock of Harvard's words and successfully concealed her desperate concern, she found that the sight of Will alive and well was curiously irritating.

'Will!' Her words came out with rather more ferocity than she had intended. 'What on earth is the meaning of this?'

Will tried to smile at her fierceness but the effort was rather strained and it was only when Annabella had had a few more moments to consider the rather greyish pallor of his face and the tight lines of pain about his mouth that she realised that he was hurt after all. His boots were covered in mud, his jacket torn and stained and he held his left arm stiffly, cradled by his other hand.

'You're injured—' she began, anger melting swiftly into concern as she stepped forward instinctively to take a grip on his good arm.

'The veriest scratch to my shoulder, but it has bled overmuch.' Will sounded weary and strangely detached. He swayed a little, leaning briefly against her. Annabella tightened her grip.

'Bandages, perhaps…' there was a trace of rueful amusement in his voice '…and do I ask too much for some food and wine? I am sorry to trouble you this way—' the blue eyes, clouded with pain, searched Annabella's face '—particularly when I am a fugitive.'

'Don't be foolish,' Annabella said shortly. 'Of course we will help you! You must come upstairs—'

'No!' Will's gaze narrowed with the effort of concentration, of holding off the faintness that threatened him. 'The servants—'

'Can be trusted.' As Annabella spoke, she heard Susan's footsteps on the stair and looking up, saw the maid leaning over the banisters. 'Quickly, Susan, to me! I think he is like to swoon…'

Susan asked no questions. With her help, Annabella managed to help the semi-conscious Will up the stairs, then paused on the landing.

'Best put him in your own room, ma'am,' Susan said practically. 'The other bed is not aired and Sir William looks in dire need of rest. Here—' she helped Annabella steer Will into the bedroom '—I will go and fetch some food—do you go to Miss Frensham's closet and bring bandages and some of that revolting ointment she keeps…' She saw Annabella's look of alarm and added, 'Never fear, ma'am, Miss Frensham is already asleep. Just the mention of a sleeping-draught was enough to do it! No need for her to trouble herself any more this night…'

Miss Frensham was a confirmed hypochondriac and had a whole collection of bandages, dusting powders and ointments in her closet. Annabella trod softly up to her door and scratched quietly on the panels. A muffled snore was the only response. Tiptoeing into the darkened room, Annabella paused only briefly to check her companion's unconscious figure, bundled up in severe gingham with the huge lace bedcap perched atop her head and her curling papers rustling beneath it. Miss Frensham wheezed again. Reassured, Annabella started to take a vast amount of pots and potions from the cupboard, Miss Frensham's regular snuffling her only accompaniment. She backed out of the room and bumped into Susan again on the landing. The maid had her arms full of blankets and a pitcher of water held precariously in one hand. She ran a careful eye over Annabella's haul of medicines and nodded with approval, holding out her own load.

'Take these to Sir William, ma'am,' she ordered. 'I'll go to the kitchens and get him some food.' And, giving no time for Annabella to wonder at her complicity, she hurried off downstairs.

Chapter Eight

Annabella found that Will had managed to prop himself against the pillows, but his eyes were closed and his colour bad, giving the lie to his earlier claims that he was not much hurt. There was dried blood on his sleeve, and a fresh, bright stain on his chest. As Annabella touched his hand, he opened those very blue eyes and tried to smile.

'Annabella... Thank God...'

Annabella poured some water with hands that shook a little, and helped Will into a more upright position so that he could drink. His head rested against the curve of her shoulder and, as she watched him, she felt a great wave of fear and tenderness overcome her. She brushed the tumbled hair back from his forehead with gentle fingers.

'I have bandages and some blankets,' she said a little gruffly, to cover her emotion, 'and Susan is bringing some food for you. I think, perhaps, that it would be a good idea to bind up that wound first...'

Will looked down and seemed vaguely surprised that the wound was still bleeding.

'Damnation…' He moved uncomfortably. 'Will you help me off with this shirt? A strange request to a lady, I know—' despite his pain, his blue gaze mocked her '—but we shall do better without it.'

Annabella was annoyed to find herself colouring up fierily. She slipped his jacket off and started on the shirt buttons with fingers which slipped slightly. The wound was to his shoulder, a deep gash that looked clean but was still bleeding slowly. Further down his arm was another, a smaller laceration that was nevertheless an angry red. Annabella's breath caught on a small gasp. She had never seen such injuries before, let alone had to dress them. She had not the first idea where to start.

'Annabella,' Will said patiently, after several minutes had elapsed, 'I would as lief not lie here forever! If you wash the wound, dust it with that powder and bind it up, I shall do well enough. The other is a mere scratch that will heal on its own given time.'

His matter-of-fact tone steadied Annabella, as it had been intended to do. She reached a little uncertainly for the cloth and dipped it in the bowl of water, dabbing gently at the gash until it was clean. She heard Will catch his breath and bit her lip in wordless sympathy, but though his face had paled visibly, he said nothing and made no further sound. The pale yellow powder from Miss Frensham's collection of medicines looked horrible, but once Will had reassured her again that it was perfectly safe to use, she dusted the wound and started to try to bind it up. Here she got herself into a considerable tangle, and it was Will who, having tended to plenty of men injured in action, took the end of the bandage and showed l how to wind it around him securely. Halfway through, Annabella became inexplicably distracted by the smooth, bronze skin of his chest beneath her fingers. She could feel the warmth emanating from him, smell the scent of his skin. She dropped the bandage, reached clumsily to pick it up again, and found her hand caught and held by his.

There was a light in those blue eyes, at once tender and demanding, which held her captive. He raised her hand slowly to his lips and kissed her fingers.

'Thank you,' he said huskily. 'You have been very kind.'

Annabella freed herself reluctantly and managed to finish tying the bandage. She found she could not meet his eyes. This sudden shyness was extraordinary, after the passion of earlier in the day. But that seemed like another world now. She busied herself in tidying up, pouring him another mug of water and fussing with his blankets.

'We will have some food for you shortly. You must be hungry...'

'Thank you,' Will said again, softly. He was still watching her with that odd mixture of tenderness and speculation. Then his expression changed. 'Annabella, I owe you an explanation. I heard what Harvard said tonight—or the majority of it, at least. I was outside... But—' the bitterness crept in '—you had heard the rumours about Lake Champlain already, of course.'

'Yes, and I never believed them!' Annabella was vehement in her need to reassure Will that she had never doubted him. 'When I heard them in Somerset I counted them as spiteful malice and nothing more.

And now I have no more reason to believe them than I did before!' She hesitated. 'The only thing I do not understand, Will…' her voice wavered, but she was determined to continue '…is why you did not agree to go with Harvard to clear your name. Surely you have nothing to fear? Surely you could establish your innocence beyond all doubt!'

A faint, rueful smile touched Will's mouth. 'You are more generous to me than I deserve, my love! What you should be saying is that a man who resists arrest rightly forfeits the claim to be treated as a gentleman and may expect to be thrown into chains! My actions suggest I have something to hide…that I must indeed be guilty! No doubt that is what Harvard will say! And all my acquaintance would expect me to have surrendered to him tonight, to be dealt with justly and considerately, escorted to London to explain myself to the Admiralty, perhaps, but not hunted as a criminal!' He turned his head away and closed his eyes for a moment.

'Then…' Annabella began, uncertainly, 'why did you choose—?'

Will's eyes opened again. They looked shadowed and very tired. 'Oh, yes, Annabella, you are right in that I could have cleared my name had I been given a chance. But that choice was never mine. Harvard did not challenge me as he claims. He shot me without warning. Oh, I do not doubt that, now he has lost me, he will tell everyone I ran from arrest. But the truth is that he tried to kill me and now he wants me dead!'

Annabella put a hand to a head that was spinning. She wondered fleetingly whether Will was delirious, but though he was clearly in pain, there was no real fever—not yet. But even so...

'You think I have run mad,' Will observed, reading her thoughts all too accurately. 'I assure you that it is true. Harvard never identified himself to me, never challenged me to stop...' He sighed. 'I had been dining with the Linleys over in Lambourn, as you know, and it was later than I expected when I rode back. It was dark, but I saw two men riding towards me. As I say, there was no challenge—they shot at me without warning. The first shot grazed my arm and, naturally enough, I rode off, thinking they were footpads. I had a pistol with me and could have taken them on, but it was dark and I could see no point in taking the risk... Then the second shot took me in the shoulder.' He shook his head. 'I fell off my horse, which was terrified and took off down the road as though the hounds of hell were after it. But I managed to scramble into cover, and in the darkness they could not find me. It was then that I heard them talking.'

The lines of anger and bitterness set deeper in his face. 'Harvard was swearing violently because they had lost me. He said that they had to find me, that I could not be allowed to live and tell the tale. I recognised his voice, for they were standing a bare twenty yards from me. And he addressed Hawes by name, which gave me pause for thought. Hawes was the Master at Arms on my last ship, but before that—and after—he was Harvard's man.'

'Then you are saying that it was quite deliberate,' Annabella said slowly, and Will nodded.

'Oh, yes, there can be no mistake. They set out to take me—and not alive, either. The tale that I was running from arrest was made up afterwards, to discredit me in case I came forward to claim Harvard had tried to kill me.'

There was a silence. The candle flame guttered. 'But why should Harvard do such a thing?' Annabella asked slowly. 'It is not that I disbelieve you, Will, but—'

Will shrugged a little irritably as though his wound pained him. 'That's the devil of it! I do not know! His original orders must have been to take me in, they can hardly have been to shoot me! And Harvard and I were never close friends, but I had no notion he bore me such a grudge! Damnation, I cannot think straight! I have spent the best part of the night since it happened trying to understand why he would do this to me!'

Annabella put a soothing hand to his forehead, concerned that it was starting to burn with a feverish heat. 'Try to sleep a little,' she counselled. 'Doubtless much will fall into place when you have a clear head! Now is not the time to puzzle yourself with this!'

Will gave her another faint smile. 'You speak much sense, sweetheart!' A shadow touched his face and he plucked a little fretfully at the blankets. 'But I should not stay here, bringing you into danger—'

'I am your future wife,' Annabella said strongly. 'Who should have a better right to look after you? Now go to sleep. You are feverish…'

She heard him laugh softly. 'So I am, but not the sort that you mean! I have been burning for you, Annabella, for a long time!' He caught her hand again. 'For a long time I have been afraid of what I would do, for I wanted you so much, and now here I am in your bed, but not in the sense I would have envisaged!'

'You *are* feverish,' Annabella reproved, trying not to smile.

She wrapped him in the blanket and left the water within reach. It seemed that Susan's food would not be needed, for Will seemed to be falling asleep before her eyes, and no doubt it was for the best. She stood for a moment, looking down on him, filled with love and tenderness as she considered the curve of his cheek, the silky thickness of those dark eyelashes, the determined line of his jaw, somehow softened now that he was so vulnerable. A faint knock at the door broke her reverie, and Susan slipped into the room.

'Sorry I was so long, ma'am. One of them oafish sailors came back asking some questions, but I sent him off with a flea in his ear!' She saw Annabella's look of alarm. 'No cause to worry, ma'am! Now, I'll sit with Sir William, for you look done up and no mistake!' She was shepherding Annabella towards the door as she spoke. 'Owen will be setting off to market early tomorrow and will get a message to Oxenham— I was thinking you'd be wanting them to help... And don't worry, ma'am—we'll take good care of Sir William, seeing as you're sweet on him!'

Annabella slept late, completely exhausted, and only awoke when Susan pulled back the bed curtains and put her cup of morning chocolate carefully down on the bedside table.

'He's proper feverish today, ma'am, I'm afraid,' she said, in answer to Annabella's enquiry about Will's health. 'Frank sat with him through most of the night. I've changed the dressing on his wound and it's starting to heal, but he's very hot and he hasn't woken. If you're going in to see him, ma'am, try to give him some more of that draught. It looks nasty, but it works well.'

Annabella dressed hurriedly and slipped quietly out of the spare room and across the landing. Though the entire household appeared to know of Will's presence and accept it with silent connivance, Annabella had no wish for Miss Frensham to stumble on a wanted man in her bedroom. The consequences of that would be too difficult to deal with. She abandoned the challenge of thinking up ways to distract her companion for the day, and pushed open the door of her room a little apprehensively.

Will had thrown back his covers and was tossing and turning restlessly. His forehead was hot and damp with fever, and he was murmuring a little in his dreams. Annabella bathed his face gently, but he did not wake, and after a moment she sat down on the edge of the bed beside him, just holding his hand in hers.

He woke suddenly a few minutes later. The blue eyes, glittering now with pain and delirium, raked Annabella's face but she was not sure if he knew who she was. She gave him some water, then the noxious black draught, which he tried half-heartedly to push away, before swallowing a small mouthful.

'Where am I…?' Will's voice was a whisper, his gaze narrowed with the effort of concentration. 'Annabella? Then it is true…' He tried to sit up and fell back with a groan, closing his eyes.

'Keep still.' Annabella pressed a soothing hand to

his cheek. 'You are quite safe, and soon you will be well again.'

Will smiled a little, his eyes still closed. 'Safe… A ministering angel…' Suddenly his eyes opened wide again and fixed on her face. 'Do you love me, Annabella? Tell me!' His hand was gripping her arm with surprising strength for one so ill, and his tone demanded an answer. A small chill touched Annabella's heart. Surely he could not have forgotten their betrothal so quickly? But then, with a fever, one might forget many things…

'Yes,' Annabella whispered, 'I love you very much, Will. I have done for a long time.'

Will relaxed almost at once, his eyes closing like those of a sleepy child reassured by her words. His hand slid from her arm and his breathing deepened into what seemed to be normal sleep. Annabella watched him, feeling her love for him uncurl inside her and expand until it felt as though it filled her whole being. No consideration of the crime of which he was accused could alter her feelings for him. But how they were to untangle this knot was less clear.

The door opened softly and Susan stuck her head around it.

'You must take some breakfast, ma'am,' she chided gently. 'Miss Frensham has just woken and is in a very delicate state this morning. I have persuaded her to stay in her room for the time being.'

Annabella sighed. Miss Frensham's delicate state, no doubt induced by the shocks of the previous night, was another trying circumstance to contend with whilst she tried to see her way clear to helping Will.

She stood up and went downstairs, her footsteps slow, her mind dogged with anxiety.

The day dragged by. Annabella, torn between worrying over Will's condition and puzzling over his allegations towards Captain Harvard, moped about the house, spent half an hour desultorily cutting roses in the garden, and watched the hands of the clock drag themselves round towards the afternoon. A hasty council of war between herself, Frank and Susan had led to the decision to move Will across to Lark Farm, where they felt he would be safer from both the attentions of Captain Harvard and any unexpected forays Miss Frensham might make into Annabella's bedroom.

The next problem was how to move the invalid, for Will had not regained consciousness and Miss Frensham was up and prowling about the house in an irritable sort of a way. In desperation, Annabella brought out the piece of embroidery which she had been working on for at least six months and which Miss Frensham had frequently criticised for its poor workmanship. The half-hour she spent going over its defects with her companion was tiresome and boring, but had to be time well spent. Fortunately, the exercise put Miss Frensham into far happier a frame of mind and after lunch she graciously agreed to arrange the roses Annabella had cut that morning.

Annabella, meanwhile, was beset by further doubts. When Susan had told her the night before that Owen Linton would take a message to Oxenham, it had seemed the best solution. Now, however, she was not so sure. James Mullineaux was, after all, a Justice of

the Peace and probably the first person Captain Harvard would turn to in his hunt for the fugitive. Will
and James might be the best of friends, but how
would that friendship be sustained when Will had
been denounced as a traitor and a criminal? Still, it
was too late now. Annabella picked up a magazine to
while away the tedium of the afternoon and almost
immediately heard the sound of a coach pulling into
the yard followed by voices in the hall.

'Annabella!' Alicia, immaculately beautiful as ever
in a gown of deep green, hurried in to greet her sister.
'We had the most extraordinary message from Owen
Linton this morning! Are you all right? What on earth
has happened?'

It was not just the Mullineauxs who had arrived,
Annabella realised, but Caroline and Marcus Kilgaren
as well. Suddenly overcome with a rush of emotion
at seeing them all, Annabella threw herself into Alicia's arms with rather more fervour than might be
expected after a separation of only five days. Her sister, however, took this all in good part and only
hugged her back.

'Oh, Alicia,' Annabella said, muffled, 'I am so glad
to see you!' She let her sister go reluctantly and tried
to compose herself. Caroline and Alicia guided her to
the chaise-longue and sat down on either side of her,
their faces showing identical expressions of woe. It
would have been amusing had Annabella not been too
upset to appreciate it.

'Well, Annabella,' James said bracingly, with the
directness for which he was well known, 'what the
hell's going on? All we have heard is some cock-and-
bull story from Linton, in which he claims Will Wes-

ton was accused of treason and shot whilst evading arrest!' He moved across to the window and propped himself against the sill. 'I'd have thought him barking mad,' he continued, 'were it not for a visit this morning from some chap—Harvard, I believe he was called—looking for Will on behalf of the Admiralty! So?'

To her surprise, Annabella discovered that this abrasive unsentimentality was just what she needed. Where Alicia's sympathy might have encouraged the tears, James's straight talking forced her to confront the problem. Nevertheless, the mention of Harvard's name caused her to shiver.

'What did Captain Harvard say?' she asked tonelessly.

James moved restlessly to look out of the window. 'Why, he told us that the Admiralty had sent him to bring Will up to London to answer the charge of treason which had been levied. He said that he and one of his men had been given the intelligence to expect Will to be returning from Lambourn last night, and they had intercepted him on the road. They challenged him, at which he shot at them and rode off. They returned fire and brought him down, but could not find him.' James's face was sombre. 'Harvard was not slow to point out that Will's actions damned him as a guilty man trying to escape. He even hinted that Will might be unbalanced. I fear I did not take to Captain Harvard,' James finished, a little grimly.

'Harvard was here last night, after it happened,' Annabella said, with another shudder. 'He said much the same to me. He was sure that Will would have made for here to seek shelter.'

James raised his eyebrows. 'Harvard seems very sincere in his wish to find Will,' he observed gently. 'He even said that he was afraid Will might be dying on a hillside and asked for my help in mounting a search party!' James smiled for the first time. 'But I thought I should save myself the trouble!'

Their eyes met. 'Will is not here,' Annabella said truthfully, looking at them all very straight, 'so you need have no fear on that score!'

Alicia stirred. 'But is he safe, Annabella? Oh, don't worry about James—' she had seen her sister's look of apprehension '—as long as he does not know where Will is, he can answer all questions put to him by Harvard quite openly! We are more concerned that Will is injured!'

Annabella capitulated. There was such genuine worry on all their faces that she could not believe they would ever betray Will. Especially when they knew the truth. 'He has a wound to the shoulder and is in a fever,' she said carefully, 'but I do not believe it to be life-threatening, unless Miss Frensham's powders and potions carry him off! He is quite safe, but unfit to move for now. But pray do not tell Captain Harvard any of that! The more time he spends out on the hills searching for Will, the better!'

Caroline leant forward, going straight to the heart of the matter. 'But what does Will have to say about this, Annabella?' She frowned unhappily. 'I do not need to tell you that none of us can believe either the charge of treason or the accusation that Will shot at Harvard and escaped. Can there have been some mistake?'

'There is no mistake,' Annabella said bluntly. 'Will

told me that Harvard tried to kill him. They shot at *him* without warning, then tried to hunt him down. I assure you—' she had seen the shocked, disbelieving horror on the faces of them all '—it is true.'

There was a stunned silence.

'The charge of treason in itself is sufficiently bizarre,' Marcus Kilgaren said quietly, after a pause, 'but this beats all else. Will is certain that there can be no misunderstanding?'

'None,' Annabella said, with another very straight look. 'But, of course, it is only his word against Harvard's, and Harvard has a witness who will back his own story. Worse, Will is currently too ill to put his side of the story and Harvard is taking advantage of his disappearance to suggest that Will is condemned by his own actions! Will cannot simply come out and accuse Harvard of attempted murder—not when the evidence looks so bad against him! And he has no notion as to why Harvard acted as he did!'

'Now we see why Harvard seemed so mighty put out to have lost Will,' Marcus said grimly. 'No doubt he would prefer to find him dead on a hillside somewhere—or captured and locked up, with no one taking seriously his counter-allegations!'

'But what is it all about?' Alicia asked plaintively, putting in to words the one thought that was troubling them all. 'The charge of treason is the start of all this, and to accuse Will of such a crime is the biggest piece of nonsense I ever heard! Why, a man of greater integrity it would be hard to find!'

'Someone has been planting poison in the ear of the Lords of the Admiralty,' James said quietly. 'You may remember that there was some foolish talk a couple of years ago about how Will had run out of a naval engagement and left another captain to face the enemy alone. It was complete nonsense, but unfortunately the story never quite died. Though how it has blown up again now, I cannot tell.'

'I heard that malicious tale myself when I was in Taunton,' Annabella said hesitantly, glancing at her sister. Marcus's words had hit precisely upon what had been troubling her, for surely a man such as George Jeffries had no influence to raise such a serious charge against Will Weston. There had to be someone else involved...someone with power, or at least greater influence.

'In Taunton? From whom?' Marcus leant forward.

'Why, from Captain Jeffries,' Annabella said, still hesitant. 'He told me of that and of other unsavoury rumours about Will making a fortune from being in league with pirates. But Jeffries has no standing—he would never be given credence!'

'Maybe not,' Marcus reflected, 'but someone else might...' He caught James's gaze across the room. 'If Jeffries had repeated the rumour to someone with both influence and a grudge...'

'Ermina Hurst has a cousin, or some such, at the Admiralty,' Caroline said slowly. 'I remember her mentioning it in passing one evening, but I was not really attending, for you know how that woman rattles on!' She caught herself up, and looked appalled at what she seemed to be suggesting. 'Oh, but surely... No! Even Ermina would not—'

'Miss Hurst did not take her rejection by Sir William in good part,' Marcus pointed out coolly. 'Perhaps she saw this as a means of revenge...'

'But we do not even know if Ermina knew this Captain Jeffries,' Caroline burst out. 'Oh no, this is too far-fetched for words! I am sure we wrong her even by thinking of it!'

Judging by the looks on the faces of the two men, Annabella thought that they were not so sure. And nor was she, when she considered it. After all, she had been a witness to the frustrated spite of Miss Hurst as she realised that both Viscount Mundell and Sir William were slipping beyond her grasp.

'Miss Hurst danced with Jeffries at the subscription ball in Taunton,' she said quietly. 'I remember thinking it odd at the time, for a man like Jeffries was far beneath her touch! But all the same…'

'It will bear investigation,' James observed, 'along with a number of other matters.'

The others looked at him enquiringly. 'Well,' James enlarged, 'it seems singular to me that Harvard should choose to seek his man in the middle of the night when he might have called at Challen in the daylight! That in itself is suspicious and suggests he wanted no witness to the encounter! I would like to know Harvard's original orders!'

'Admiral Cranston could probably tell us that,' Marcus said speculatively. 'Harvard mentioned this morning that he was acting under Cranston's authority—although he appears to have exceeded it somewhat!'

'But why did Harvard try to shoot Will?' Caroline said crossly, in the tone of voice that suggested the attempted murder was a tiresome parlour game. 'If only we knew…'

'If we knew that, my love, we would have solved the whole case,' Marcus said with a twitch of his lips.

James stirred in his chair. 'There's plenty we *can* do, however, whilst we wait for Will to recover and state his case! We need to trace some of Will's colleagues—those who could give testimony and clear his name of the treason charge. Then we can try to discover the background to all this from Cranston. And I will try to find some witnesses—any witnesses—to last night's events. It's a long shot, I know, but it's possible... When we've turned up anything useful I'll send word,' he added to Annabella. There was an irrepressible twinkle suddenly in his dark eyes. 'You have to hand it to Will—he has certainly hit on a novel way to effect a reconciliation!'

Annabella looked flustered. She had forgotten that she had yet to impart what had previously been the most important piece of news of all. She turned to Alicia, her green eyes suddenly bright. Despite their situation, nothing could dampen her happiness in her engagement to Will.

'Oh, Liss, the most marvellous thing! Will and I became betrothed yesterday afternoon! I had almost forgot!'

Announcements of marriage were usually followed by a flurry of exclamation and congratulation, Annabella thought with irony. Twice she had declared her intention to marry, and on both occasions the news had sunk like a stone. The first time, her father had stormed and raged, refusing his consent until she had lied that she had already given herself to Francis in the most intimate of ways. This time was little

better, for no one said anything at all until Alicia rec-
ollected herself and got up to kiss her.

'I am glad that you have settled your differences,
Annabella,' she began carefully, 'but—'

'I know!' Annabella sighed. 'You do not think it
wise to contemplate a betrothal to a man who is under
suspicion of treason and attempted murder!'

'Well, not precisely—' Alicia caught her husband's
eye and fell silent just as the door opened.

'Mrs St Auby,' Miss Frensham said peevishly, 'the
mildew has taken those roses and they are quite unsuitable! I have done my best, but no one will dispute
that they are not up to scratch! And,' she added as an
afterthought, 'that tiresome Captain Harvard is here
again, poking about in the kitchen and asking questions! It's enough to give me a megrim! I am retiring
to my room!'

Harvard was already lurking in the corridor, even
as Frank, wooden-faced, made the unnecessary an-
nouncement of his presence.

'Captain Harvard is here to see you, ma'am.'

Annabella saw the mingled speculation and concern on the faces of her companions, and felt them
range themselves behind her in a wordless show of
solidarity. She got up and faced the door, a martial
light in her eyes.

'Please send the captain in, Frank,' she said
sweetly. 'Does he have his band of merry men with
him?'

It was evident that the Captain had heard this last,
for his colour was high as he came into the room and
there was an angry look in his eye. This turned to
greater annoyance as his gaze took in Annabella's

visitors, especially when James came forward cordially to shake his hand and remind him of his fruitless trip to Oxenham earlier in the day. It was clear that Harvard had neither expected nor sought such an audience, and he too could feel the unspoken unity of the group ranged against him. He bowed a little abruptly.

'If you will excuse me, ladies and gentlemen, I have private business with Mrs St Auby...'

This did not have quite the desired effect. There was just the right degree of hauteur in Alicia's raised eyebrows to make him feel uncomfortable, and Annabella was quick to capitalise on this.

'I have no secrets from my sister, sir,' she said in honeyed tones, 'nor indeed from any of my friends. You may speak freely.'

It was obvious that the Captain did not wish to speak freely before everyone. He ground his teeth. 'If you would grant me a private interview, ma'am—' he began, but this time it was Alicia who intervened.

'Come, come, sir, it would not be at all proper for me to permit my sister to speak with a gentleman alone,' she chided. She settled herself more comfortably in her chair as Annabella gestured the irate Captain to join them, turning wide, innocent eyes on the Captain she did so.

'Well, sir? You find me positively agog... Have you had any success in your hunt for Sir William Weston?'

Captain Harvard swallowed hard. 'No, ma'am, we have not. Which is why I am here once more. You did not disclose last night that you are betrothed to Sir William! We have reason to believe that he is hiding here and I have a warrant to search these premises!'

This assertion was met with veiled amusement by Caroline and Alicia, and James turned aside to hide a smile, as though they thought Harvard was playing a part in a bad melodrama. Captain Harvard looked put out.

'This is no matter for jest, madam—'

'No indeed!' Annabella tried to look suitably grave. 'I do apologise! Only you see, sir, we have so little excitement out here in the country that I fear you have quite overset us! Please search to your heart's content! You will find the attics sadly dusty, I fear, but you must not neglect them! And we have cellars, too... Oh!' Inspiration hit her. 'And make sure you include the farm outbuildings in your search! Mr Linton will not mind!'

Larkswood was a relatively small house, but Captain Harvard was determined to be thorough and the search took three hours, during which time he became progressively more bad-tempered as his men found nothing. Nor could he get Annabella on her own as her guests settled down to play a game of whist in her drawing-room.

From the house they progressed to the farmyard where a furious Owen Linton, protesting volubly, was ordered to give the sailors access to his outbuildings. Annabella's confidence in him was not misplaced as he deliberately forgot to warn them of the uncertain temperament of the horse tethered in the far barn. Having sustained bruised shins from kicking, and painful bites to arms and shoulders, the search party shot out of the building straight into the cow byre where the floor proved unpleasantly slippery. Liberally smeared with dung, they assembled in the yard under the frosty eye of the Captain, who certainly could not see the funny side of the situation.

'I did warn you last night that it was all a hum,' Annabella remarked helpfully after Captain Harvard had admitted defeat and was standing in the hall calling his men to order. She brushed some straw and a few cobwebs off his uniform, smiling sympathetically at him. 'You will not find Sir William Weston here, sir. You would do better concentrating your attentions elsewhere!'

'I will be over tomorrow morning to pay my respects to Admiral Cranshaw,' James said, appearing in the drawing-room doorway and giving Harvard a civil nod that made him feel even more uneasy. 'I shall be interested to hear of the progress of your enquiries!'

Harvard shifted uncomfortably from one foot to the other. To have his incompetence rehearsed before his senior officer was almost more than he could bear, but he could not afford to antagonise a man of James Mullineaux's position and influence. He swallowed hard.

'You will find the Admiral at The Old Crown in Faringdon, my lord,' he said, as politely as he was able. 'I shall hope to join you there with good news of the hunt as soon as I am able.'

James allowed the faintest flicker of a disbelieving smile to lighten his face. 'Good man! Then we must not keep you from your search, Harvard! Have you tried the caves on the far side of Weathercock Hill?

They used to be used by highwaymen preying on travellers from Lambourn and might be worth a look!'

The Captain nodded his thanks and marched off down the drive as James said softly, 'What a pity I forgot to warn him about the marshes over that way! My tiresomely bad memory…'

It was late when Annabella trod softly down the garden, across the yard and up to the farmhouse door. A full moon had risen, shedding its bright white light across the gardens and accentuating the black shadows. Susan was waiting for her.

'He's still feverish, ma'am, I'm afraid.' Somehow she still managed to sound reassuring. 'If you could sit with him for a few hours, ma'am, Owen will come along to be with him through the night.'

'Of course.' Annabella paused, her hand on the doorpost. 'What happened when the sailors came, Susan?'

In the candlelight she saw the maid smile. 'Oh, Owen showed them round the farm before they went out to the barns… He had secured the door somehow—he claimed it was bricked up and even kicked it to prove his point! He's a fly one, is Owen! I could hear them talking outside, but they didn't suspect nothing, and Sir William never stirred. All's well, ma'am!'

Annabella looked at her, wondering at the unquestioning loyalty the servants seemed to have towards Will Weston. They had slipped into connivance without a word, just as James and the others had done earlier. It was extraordinary, considering that Will

Weston was a wanted man, yet no one, it seemed, doubted Will's innocence...

'Sir William is a good man,' Susan said stolidly, in answer to Annabella's unspoken question. 'Owen says that he was always a fair and just man, and his father the same before him. And Frank says that any friend of Lord Mullineaux must be in the right of it, so that's good enough for all of us, ma'am.' She bundled up the soiled bandages and picked up the lantern. 'There's fresh candles over by the wall, ma'am, and some water in the pitcher. If he wakes, give him some more of that draught. And if he's too hot, try sponging him down!'

The attic room of Owen's farm was painted white with a makeshift bed against one wall, tucked under the sloping eves. Annabella knelt down beside Will, attempting to bring some order to his tumbled sheets as he tossed and turned uneasily. Each time she tucked him back in he would throw the covers back as though burning up with the fever and desperate for cooler air. His skin was scorching hot. Try sponging him down, Susan had said. Annabella picked up the sponge a little gingerly. She had never considered herself to be a missish girl, but bandaging Will's wound the previous night had shaken her, and now she was not sure she could help him.

Will threw his covers off again, intolerably hot, and Annabella stared transfixed at his powerfully muscled torso, tapering with perfect symmetry to the flat stomach and narrow waist. Just like the previous evening, his smooth, tanned skin fascinated her. She began to gently soothe it with the cool sponge, encouraged as his restless movements slowed and he seemed calmer.

The blankets lay low across his flat hips and a little colour came into Annabella's cheeks as she tried to continue her ministrations and preserve his modesty at the same time. For a widow she was very prudish, she told herself severely.

The change in Will happened abruptly. It was not cold in the little room, for the evening was mild though clear, but suddenly he started to shiver violently as though all the heat had drained from his body. Annabella hastily pulled all the blankets over him, wrapping him up as tightly as possible, but it did no good. He was racked with shaking, his teeth chattering. Try as she might, Annabella could not kindle any warmth in him.

'I'm so cold...' Will's eyes had not opened, it was not possible to tell if he were really conscious, but the pitiful whisper seemed all too true. Without thinking, Annabella lay down beside him, wrapping her arms about him in an attempt to put some warmth back into his body. She burrowed under the covers, pulling them back over both of them to cocoon them around. It was not long before she was very hot indeed, whilst Will appeared scarcely less cold. Her clothes, whilst keeping her warm, prevented the heat from reaching Will. Annabella sighed with irritation. There was only one solution to both problems.

She got up, blowing out the candle and taking off her dress with brisk, practical movements. Her shawl made an excellent additional blanket, and in her shift she was able to curl up closer to Will and transmit her body heat to him. It was cosy and relaxing in their retreat and Annabella felt herself drifting into sleep. At the back of her mind she was wondering what on earth Owen Linton would think when he came in to sit with Will, and what Miss Frensham would say if she found her missing. Neither thought seemed to trouble her sleepy mind much. She slid into dreams.

Annabella woke to find herself cradled in Will's good arm, her face turned into the curve between his shoulder and his neck. His skin felt cool and fresh, and he was not tossing with fever or shivering with cold. Bright daylight was creeping into the attic room and with horror Annabella guessed it must be at least seven in the morning.

Worn out with emotion and worry, she had slept the night through and never even stirred. But Will seemed better, and that was the important thing. Better still, he had not woken and she was likely to be spared any difficult explanations of her presence. Annabella slid carefully out of his warm embrace, wincing as her bare feet touched the cold boards of the floor, and bent a little stiffly to pick up her dress.

'What the *devil* is going on?'

She had not heard Will move, but now she saw that he had raised himself a little against his pillows and was regarding her with amazement and disbelief in the pale light. Annabella was acutely aware of her semi-naked state, the transparent lawn of the low-cut shift. She clutched her dress in front of her.

'Oh! I had no notion you were awake! Are you feeling better now?'

'I feel much recovered, thank you!' Will's tones were clipped, but with a hint of puzzlement as though he could not recall precisely what either of them were doing there. 'Annabella—'

'I am so glad the fever has broken,' Annabella gabbled desperately. 'You have been ill for a day and night and we feared you would remember nothing—'

'I remember nothing of the past day, but I am not so ill as to think I am imagining the sight of you standing there in your shift,' Will said sharply. 'What's going on, Annabella?'

'I…we…' Annabella made a hopeless gesture with the dress, saw Will's gaze follow the curve of her breasts as revealed by the flimsy shift, and gave a squeak of desperation.

'Please, Will! Could you look the other way whilst I put my clothes on?'

'It seems a little late for modesty,' Will said grimly, but he turned over heavily and waited whilst Annabella fumbled clumsily with the fastenings.

'Now—' he turned swiftly back and caught her wrist as she would have scuttled past him '—you will oblige me by explaining exactly what you are doing here!' He looked at her scarlet, defiant face, and added, 'It does not take much thought to realise that you have just spent the night in my bed!'

'You were cold,' Annabella said crossly, 'and I could think of no other way to help you!' She saw his raised eyebrows and added, 'I did not expect my ministrations to be met with such ingratitude!'

'You were fortunate not to be in receipt of any ministrations from me!' Will said dryly. 'I may be sick, but you are enough to tempt a saint!'

Annabella snatched her shawl up. 'I am glad to find you so restored to health and bad humour!' she said, still cross. 'I will send Owen in to help you wash. I have no wish to offend your sense of propriety still further!'

* * *

'Mrs St Auby!' Miss Frensham's thin figure was stiff with outrage. 'As your companion, I feel I must make a stand against these night-time walks you persist in taking! I sought you out last night only to find you gone—'

'And I explained to Miss Frensham that you had thought to take the air, ma'am!' Susan finished, her impishly pretty face for once expressionless.

Miss Frensham rustled her magazine irritably. 'I shall be glad to see you married and off my hands,' she said, as though Annabella was a troublesome sixteen-year-old. 'Your sister was just as difficult—I fear it is the Stansfield blood!'

'So I have been told, ma'am,' Annabella returned politely, slipping into her seat at the breakfast table and applying herself to her food with enthusiasm. The sight of Will recovering from his fever had lifted such a burden from her that she felt ravenous.

'Sir William fancies himself recovered, Susan,' she later told the solemn-faced maid. 'Please ensure that Owen keeps him indoors for at least another two days to give his wound time to heal. I shall stay here to allay Miss Frensham's concerns and in case Captain Harvard returns.'

The day dragged by as slowly as the previous one. Annabella, prudently keeping out of Will's way to give his temper time to cool, went riding in the afternoon and came across a small party of sailors toiling through the heather on the hill, gloomy and streaked with mud and slime. She greeted them cheerfully and watched in satisfaction as they headed away from Larkswood. That night she resisted the urge to go to see how Will progressed, and slept soundly alone and in her own bed.

'He's asking for you, ma'am,' Owen Linton said the next morning, and with a little apprehension Annabella thought it was perhaps time.

She found Will up and dressed in an old frieze coat and pair of breeches which were clearly Owen's cast-offs and had seen better days. There was three days' stubble darkening his jaw, which Annabella inexplicably found rather attractive and, though he was still rather pale and moved carefully, he looked so much better that she found tears of relief prickling the back of her throat. His tousled brown hair added to his air of general dishevellment, but his eyes were alert and unclouded by pain or fever. He took Annabella's hand and gave her the searching look she was coming to know well. He drew her across to sit beside him on the bed, his eyes never leaving her face.

'I did not have the chance yesterday to thank you properly for your care of me,' he said, with a hint of a smile. 'I understand that you have been nursing me and it can have been no work for a lady. I am sorry—'

'I am not made of spun sugar, sir!' Annabella said sharply, taken aback a little by his formality. This was not the Will Weston she had come to know; that man would have taken her to task, perhaps, for her unconventional behaviour, but would not have treated her with this painful correctness.

'No, but…' Will frowned. 'Forgive me, I cannot remember anything about that night…I hope that I did not take advantage, or behave improperly.'

He looked so concerned that Annabella burst out laughing despite herself.

'For shame, sir!' She wiped her eyes. 'What can you be thinking of? You were a sick man, and I did nothing but try to make you comfortable! Neither of us should feel concerned by the situation!'

Will did not smile, and Annabella began to wonder what was wrong. Something was clearly worrying him.

'I know I have compromised you, but I fear I cannot offer you marriage whilst my name is under a cloud,' Will said, in a rush.

Annabella was silent, looking at him. The concern and misery was clear in his blue gaze; he looked as though he was begging her to understand. And the hurt and anger his words had caused melted away as Annabella realised what he was trying to tell her. His code of honour simply did not permit him to marry her when he felt he had nothing but ignominy to offer her.

She moved closer to him, until she was brushing against his body and could reach across to graze her mouth against his. She heard his breath catch in his throat as her lips traced a warm line down the strong brown column of his neck. It filled her with excitement to think that she could do this to him. She could feel his tension, the control he was desperately trying to exercise. Her fingers untied the laces of his shirt so that she could spread her palms gently against his chest, careful of the wound to his shoulder, but questing, searching, nevertheless.

'Annabella…' The word came out as a groan as Will fell back against his makeshift pillows.

'It is not acceptable for you to spend the night with me and then change your mind and refuse to marry me,' Annabella said, her voice prim but her drifting hands demanding as they moved lower. 'It is not the action of a gentleman, sir… I insist,' she added softly, 'that you give me demonstrations of your good intentions.'

Will was evidently not as weak as she had at first supposed. He moved swiftly to tumble her beside him on the bed, his mouth claiming hers ruthlessly. Their lips met and clung tenderly, sweetly, until he let her go reluctantly and sat up with a rueful smile.

'Enough of this! I have to think, and you have to help me, and it simply cannot be done when you distract me so. That was a very wicked trick, Annabella!'

Annabella snuggled closer to him. She had heard the amusement in his tone and pressed a lazy kiss against his throat.

'You did not want to resist me,' she said perceptively. 'If you had chosen, you could have done so! You wanted me to persuade you to keep your word!'

Will looked at her with his searching blue eyes. 'You are right,' he agreed slowly, 'and how well you understand me already, my love! As a gentleman I should not press my suit with you for you deserve better than this. But I shall take what I want, nevertheless! I love you and I will marry you as soon as I can.'

'It does not matter,' Annabella said stoutly, 'for we shall soon clear your name.' She reached for the food basket. 'Let's eat,' she said, ever practical. 'Susan has prepared you the most marvellous breakfast!' She gave him a naughty smile and stretched luxuriously. 'I am so hungry…'

'Minx!' Will said, his mouth full of one of the

freshly baked rolls and honey which Susan had packed for him. He ate ravenously and drank a fair draught of the new milk from Owen's herd, before settling back against the wall with a contented sigh.

'Ah, that's better!' Will's tone changed, became intent. 'Now, Annabella, you must tell me what has been happening these three days past. I need to try to piece it all together.'

Annabella obediently related the visit from Captain Harvard and also the call made by James, Alicia and the Kilgarens.

'James has been working on your behalf and said that he would be in touch when he had some information to impart,' she finished. 'Oh, Will, you do not think that this whole matter could be some outrageous mistake? I have been thinking about it the whole time and can make no sense of the matter!'

She heard Will sigh. 'I wish I could say it was easy to explain,' he responded heavily. 'I truly wish I could claim it all as a misunderstanding. But I know what happened that night, Annabella.' The conviction rang in his voice. 'Harvard set out to kill me. When he knew that I had somehow got away, he was determined to find me and silence me. I do not know why, but I know it is true.'

'When they came here that night, Harvard had a whole troop with him,' Annabella observed suddenly. 'Yet you say that there were only the two on the road...'

Will was looking at her with sudden concentration. 'I had not thought of it before, but that is both true and also suspicious. Now I come to think of it, I heard the troop approaching up the road just after I had reached Larkswood land. It would be interesting to know just what orders he had given to them. I imagine he intended to present them with my corpse, telling them that he and Hawes had courageously tried to arrest me whilst they waited for reinforcements to arrive, and that I had been shot trying to evade capture!'

Annabella shivered, folding her arms for warmth. 'You mean to imply that Harvard would not have wanted an audience for what he planned,' she said quietly. 'But Will, this is monstrous! What can we do?'

'Get to Oxenham as soon as James sends word,' Will said, a little grimly. 'There's strength in numbers and this house is already under suspicion. Then, perhaps, we may untangle the threads and try to work out what to do. Is your carriage ready?'

'Yes—Frank has it all prepared, but it is only a surrey, Will, little more than a cart and with nowhere to hide you!' Annabella desperately tried to think of a solution. Suddenly a feeling of melancholy assailed her as her doubts of the previous day returned. If they could not clear Will's name...

Will caught her wrist, pulling her to him. 'Remember I love you,' he said softly. 'You are bright and brave and beautiful, and I love every little bit of you, Annabella, not just the beauty on the outside.' He kissed her hard and let her go. 'Now, this is what we will do...'

They spent the rest of the day playing chess to pass the time and in the evening Owen came to tell them that Captain Harvard had set a watch on the house.

* * *

'Good morning, Captain!' Annabella, a wide-brimmed straw hat crammed hastily on her head and a shawl about her shoulders, sallied forth from the house with the breezy greeting on her lips. It had been somehow inevitable that Harvard had materialised as the carriage was brought out into the yard and he was surveying them all with deepest suspicion. His cold grey gaze took in Annabella's appearance, then moved on to Susan, who was carrying a large case, and finally came to rest on Miss Frensham. The companion, trailing yards of scarves and jingling beads, was exhorting Frank to be careful with her baggage and had barely noticed the throng of men and horses coming into the yard. When she finally looked up and saw the Captain's inimical gaze, she drew back with a start of alarm.

'Oh, you startled me, sir! Whatever can be going on?'

Annabella took her arm in a firm grip. 'This is Captain Harvard, Emmy—you remember him, of course?'

Miss Frensham drew herself up. She had indeed remembered the Captain. 'I recall the gentleman bursting in twice and making rash accusations,' she said haughtily, 'on the first occasion at some ungoldly hour of the night! I hope, sir, that you are not about to repeat the exercise!'

Emmy could be surprisingly robust, Annabella reflected, with a slight smile, noting the Captain's discomfort at having to upset so proper and elderly a gentlewoman.

'I apologise for discommoding you, madam,' he said abruptly, making a stiff bow. 'I am only doing my duty.'

'Still chasing shadows, Captain?' Annabella enquired sweetly. 'You are wasting your time with us, I fear! Still, if you have nothing better to do…'

Harvard did not rise to this calculated provocation. 'You are going away, ma'am?'

'As you see.' Annabella watched as Frank stolidly continued to put the baggage into the cart. 'A visit to my family for a few days, that is all. It has been planned for some time. Nothing exciting, I fear…' And she turned her limpid green gaze on the Captain.

Harvard was also watching the bags being stowed. It was obvious that there was nothing—or no one—else hidden in the cart, for there was no room. His distrustful glance swept over them all again: Frank, poker-faced as he carried on with his work, Miss Frensham glaring at him with mistrust equal only to his own, Susan waiting respectfully for her mistress to ascend into the surrey, and Annabella, still smiling with carefree charm.

'Sir William Weston—' he began.

'Is not concealed about my person, sir,' Annabella said, smiling widely, 'as you can see. Nor is he disguised as my companion or my maid!'

Miss Frensham looked affronted. Susan giggled delightfully.

Harvard lost his temper. He seized Annabella's arm. 'I do not trust you, madam! It seems to me that you have something to hide—'

'Unhand me, sir!' Annabella said, green eyes flashing. 'I am not to be manhandled thus! Your commanding officer shall hear of this!'

There was a rumble of wheels on the cobbles as Owen Linton's haywain started its ponderous journey out of the farmyard, weighed down not with straw but with a load of root vegetables on their way to market. In the next field, his cowhand was guiding the herd out of their pasture and down the track towards Oxenham. In a flash, Harvard had dropped Annabella's arm and swung round on the cart.

'Stop that cart!' He ordered. 'You men, bayonet those vegetables! *That* will be where he is hiding!'

Susan started to giggle uncontrollably as the sailors began to stab randomly at the turnips. There was an outraged shout from Owen as the vegetables started to roll out of the back of the cart under this assault. Turnips and swedes tumbled to the ground and surged across the yard in a yellow tide. Owen was struggling in the grip of two burly sailors, swearing and shouting. And no one was hiding under the vegetables. As the cart emptied and the blank space stared back at him, the colour suffused Harvard's face in a rich tide. Annabella was watching him with the sort of detached interest that could only add to his embarrassment and his men were sniggering behind their hands.

'Well,' Annabella said brightly, into the pregnant silence, 'we will be on our way then, Captain. I trust that you will be compensating Mr Linton for the damage to his crop. If you are fortunate, he may permit you to take some of the less-damaged vegetables for your supper! Good day!'

Harvard watched the surrey down the road before ungraciously ordering his men to help a grumbling Owen pick up his load. A few fields away, the cowhand was driving the animals through the gate to a buttercup meadow. But no one was watching him, and no one saw the figure that crept away from the comfortable cover of the cows' heaving flanks, slipped along the hedgerow and disappeared in the direction of Oxenham.

Chapter Nine

'Oh, it was priceless!' Annabella said, several hours later, wiping her eyes. 'There was Owen, his face as black as thunder, and Miss Frensham muttering that Captain Harvard was clearly deranged, and turnips rolling everywhere… And I have always wanted to say 'unhand me'! It's such a theatrical phrase!'

'Poor Harvard,' James said, with patently false sympathy. 'He must have known that there was something afoot! You clearly have a talent for pretence, Annabella!'

'Well,' Annabella said pertly, 'if I need to earn my living I could always go on the stage, I suppose!'

'Rather than open a confectioner's?' Will murmured, with a bright, enquiring look. 'Will you, perhaps, settle for a smaller enterprise? A husband and family?'

Annabella's lips twitched. 'A greater enterprise, you mean! But the whole idea was of your making, if the truth be told! How did you fare with those cows, Will?'

'They were very amiable creatures,' Will said. 'So what do we do now, James?'

They were all gathered in the library at Oxenham, James and Alicia, Caroline and Marcus and now Annabella and Will. Alicia had drawn the curtains against the fading light and prying eyes, and they were all sitting in a circle before the fire.

The first thing that Will had been at pains to explain was Harvard's unprovoked attack, and his determination to find Will and contrive his death. Despite Annabella's assertions that they all knew and understood, Will clearly felt he had to make his friends believe in his innocence. He had sat defiantly staring them down, almost daring them to contradict him. But no one had suggested that they disbelieved him, and gradually the tension had left him.

Then James had said feelingly: 'You'd damn well better be innocent, William, for I've spent the best part of two days buttering up that old duffer Cranshaw on your behalf, and Marcus has had to go to Portsmouth, a town he swears he hates more than any other in the country! We don't expect to be told now that it's all a mistake and you're about to turn yourself in!'

There was a pause, then they all burst out laughing.

'I pity you trying to pump Cranshaw for information, James,' Will said with feeling. 'The fellow's a tight as a clam when it comes to business!'

A grin lightened James's face. 'Oh, at first he was reticent, but after we had broached our second bottle he became more loquacious!'

'James!' Alicia was trying to look disapproving. 'I

hope you are not suggesting that you got poor Admiral Cranshaw drunk just to gain information!'

James gave her an unrepentant smile. 'All's fair in love and war, as they say, my sweet, and this is definitely war!'

'So...?' Alicia invited.

'Well...' James settled more comfortably and stretched his legs out before him '...Cranshaw said that someone at the Admiralty—unfortunately he was not quite drunk enough to name them!—had been stirring up trouble by raising the old rumours against Will. The Lords of the Admiralty, more with the intention of exonerating Will than anything else, decided to ask him to come in to answer the charge, all very gentlemanly and without any hint of arrest. Harvard was the man they chose for the commission.' James shifted slightly, his dark gaze resting on the intent faces of his audience. 'Now this is where the tale becomes particularly interesting. According to Cranshaw, Harvard was violently opposed to the plan. He said that the rumours were nothing but spite with no basis in fact, and that Will should not be called on to defend himself against such base allegations. He was most vehement on the subject, Cranshaw said.

'And yet,' Marcus continued softly, 'a few days later, Harvard tried to shoot Will dead—with only one witness to the deed, and a witness, moreover, he trusts to support him. They failed and then tried to hunt Will down to kill him... It is far removed from Harvard's impassioned pleas to his masters at the Admiralty that Will is innocent of all iniquity!'

'It doesn't make sense!' Caroline said despondently. 'How can the man argue in Will's favour one minute and try to murder him the next?'

'And then brand him a criminal and outlaw!' Annabella finished indignantly.

Everybody exchanged glances. There was silence.

'My head is spinning,' Alicia complained, voicing the feelings of all of them. 'I feel as though I am looking at a mirror which turns everything back to front—'

Marcus gave an exclamation. 'Back to front! Of course!' He looked around their intent faces, his eyes suddenly bright with suppressed excitement. 'There is one possible theory that makes sense!'

Everybody waited patiently.

'Suppose for a moment,' Marcus continued in the same thoughtful tone, 'that the rumours are true.' There was a quick, collective intake of breath. 'I do not mean that they are true in relation to Will,' he added quickly, seeing the militant light in Annabella's eyes and smiling a little, 'so there is no need to glare at me! But suppose that there is a grain of truth in them. It is often the way with gossip and scandal. It has its origins in fact, but the real details become obscured.'

'I collect that you mean to imply that the rumours relate not to Will but to someone else,' Annabella said carefully, feeling her way towards the solution Marcus was proposing.

Marcus leant forward. 'Precisely,' he said in the same quiet tones. 'I suggest that we have been looking at this the wrong way up—or back to front, as Alicia said. We have assumed that the rumours are untrue, because we know that Will never abandoned battle as he has been accused. But what if it was true that a Navy captain *had* turned tail in the heat of battle and left his colleagues to fight on alone? And how if that captain was not Will Weston, but Charles Harvard?'

'And Harvard,' James added, 'knows what he has done, knows that he was safe whilst the rumours blamed Will, and knows that any investigation might exonerate Will and point the finger of blame elsewhere!'

'So,' Marcus finished, 'he tries to remove Will first, and with him the possibility of the truth coming out!'

There was a silence.

'Oh Marcus, what a splendid idea!' Caroline burst out, her eyes shining.

Marcus smiled modestly. 'It is good, isn't it! The point is whether or not it could be true!'

'Would it be possible, Will?' Alicia asked, a little hesitantly. 'I mean, would it be possible for one ship to be mistaken for another in the heat of battle? After all, most of us have no idea of how a sea battle is conducted!'

Will had been sitting back in his chair whilst Marcus propounded his theory. His pose was relaxed but his gaze was watchful, although a blue light had started to blaze in his eyes at the suggestion of Harvard's culpability. Now, he put his empty glass down gently and sat up.

'Yes, it's possible,' he said slowly. Everyone caught their breath. 'But unlikely,' he finished. Everyone sighed. Seeing their blank, disappointed faces, Will tried to explain. 'Even in a naval battle where you're intent on your own ship's position and that of the enemy, even with all the smoke that's generated and the hideous noise and confusion, a good captain is aware of the tactical movement of the fleet around him. If a ship of the line were to slip away and abandon the action, it would surely have been noticed!'

He sat back and took Annabella's hand in his, aware of the way in which her face had lit up with hope at the possible explanation, and fallen with disappointment a moment later.

'But surely that's the point,' she said, after a moment's silence. 'Someone *did* see something suspicious and that is where the rumour came from! Maybe not something conclusive, such as a ship just sailing away, for no doubt that would have ended in court martial! But something odd, something questionable…'

'You are very hot in my defence, my love,' Will said with a slight smile. 'Believe me, if I could make the facts fit…! But what of Harvard's crew? They would have known if he had abandoned the fight!'

'Not necessarily!' Annabella urged. 'Why, I read in the papers only recently of a ship that had run aground on Lundy Island when its entire crew were convinced it was still off Cornwall! They did not even believe the lighthousekeeper who rescued them when he told them where they were! So you see, Harvard's crew might never have realised precisely where they were!'

'I had no idea that you had such an interest in naval matters, Annabella,' Alicia teased slyly, watching her younger sister colour up.

'But Annabella's right,' James interposed. 'It could happen!'

Will was still looking sceptical. 'I'd like to believe it,' he said slowly, 'but—' He broke off.

'What is it?' James asked sharply. 'You've remembered something, haven't you, Will?'

'It may be nothing,' Will said slowly, 'but Harvard and I were next to each other in the line. Towards the end, when it was clear that all was lost, I went to the aid of the *Bellepheron,* which was under heavy fire. Harvard broke line at almost the same time. I did not see where he went, for there was much smoke and a mist coming up, but I assumed he had gone to the rescue of another ship just as I had. That was what he *said* he had done.'

'But surely the captain of the *Bellepheron* could exonerate you—?' Annabella began, only to break off at the bleak look on Will's face.

'Dunphy died,' Will said, 'and the ship went down.'

There was a gloomy silence.

'Then surely we could find out which ship *Harvard* claimed to have helped,' Caroline said bracingly, after a moment, 'and prove that he did no such thing! I'll wager that he lost his nerve and chose to run, pretending later that he was answering a call for help from another ship.'

'And then he hears that there are rumours that one of the ships was seen breaking the line, and is afraid that he will be correctly identified as the defaulter. So he decides to blame you, Will,' Marcus continued. 'He simply reverses your roles. In fact, I'd guess he was one of the first to stir the scandal, subtly of course, suggesting by implication that you had deserted. Nothing could be proved either way, for the

Bellepheron's captain is not alive to defend you, and equally no one identified Harvard as the real deserter. But the mud sticks, and Harvard knows that for as long as you are suspected, he is safe.'

'It's a good theory,' Will admitted, a little grudgingly. 'But we will never be able to prove it!'

'Could we get Harvard to implicate himself, perhaps?' Caroline suggested hopefully.

'A trap…' Marcus and James looked speculatively at each other. 'Perhaps if we were to tempt him by letting him know Will is here—'

'No!' Annabella spoke strongly, her fingers clutching at Will's sleeve. 'It's too dangerous! Harvard does not trust us, he will be suspicious, wary… It's too much of a risk!'

'I'm afraid you're correct, Annabella,' Will said reluctantly, covering her fingers reassuringly with his own. 'Harvard would sense the trap, I think, if we were to use me as bait. No, there must be another way, though I cannot for the life of me think of it for now!'

'Do you remember which ship Harvard claimed to have rescued?' Annabella asked tentatively, determined to exhaust every possible possibility. 'If we could find the captain—'

'It was Dowland in the *Détente*,' Will said thoughtfully, 'but he is away at sea and has been since '14—' He broke off, seeing the triumphant look which flashed between James and Marcus. 'What is it? What have I said?'

'That's where you are wrong, old chap,' Marcus said, with satisfaction. 'Dowland isn't at sea any more. He's in Portsmouth. I should know—I saw him yesterday!'

This riveting piece of news seemed to call for another drink, and James refilled their glasses. The atmosphere in the room had lightened considerably.

'Why did Dowland never say anything?' Caroline enquired. 'If our theory is correct, one would have expected him to have exposed Harvard's fabrication.'

Will was shaking his head. 'You must remember, Caro, that Dowland probably never even knew what Harvard was saying. Immediately after Champlain, Dowland was given another ship and sent to the Indies. The rest of us were stationed off Canada until the end of hostilities. Until now, no doubt no one has asked him the right questions!'

'And neither did I yesterday,' Marcus admitted. 'But the one thing I did ask him was to come up to Oxenham as soon as he was able. I thought he might be able to help us. He arrives tomorrow!'

'So, James, do you have any further surprises to spring?' Will asked. He had changed completely, his blue eyes sharp and alert, the pain in his shoulder forgotten in this new excitement.

James grinned, catching the atmosphere. 'Just one! I had been trying to find a witness to Harvard's actions on the night he shot you, Will. And against all the odds, I have got one!'

The news was electrifying. 'But who on earth would be out at that time of night?' Annabella marvelled.

'Not you, then, my love?' Will asked, with a teasing look which suggested that he remembered Annabella's peregrinations at two in the morning.

James laughed. 'As it happens, Will, I know you will appreciate the poetic justice of this! You may remember that you were after a certain poacher who had dealt heavy losses to both the Challen and Oxenham estates. Well, last night we caught him! And last week he was in the vicinity of Larkswood... So, it is fortunate you did not catch him on the night you met Annabella!'

'Annabella!'

Annabella was still asleep when the knock came at her door. The lights had burned late in the library the previous night and she had not seen Will again. She and Alicia and Caroline had sat with Amy Weston, Miss Frensham and Lady Stansfield, chatting in desultory fashion, each trying to preserve the illusion that all was as normal. Amy had not suspected anything, but Lady Stansfield, with her sharp perception, had scanned the faces of both her grand-daughters, noted some hint of tension and kept her own counsel.

'Annabella!' The scratching at the door was insistent, as was the whisper outside. Annabella slid out of bed and went across to the door. The light had begun to seep around the bedroom curtains but it was still very early.

'Who is it?' she whispered, suddenly nervous.

'It is I. Alicia.' Her sister slipped into the room, fully dressed. Behind her was Caroline Kilgaren. Both were smiling, almost radiant with bright excitement. It struck Annabella as most inappropriate given the somewhat grim circumstances.

'What on earth—?' she began crossly, only to be

shushed by Alicia. Caroline shut the door with exaggerated care.

'We have come to help you get ready for your wedding,' Alicia said, her eyes sparkling. 'Will would
have come to ask you himself, but James and Marcus
would not let him out of his room lest he were seen!
But he says that if you refuse he will come for you
anyway! He gave me a message for you, Annabella.'
She frowned slightly in an effort to remember the
words precisely. 'He said that he had told you he
would marry you as soon as he could, and the time
is now. Will you come?'

She watched as Annabella's green eyes filled with
tears. 'I think he loves you very much,' she said
gently, adding as the tears started to overflow, 'Caroline and I have been discussing it and we really feel
you should agree to marry him!'

That fortunately had the happy effect of making
Annabella laugh, although the sight of Caroline bringing forward the silver and gold dress she had worn
for the ball at Mundell almost made her cry again.
The two girls worked silently, helping Annabella into
the dress and arranging her hair in an elegant cascade
of golden curls. At the end, Alicia stepped back and
sighed.

'Oh, you look so beautiful!' She had a lump in her
own throat now. 'And here—' she produced a battered jewel case '— are the Stansfield diamonds. A
fitting occasion for them to be worn again!' She
hugged her sister. 'Our grandmother gave them to me
to give to you specially. She is to be there this morning, for she says that, having missed my marriage to
James, there is no chance that she will miss yours as

well!' She clasped the jewels around Annabella's neck where they glowed softly with pale fire.

The little chapel at Oxenham had not been used for many years and the old priest was in retirement on the estate, but he had answered a summons from James Mullineaux to come to officiate at his sister-in-law's wedding. There, with two candles burning on the altar, Will Weston took Annabella St Auby as his wife.

At the last minute, descending the faintly lit stair, Annabella had clutched at Alicia's arm. 'Oh, Liss, is it not rather dangerous?'

Alicia had paused. 'Not really. Marriage is difficult sometimes, perhaps, as you well know, but not dangerous precisely...'

'No...I meant this...now. It is morning and if anyone were to be about...'

'Oh, yes...' Alicia was preoccupied with keeping her footing in the dark. 'But if Will is prepared to do this for you, Annabella—'

'I know, but suppose Harvard were to guess and burst in!'

'This isn't the Middle Ages, you know! This is a private house, and I doubt that even Captain Harvard would be prepared to risk everything by attempting to raid the premises!'

There was a moment's silence, then Annabella stopped again. 'Liss...'

'Yes?' Alicia had started to sound quite irritated.

'How can Will and I be married when the banns have not been read?'

'Because Will has a special licence, Bella! I believe he procured one a while ago—'

'Oh, I see! Will *assumed* that I would agree to marry him—'

'Yes, he did! And he was right, wasn't he?'

And now they were indeed man and wife, and the priest was saying the blessing, his benign face wrinkled in a smile. Behind them, Alicia and James were looking besottedly at each other, Caroline and Marcus were holding hands, and even Lady Stansfield had a misty look on her face. Annabella stood on tiptoe to kiss her new husband.

'Now you have Larkswood back again,' she whispered irrepressibly, and saw him smile, but he did not answer.

Lady Stansfield, trying not to yawn at the earliness of the hour, kissed her grand-daughter and her new grandson-in-law, and then Alicia and Caroline escorted Annabella back up the stair to her room and helped her out of the wedding dress.

'Well,' Annabella said, a little inadequately, 'what shall I do now? It can only be nine o'clock, but I suppose I should get dressed properly.'

'Why not go back to bed for a little?' Caroline suggested pragmatically, but with a twinkle in her eye. 'You had a very tiring day yesterday, and Will has been ordered to rest, but perhaps he would like to share a breakfast here with you first...'

She dismissed Annabella's high-necked cotton nightdress with a wave of one hand, bringing forward one of Alicia's delicious gauzy creations. To Annabella's mind this was rather filmy, revealing far more than it concealed, and she was suddenly overcome by an extraordinary wave of shyness.

'Oh, but surely—' she could feel herself colouring

up '—is this not a little impractical for breakfast? Something more modest…'

Caroline raised an expressive eyebrow at Alicia.

'There will only be yourself and Will here,' Alicia said, trying not to laugh, 'and there is a wrap to go with the nightdress…here…'

The wrap was no more concealing than the night-gown, Annabella thought, obediently putting it on. She was suddenly beset with nerves. It did not appear to help when she told herself that she was no innocent, and that she had already spent a night with Will, albeit in different circumstances. She had longed for this moment, but now she was afraid. Her experience of Francis's lovemaking had not been a pleasant one, after all, and despite the pleasure she had found in Will's kisses, there was no guarantee that matters would be any easier with him… She managed to frighten herself so much that when Will came into the room some fifteen minutes later, he found his bride huddled under the blankets and looking at him with distinct nervousness.

Will smiled a little, bringing a bottle of champagne and two glasses over to the bedside and sitting down on the edge of the bed as though it were the most natural thing in the world for Annabella to suddenly find him invading her bedroom. He poured for them both and raised the glass in a toast to her. The champagne bubbles tickled Annabella's nose as she looked at him warily over the rim of the glass, the sheet tucked tightly around her.

As well as the champagne, Will had brought soft bread rolls, still warm from the oven, with rich golden butter and honey. Annabella, surprised to find herself hungry, ate and drank her fill and finally set her glass down rather reluctantly. Will yawned suddenly.

'Lord, I'm still so tired! My shoulder aches... Could I...would you mind if I were to rest for a while...?'

Annabella immediately felt guilty. 'Oh! Your shoulder! I almost forgot. Of course...' She turned away, deliberately averting her gaze in an agony of shyness as Will wearily stripped off his clothes, slid into bed beside her and blew out the candle. There was a moment of tense silence, then Will sighed again.

'Annabella, I'm so sorry, would you mind if I just hold you gently? I feel a little cold...' He did indeed sound very fatigued and Annabella reproached herself for her self-consciousness when Will was evidently too tired to care about anything other than his physical discomfort. The flimsy, transparent nightdress need not matter, she reassured herself. He would not see it, and at least it would provide a barrier between them...

Will moved closer to her and Annabella was suddenly acutely aware of his body curved against hers, even through the almost non-existent encumbrance of the nightdress. Contrary to what he had said, he actually felt very warm. She could feel his chest brushing against her back, his thigh just touching hers, the gentle caress of his lips against the sensitive skin of her neck. He slid his good arm around her, pulling her closer, and settled down with a relaxed sigh.

Annabella found herself unable to rest. She was acutely and intensely aware of both him and the inconvenient demands of her own body. Her mouth was dry and it was not nerves that quickened her breathing now. The more she tried to distract her thoughts, the more they obsessed her. She imagined Will lifting the swathe of honey-coloured hair from her shoulder and sliding the silky material away so that he could press his lips to her naked skin. Suddenly she wanted him desperately. She gave an involuntary moan. Will shifted irritably.

'Whatever is the matter, Annabella?'

Annabella wriggled frantically to try to get away from him but he held her still. A delicious ache of anticipation in the pit of her stomach now threatened to overwhelm her. Her nerves had fled but she was frantic that Will should not guess her state, not when he was tired and hurt, and needed only to rest. She wriggled again.

Will rolled away from her, pulling her over on to her back in the process. Annabella opened her eyes to see him leaning on one elbow looking down at her. It was very dark in the room and she could not discern his expression. His fingers were absentmindedly entwining themselves in the curls of hair that nestled at her throat, just grazing her skin with the lightest of caresses. Annabella tried to ignore the tiny tremors of sensation which his touch was awakening.

'I'm so sorry,' she said in a rush. 'I know you are tired, but I find I cannot sleep. Perhaps I should read for a while, or get up and dressed—'

Will's mouth coming down on hers cut off any other inanities that she might have chosen to utter. Annabella's gasp of mingled surprise and pent-up relief was lost, as were any coherent thoughts that had previously been in her mind. She was helpless with desire, weak with the taste and feel of him. And he lingered over the kiss, prolonging their pleasure until Annabella was almost begging him to move on, digging her fingers into his back, pressing against him with abandonment.

It was then that Annabella discovered just how wickedly erotic her borrowed nightdress proved to be, for it fastened with a series of small buttons down the front which Will was now proceeding to undo with thorough and tormenting slowness. His lips brushed the hollow of her throat, pressing a trail of tiny kisses downwards. The material parted slightly, tantalisingly, and he traced its progress to the cleft between her breasts, sliding the silky fabric away slowly so that he could bend his head to her sensitised nipples. Annabella writhed beneath him, pulling him hard against her, but he resisted her blandishments.

'Oh, no, sweetheart... I've waited a long time for this and I don't intend to hurry...'

Annabella twined her fingers in his hair as his hands and lips continued their wicked provocation. The nightdress finally slid away from her shoulders and arms, leaving her naked to the waist. And Will had finally lifted his head from her breasts and was moving downwards again, hesitating once more over each button, his mouth still following the path of his fingers to stroke and caress and tease. His fingers skimmed the soft skin of her stomach, and the fluttery, demanding ache within Annabella intensified. She arched against him, desperate with need. With a gentle movement, Will turned her on her side so that she had her back to him and they were lying as they had been at the start. But this time Annabella was shock-ingly aware of his arousal, the hardness of him pressed against the curve of her bottom. She gave a little gasp.

Will's fingers moved to cup her breast and she gasped again, willing him to end this torment. The nightdress was unfastened as far as her hips, but its slippery folds were entwined about them in a manner which suddenly seemed excessively stimulating. Then she felt Will's hands move to undo the last buttons and the material fell away.

His leg slid between hers, his fingers straying across the softness of her inner thighs. Annabella's eyes were open wide as she drifted with the unimaginable pleasure of Will's touch. She slid onto her back again, her lips parting as Will raised himself above her to reclaim her mouth in a kiss as deep as it was protracted. His hands were on her hips as he moved her beneath him. And when he finally put an end to all waiting, taking her with a fiercely gentle demand, Annabella thought nothing of the past and was enveloped in the exquisite fulfilment of the present.

Later, lying amidst their tangled sheets, with the candle relit and the champagne consumed, she looked somewhat accusingly at her husband.

'I thought that you were tired, Will! I was at great pains not to disturb you—'

With one swift gesture, Will pulled back the tumbled bedclothes and considered her naked body, holding the sheet out of her reach when she would have snatched it back.

'I defy anyone not to be disturbed by the feel and the touch of you,' he said softly. 'And if I was a little less weary than you imagined, well… No—' as she made another determined grasp at the sheet '—you denied me the sight of you before, Annabella—I insist that now I make up that deficit.'

Annabella shivered a little before the concentrated desire in his face. She put out a hand and tentatively touched his shoulder. 'But your arm… Should you not be resting?' Unconsciously, her fingers brushed across the bronzed skin of his chest, revelling in the feel of him.

'The doctor tells me that I should spend some time in bed,' Will said with the shadow of a smile, 'and we have an entire day before we can put our plans into practice tomorrow night, so I intend to take his advice…'

Charles Harvard was ill at ease in the elegant dining-room of the Marquis of Mullineaux's house at Oxenham. It was not the grandeur of the company or the estate that overawed him, but the uncomfortable feeling of walking into the lion's den. At first, when he and Admiral Cranshaw had received their invitation to dine, Harvard had begged his superior officer to excuse him, arguing that his duty conflicted with the occasion. Cranshaw had called him a damn fool and looked at him as though he really believed Harvard to be mad.

'Can't afford to offend an influential man like James Mullineaux,' he grunted, shovelling his breakfast kedgeree down his throat as he spoke. 'Besides, Mullineaux's sound—may be a friend of Will Weston, but wouldn't do anything to prejudice the course of our investigation! Damn it, the man's a justice of

the peace and a damned fine shot besides! Would
have thought an ambitious young officer like yourself
would be glad of an opportunity to further your acquaintance!'

Faced with his Admiral's monumental displeasure
and utterly unable to explain himself, Harvard had
been persuaded to attend for dinner, and had almost
immediately felt vastly uneasy. He found himself next
to Lady Stansfield at dinner, an unkindness on the part
of his hostess which could scarcely be matched.

The old Countess had eyed him up and down with
disfavour and said, 'Harvard? Of the Yorkshire Har-
vards?'

It was impossible to tell from her tone whether it
would be a good or bad thing to claim kinship with
the unknown Yorkshire cousins, so the Captain had
explained that his was the Sussex branch of the family. Lady Stansfield had sniffed her disapproval but
offered no comment. As a fine turbot stuffed with
spinach and ham followed the soup, Harvard began
to relax infinitesimally. Lady Stansfield spoke again.

'Making any progress on your wild-goose chase?'
she enquired affably.

Before the Captain could think of a tactful response, Alicia had interrupted from further down the
table.

'Grandmama, it is not really appropriate to ask poor
Captain Harvard about business whilst we're at dinner!'

'I should say not,' James agreed with deliberate
tactlessness. 'I'm the sure the Captain don't want re-
minding of his lack of success!'

Harvard flushed.

'Have you seen the Regent's Pavilion at Brighton?' Lady Stansfield enquired, with suspicious affability.

'Yes, ma'am,' Harvard decided to risk it. 'I thought it most attractive.'

'Monstrosity! Carbuncle!' Lady Stansfield spoke through a mouth of spinach. Harvard thought he also heard her say 'Stuffed shirt!' but he could not be sure.

Further down the table, as far away from Captain Harvard as possible, Annabella sat watching her grandmother bait him. Seeing Harvard, knowing what he had tried to do to Will—to her husband—made just sitting in the same room with him a trial for Annabella. But she understood the necessity for a cool head. Just as she had helped Will by hiding him through the time at Larkswood, now she would help them trap his would-be murderer.

Marcus was talking to Admiral Cranshaw, who was in high good humour as his glass was filled and re-filled and a loin of beef succeeded the turbot.

'I hear that John Dowland is back in port,' he was saying casually.

'Ah,' Cranshaw nodded sagely. 'Dowland's back, is he? Sound man, sound man. Bruising rider to hounds, too!' He took a swill of his wine. 'D'y hear that, Harvard? Dowland's back! Must be all of two years since you saw him, eh?'

Harvard dropped his fork on the floor and snapped at the footman who bent to retrieve it. He appeared to have gone very pale.

'Bad *ton* to blame the servants,' Lady Stansfield observed malevolently. 'Very bad *ton,* young man!'

Harvard ignored her. 'Are you sure, my lord?' He

was addressing Marcus Kilgaren, who looked rather surprised.

'Why, yes, I heard it from Will Weston before he disappeared! I remembered it particularly, for Will said he planned to go to Portsmouth to see Dowland…'

Harvard was already half out of his chair when he realised that all eyes were upon him and he sank back, reddening.

'Extraordinary behaviour!' Lady Stansfield said, looking down her nose.

Cranshaw, his face as red as the wine, seemed to have noticed nothing amiss. 'Aye, a good captain, Dowland was,' he reminisced. 'It would have been at Lake Champlain that you last saw him, eh, Charles? His was the only other ship the Americans couldn't take, apart from yours and Weston's…'

'Yes, sir,' Harvard said woodenly.

'I expect Dowland remembers Champlain well,' James said pleasantly. 'I'm sure he'd be an interesting man to talk to…'

'Oh, fine fellow!' Cranshaw agreed enthusiastically. 'Of course, he's been out of touch a long time; after the battle at Champlain he was sent to the West Indies… Portsmouth, you said, Kilgaren? Well, well, he'll be glad of some shore leave, no doubt… What's the matter, Harvard?' Cranshaw had flushed even more red with annoyance as his junior officer had stood up. 'Meal's not over yet, y'know!'

'Perhaps the Captain has been at sea too long,' Annabella murmured *sotto voce*. 'Here on land it is the *ladies* who retire first!'

There was general laughter. Cranshaw waved aside Harvard's impassioned 'Sir!'

'Later, man, later!' He was not to be denied his pudding. 'I declare, you're behaving damned oddly tonight!'

Harvard subsided again. But they had not finished with him yet.

'Heard an extraordinary story from my gamekeeper today,' James said, his eyes meeting Alicia's briefly with a wicked twinkle. 'Apparently he apprehended a poacher last night, a man from Challen, whose enterprises have taken him as far afield as the borders of Sir Dunstan Groat's land. Anyway, the man told a story that might interest you, Cranshaw.'

The Admiral grunted through a mouth of pudding. Harvard had gone a pasty white.

'Seems he was out the night Will Weston disappeared,' James continued, with blithe disregard for Harvard's sickly countenance, 'and says that he has some information that might be of interest. I promised to go to hear his tale tomorrow...'

Harvard raised his wineglass with a hand that shook slightly. Some wine splashed on to the white cloth.

'If he has information germane to our enquiry—' his voice sounded strained even to himself '—then he should be turned over to our authority...'

There was a sudden silence. James, who had been helping Annabella to some more dessert, turned and raised his black brows.

'My dear Harvard,' he spoke quite gently, 'the man was caught armed and resisting arrest, and with some of my deer! He is on a capital charge! But I am happy

for the Admiral to accompany me if he wishes to hear
the fellow's tale—'

'No!' Harvard caught himself. 'That is, a criminal
such as that cannot be a reliable witness—'

'Nonsense, Harvard!' Cranshaw wiped his mouth
on his napkin and laid it down with a sigh of satisfaction. 'If the fellow's got some information about
Weston, I should be pleased to hear it!' He was feeling more generous now, more expansive. 'Tell you
what, Harvard, you're always set on work, that's your
trouble!' He waved an arm in effusive appreciation.

'Fine food, excellent cellar, pretty women...' he
approximated a courtly bow at Annabella, who smiled
back '...and all you can think about is questioning
prisoners! Dashed dull, what!'

The door opened. Fordyce trod softly into the room
and whispered urgently in James's ear. James threw
down his napkin and stood up.

'Seems you will have a chance to speak to Dowland sooner than you might have expected, sir,' he
said pleasantly to Cranshaw. 'He is here now, in fact,
and asking to see you urgently. And I understand that
he has Sir William Weston with him! Why, Harvard—' James's voice was suddenly as cold as ice
'—wherever can you be going in such a hurry? Fordyce, Liddell, please detain the Captain for a moment.
There is something I am sure he must be interested
to hear...'

'Here we are like three grass widows,' Caroline
complained disconsolately, two days after the gentlemen had left for London. She cast aside her magazine
with a grimace. 'Why must we sit here tamely waiting

for them to come back to us? Can we not entertain ourselves?'

Annabella sighed. It was raining, which seemed peculiarly appropriate. To have had Will snatched from her arms so soon after their marriage was particularly hard to bear, but she knew he had to go to clear his name and sort out all the unpleasantness occasioned by Harvard's own arrest for both treason and attempted murder.

When the Master-at-Arms, Hawes, had become aware of his captain's arrest he had hastened to vindicate himself and blame all on Harvard. His testimony, taken with that of James's poacher, was sufficient to clarify the matter of the attempted murder. Captain Dowland's assertion that he had seen Will Weston go to the aid of the stricken *Bellepheron* and that he had neither needed nor gained Harvard's aid at Champlain, was even more damning. It became apparent that Marcus's theory had been correct and that Harvard had lost his nerve in the dying stages of the sea battle, fearing capture so much that he had abandoned the conflict and fled. In the heat of the action no one had clearly seen or even guessed his deed, except for Hawes who was as guilty of treason as his master. And when Harvard had heard the first rumours swirl that a captain had abandoned the fight, he had been quick to pin the blame on Will Weston.

That left only the small matter of identifying the person who had stirred up the rumours again two years later and Will had been confident that he could find that out when he went to the Admiralty. It was ironic, Annabella thought, that Harvard had had more reason than anybody to prevent the Admiralty taking the rumours seriously, and that when they had done so he had been forced to revert to his murderous plan to try to save his own skin...

'So what do you suggest, Caro?' Alicia asked, cutting across Annabella's thoughts.

'Why, that we too should go up to London!' Caroline jumped to her feet. 'The Little Season will have started and anything is better than moping around here! Mrs Weston may not care to accompany us, but I'll wager Lady Stansfield would be game! Come, what do you say?'

Annabella felt a sudden rush of excitement. She had never been to London and it would have the added advantage of bringing her nearer to Will.

'Well...' Alicia said cautiously, trying not to smile as she saw her sister's bright eyes fixed on her pleadingly, 'perhaps...'

'Capital!' Caroline clapped her hands. 'I will make arrangements at once! And,' she added, with a very naughty smile, 'we shall not send word to the gentlemen, I think! They will hear soon enough!'

The ballroom at Stansfield House had seen many a spectacular social occasion but none so impressive as the ball given by Lady Stansfield a week later. The *haut ton* had been stunned to discover her ladyship back in Town, accompanied by not one but both of her beautiful granddaughters. That those granddaughters appeared to be unaccompanied by their husbands was an even greater bonus.

In the days preceding the ball, Annabella had had to be almost forcibly restrained from going out to see the sights of the city and in particular to acquaint herself with the delights of the Bond Street shops. The impact of their arrival would be all the greater for having kept themselves hidden away, Alicia and Caroline argued, and Annabella acquiesced reluctantly, having extracted a promise from her sister that they would go on a shopping expedition as soon as possible. But on the night of the ball Annabella was forced to admit that her sister's strategy had been sound. The ballroom itself, decorated with tiny coloured glass lanterns and stained glass panels which cast ethereal coloured shadows, was the perfect foil for herself and Alicia. In a rich strawberry silk and lace dress Annabella felt more elegant than she had ever been, and the distinction of the company made the event a far cry from the provincial assemblies she was accustomed to.

Hugo Mundell, accompanied by his sister and her fiancé John Dedicoat, were amongst the first arrivals. Mundell seemed in high good humour to see Annabella again, pressing a leisurely kiss on her hand and complimenting her on her appearance.

'I understand that it is customary to congratulate a lady on her marriage,' he added with a smile. 'Alas, Lady Weston, I find I can only be sorry to hear of yours! Will has snatched you away before the rest of us had a fair chance!'

Annabella, diverted by the novelty of being addressed by her married name, thanked him prettily for the compliment and agreed to grant him two dances later in the evening.

'But where is Will this evening?' Mundell pursued, looking round. 'Surely he cannot have been foolish enough to leave you alone so soon after the wedding?'

Annabella smiled. 'Alicia, Caroline and I are all without our husbands this evening,' she confirmed. 'They have far weightier matters to contend with! Will has been at the Admiralty these ten days past over this business of Harvard and the treason trial!'

'Yes, I heard of that.' Mundell frowned. 'Extraordinary business, but I am very glad Will has finally been able to settle matters. Do you have any idea how the rumours started up again?'

Annabella had just seen Miss Hurst enter the ballroom on the arm of a very distinguished-looking elderly gentleman. 'I have a suspicion...' she murmured.

Mundell followed her gaze and raised his eyebrows. All he said was, 'I see Miss Hurst has her latest quarry in tow! She has great hopes of bringing him up to scratch! That, Lady Weston, is the Duke of Belston, and if he is not in the first flush of youth and does not have any land or fortune left, he is at least sufficiently important to engage her interest!'

It was much later in the evening that Annabella found herself in the ladies' withdrawing room at the same time as Ermina Hurst. Miss Hurst's bright brown eyes appraised her with dislike, taking in the beautifully cut pink dress and the elegant tumble of Annabella's honey-coloured curls.

'Lud, Mrs St Auby—or, Lady Weston, as I suppose I must call you now—who would have thought that you could have been transformed from country mouse to society matron so easily!' she gushed. 'To become your grandmother's heiress, and to catch Will Weston into the bargain! But...' her eyes sparkled with the malicious pleasure Annabella remembered all too well '...I hear Will has forsaken you already!'

'Only to pursue an important matter of business, Miss Hurst,' Annabella said sweetly. She swung round suddenly. 'A matter which you, perhaps, have some knowledge of? Gossip always was one of your accomplishments, was it not, albeit one you did not mention when we first met?'

Miss Hurst had started to flush brick red. 'I have no notion—' she began.

'No?' Annabella was still smiling pleasantly. 'No notion of a conversation at a ball in Taunton with a certain Captain Jeffries? No notion of some poisonous slander he passed on to you and you in turn saw fit to tell your cousin at the Admiralty? No notion of the misery and trouble your spite has caused? I envy you your ignorance!'

Ermina Hurst pushed past her to leave the room, her face a mask of twisted malice. 'You upstart little Cit!' she flashed. 'I wish I had spoiled sport for you! Will Weston deserves no better, and as for you, you will find that it takes more than a pretty face and a rich grandmother to be accepted in Society!'

She turned back to the door only to find it open and Alicia, Caroline Kilgaren and Lady Stansfield standing in the aperture. Behind them were the outraged faces of half a dozen of society's most influential hostesses.

'Appalling behaviour!' Lady Jersey said to Lady Sefton. 'One only hopes that Antony Belston will see fit to take her on a *very* long wedding trip!'

* * *

After the best part of ten days, Will, Marcus and James finally walked out of the Admiralty in Whitehall into the crisp wintry evening air. London appeared to be awakening for the night; lanterns flared, carriages trundled by and couples in evening dress strolled towards the first fashionable crush of the night. None of the gentlemen paid much attention. Their minds were still full of the events of the past week, the testimonies taken from Captain Dowland and others, the statement made by Lynch the poacher, the impending court martial and trial of Harvard for treason and attempted murder.

They turned the corner into Horseguards and bumped into two slightly inebriated young men who hailed them with delight.

'Kilgaren! Mullineaux! Weston! I'll be damned!' The slighter of the two gentlemen clapped Will on the shoulder. 'Had no idea you were in Town! Thought the lovely ladies were all alone…'

The second young man blinked owlishly. 'Saw them at Lady Stansfield's ball last night,' he confirmed enthusiastically. 'What an entrance! What style! Had no idea Lady Mullineaux had a little sister! Would've made it my business to meet her sooner if I had!' He shook his head regretfully.

'Patrick O'Neill seemed damned pleased to see Lady Mullineaux again,' the first said slyly. 'Never forgave you for stealing her from under his nose, Mullineaux! Still,' he shrugged, 'no doubt we'll see you later? We're for Lady Cassilis's masquerade— should be a crush—word is Lady Kilgaren intends to go as Diana the Huntress!'

And so saying, they wove their way off towards Pall Mall.

James Mullineaux, Marcus Kilgaren and Will Weston stood stock still, staring at each other.

'What the devil—?' Marcus began, breaking off as he saw Will's rueful smile.

'I believe we have made a tactical error,' Will said slowly, 'in leaving our wives languishing alone and unattended—'

'It doesn't sound to me as though they have been unattended for long,' James finished grimly. He set off purposefully. 'Damnation! Why can Alicia always do this to me?'

'Always could, always will!' Marcus said laconically, half his mind already preoccupied with the thought of Caroline attired as the Goddess Diana. 'As for Will, seems he must claim his bride before half of London tries to be before him!'

Annabella had just begun a waltz with the Earl of Manleigh when Lady Cassilis's butler announced the Marquis of Mullineaux, the Earl of Kilgaren and Sir William Weston. She had been having the most marvellous few days… From behind the disguise of domino and mask, she smiled a little and watched the proceedings with no little interest. There was no denying that the three men looked magnificent. They were in evening dress, which immediately singled them out amongst the coloured dominoes and fancy dress of her ladyship's other guests. Then there was about them a certain air of purpose, almost of sternness, as the set about tracking down their errant wives. Annabella's heart skipped a beat. Despite the concealing domino Will had been making a straight line for her when, fortuitously, he was delayed by an old acquaintance who had insisted in engaging him in conversation.

Marcus Kilgaren had come upon his wife chatting to a very old flame of hers, Lord Cavendish. Marcus was surprised to feel a real possessive jealousy stir within himself at the sight of Caroline, so exquisitely pretty, draped in a dress so diaphanous it should not have been allowed out of the shop. And Cavendish was certainly enjoying their reunion, leaning towards her, his eyes bright with admiration and something else which set Marcus's teeth on edge. He gave the unfortunate peer a nod that was barely civil and addressed his wife.

'I believe this is my dance, madam.'

Caroline's eyes widened in the flirtatious way he remembered from their courtship. He could not believe she was about to do this to him. 'I think you mistake, sir,' she said sweetly. 'I am not engaged for this dance—'

'You are now,' Marcus said grimly, grasping her wrist and almost pulling her to her feet. 'And, dear Caro,' he added in an undertone for her ears only, 'my preference at this moment would be to make love to you rather than dance with you! I am only conforming to propriety for the sake of Lady Cassilis's guests!'

For James Mullineaux, approaching Alicia was very reminiscent of the days before their marriage when his beloved had been besieged by a sea of admirers and it had been difficult even to get near to her. He cut a path ruthlessly through the crowd, not even pausing to respond to the greetings of his friends, and found Alicia at the centre, sensational in an emerald-green domino and black velvet mask, Captain O'Neill lounging by her side. The dazzling Lady Mullineaux, very sure of her power... *His* Lady Mullineaux...

He took her hand and, with the wicked smile that had always made Alicia's heart turn over, pressed a kiss on the palm. He did not even speak, simply drawing her out of the group and guiding her expertly towards a secluded alcove. Several ladies in their vicinity exchanged rueful looks. No point in wondering whether the Marquis of Mullineaux would be interested in a flirtation. The Marquis and his wife were giving off so much white-hot intense heat that to get close would be to risk burning! So much for the dictum which said that a husband and wife paying each other attention in public was unfashionable!

Annabella was scarcely aware of the moment that Will cut out Frederick Manleigh, so dextrous was his manoeuvre. One moment, the besotted Earl had been smiling down into her eyes, the next he appeared to have vanished completely. Will's arm slid about her waist, his thigh brushed against hers, hard muscle against sliding silk, and she almost lost her step through sheer sensual awareness.

'Well, madam?' Will was unsmiling, but Annabella was up to the challenge.

'I am very well, I thank you, sir.' She gave him a melting smile. 'I have been having such a delightful time!'

She saw Will's blue eyes narrow. 'So I see. I have

heard that Lady Mullineaux's little sister is the toast of the Town!'

Annabella smiled again, lowering her eyes so that their expression should not betray her.

'No doubt,' Will pursued, 'it slipped your mind to inform these gallant gentlemen that you are, in fact, my wife of only ten days!'

Annabella almost laughed. She was nearly certain that his stern tone was assumed, just as her flirtatiousness was. How could it be otherwise, when his body against hers was giving a very different message?

'Alas,' she said with every appearance of regret, 'it has often slipped my mind, given my neglect by my husband!'

She saw the expression flare in Will's eyes, the mixture of desire and challenge that set her blood racing, heady as a draught of wine.

'Do I understand you properly?' he asked musingly. 'You fear that your attention may wander, given the delightful distractions of town and the lack of attention paid to you by your lawful husband?'

Annabella lowered her gaze again, managing a modest smile. 'It is all so new and exciting,' she said, by way of excuse. 'I am sure I could be forgiven for thinking I might be missing something, were I to settle into dull married life...'

She gasped aloud as Will turned them so that Annabella's back was suddenly against one of the ballroom pillars.

'I am minded to demonstrate to these poor, love-sick fools that they are wasting their time,' he said, his mouth an inch away from hers. 'Which would be the greater scandal, do you think, my love, to kiss you here and now, or to carry you out of the ballroom to make love to you?'

'Why don't you find out?' Annabella asked provocatively, as she raised her mouth to meet his.

* * * * *

MILLS & BOON®

*M*akes
any time
special

Enjoy a romantic novel from
Mills & Boon®

Presents™ *Enchanted*™ *Temptation*®

Historical Romance™ *Medical Romance*™

2 FREE

books and a surprise gift!

We would like to take this opportunity to thank you for reading this Mills & Boon® book by offering you the chance to take TWO more specially selected titles from the Historical Romance™ series absolutely FREE! We're also making this offer to introduce you to the benefits of the Reader Service™—

- ★ FREE home delivery
- ★ FREE gifts and competitions
- ★ FREE monthly Newsletter
- ★ Exclusive Reader Service discounts
- ★ Books available before they're in the shops

Accepting these FREE books and gift places you under no obligation to buy, you may cancel at any time, even after receiving your free shipment. Simply complete your details below and return the entire page to the address below. *You don't even need a stamp!*

YES! Please send me 2 free Historical Romance books and a surprise gift. I understand that unless you hear from me, I will receive 4 superb new titles every month for just £2.99 each, postage and packing free. I am under no obligation to purchase any books and may cancel my subscription at any time. The free books and gift will be mine to keep in any case.

H9EA

Ms/Mrs/Miss/Mr ....Initials......................................
BLOCK CAPITALS PLEASE

Surname ....

Address ....

....

....Postcode ....

Send this whole page to:
THE READER SERVICE, FREEPOST CN81, CROYDON, CR9 3WZ
(Eire readers please send coupon to: P.O. BOX 4546, DUBLIN 24.)

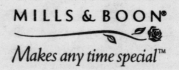

MILLS & BOON®

Makes any time special™

The Regency Collection

Mills & Boon® is delighted to bring back, for a limited period, 12 of our favourite Regency Romances for you to enjoy.

These special books will be available for you to collect each month from May, and with two full-length Historical Romance™ *novels in each volume they are great value at only £4.99.*

Volume One available from 7th May